RED CITY REAPER

Book 0 - Dead in Red City*
Book 1 - A Shot For Death - March 26, 2024
Book 1.5 - Death Uncaged - March 21, 2024
Book 2 - Death Orders a Double - July 23, 2024
Book 3 - Death With A Twist - November 7, 2024
Book 4 - Death On The Rocks - February 25, 2025
Book 5 - A Fifth Of Death* - Fall 2025
Book 6 - A Dash Of Death*
Book 7 - A Chaser of Death*
Book 8 - A Nightcap of Death *

*Forthcoming
Titles and release dates may be subject to change.

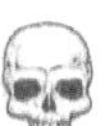

DEATH ON THE ROCKS

AN EXILED GRIM REAPER URBAN FANTASY NOVEL

RED CITY REAPER
BOOK 4

C. THOMAS LAFOLLETTE

BROKEN WORLD PUBLISHING

DEATH ON THE ROCKS
C. Thomas Lafollette

A Broken World Publication
13820 NE Airport Way
Suite #K395495
Portland, OR 97251-1158
Death On The Rocks
Copyright © 2025 by C. Thomas Lafollette
ISBN 978-1-960766-20-5 (ebook);
ISBN 9978-1-960766-21-2 (paperback)

Cover Design: Ravven
Editing & Proofreading: Amy Cissell

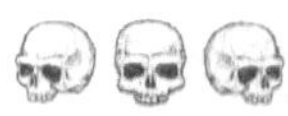

CONTENTS

AUTHOR'S NOTE

This story contains words and phrases in Louisiana Creole and Haitian Kreyòl. They are spelled according to Creole and Kreyòl standards.

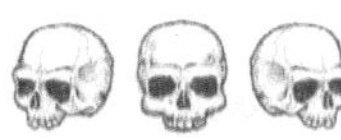

ONE

JAMIE

Jamie stared out over the basin Redemption City sat in. The lights at night always made the place look nicer than the actual dirty, crime-ridden reality. Reaching down, she patted the hood of the older Toyota Corolla she currently sat on, leaning against the windshield. It was the first time she'd had something so nice in her entire life.

Technically, it wasn't hers. It belonged to Dax, Tomi, and Mama Adele—as she asked to be called—and it came with a job. Their New Orleans soul food restaurant had taken off, but the seating area wasn't that big compared to the production capacity the kitchen had, and the crowd at Dax's bar hadn't adopted the restaurant in large numbers quite yet. But the restaurant received a lot of phone calls asking if they did deliveries. So, their friend Boudreaux "hooked them up" with the used Corolla.

She wasn't sure what that meant, and she didn't ask. She'd been around Dax's crew enough to realize Dax, Tomi, and Boudreaux might be getting up to some shady stuff. Though from what she'd seen after they'd retaken Tallulah's bar from the bikers, the shady stuff seemed to mostly involve stealing whatever they could from the

Nazi bikers. Therefore, it wasn't really stealing in their book. Or hers, for that matter.

For as much trouble as the racist assholes had caused her, Dax, and his people, they all deserved some recompense.

She pulled her phone from her pocket and checked the hour. It was time to report in with Mama Adele and start delivering orders. Gathering up her empty fast-food containers, she tossed them in a garbage can and climbed behind the wheel, dropping her half-full soda cup into the cup holder. A smile spread across her face as the engine purred to life.

It wasn't the roar of a sports car or the rumble of a motorcycle. It was a Corolla and sounded like one. But to her, it was the best sound. Freedom. It also meant a steady paycheck, occasional tips, and a bank account slowly increasing its size. And that would lead to her own apartment.

She owed Suzie big time for letting her crash on her couch until she could save up enough to get her own place. Jamie was tired of being dragged around to cheap hotels by her mother. More so, she was exhausted with the constant tension between them. It was a new and strange feeling to be around people who looked out for each other and helped those they could, even if they didn't have much. It definitely stood out from how things usually went in Red City and in her own family. She liked it.

She was still wary and cautious, but for the first time in a long time, she felt mildly optimistic about her life.

Turning the music up, she reversed and exited the parking lot of the scenic overlook. A pleasant thirty minutes later, she parked in front of Mama Adele's Soul Food and walked in.

"Ah, excellent timing." Berta, a thin Black woman of medium height, stapled a brown bag shut and set it on the counter. "First order of the night is ready to go."

Jamie grabbed the bag and inspected the order ticket to get the address, which she put into her phone's map app. "Alright, it's a short one. I'll be back in fifteen."

Berta smiled then picked up the phone. "Mama Adele's. Yes, we deliver." She winked at Jamie and shooed her out the door.

With a bit of pep in her step, she pushed the door open, held it for some customers as they entered, and returned to the car. It was a job, and it was hers. It was the first time in her life she'd felt like she held a bit of control over her own destiny. At least a little.

TWO
JAMIE

Jamie had just dropped off another order and was about to walk back to the car when she heard an all-too-familiar rumble growing louder—several motorcycles coming her way. They had the telltale obnoxious growl of Harleys and other large, custom road bikes. It might be any number of possibilities. There were a few biker gangs that operated in and around Red City besides the Black Suns, though they'd been the baddest. At least they had been until Dax decimated them.

Hell. It could be a friendly motorcycle club. Some middle-aged guys trying to capture a rebellious youth they'd never had. She snorted and pushed down a cynical chuckle. That was as likely as her winning the lottery without buying a ticket. Especially this time of night. And although this wasn't the worst neighborhood in the north part of Red City, it definitely wasn't rich-guy-motorcycle nice.

She stepped behind a tall, skinny evergreen tree next to the sidewalk and peeked around it in the direction of the rumble. The lights appeared to be coming toward her but were still off in the distance.

Making sure the coast was clear, she crouch-ran around the car, climbed into the driver's seat, and started the car, leaving the headlights off, though she couldn't help the brake and reverse lights.

As quickly as she could, she pulled away from the curb and goosed the gas pedal. The small car zipped along. She wished it was souped up like Suzie's Civic. Then she could haul ass. But the Corolla did well enough.

Fortunately, the road dipped as she drove down a slight hill, and she lost sight of the headlights of the bikes, which meant they could no longer see her. Spotting a decent option, she turned right, drove slowly until she had enough space to turn around, and parked behind a tall pickup truck that had been jacked well beyond utilitarian needs.

She killed the ignition and slipped out, shutting the door quietly to avoid drawing the attention of any nosy neighbors. With a wary eye, she looked at the windows of the nearby houses to ensure no one was peeking around a curtain. Once she felt sure she hadn't been noticed, she walked up next to the truck, dropped onto her belly, and rolled under it. The high clearance made it easy. It also provided a nice clear view of the road she'd just ducked off.

Her timing was perfect. The rumble grew louder, and the road lit up with headlights. As they rolled by, she lost count of how many there were. And despite how good her supernaturally enhanced wolf-shifter eyes were, she couldn't pick out any distinguishing marks on either the bikers or their bikes in the back and forth of light and shadow.

She groaned quietly as a thought intruded on her. If she was smart, she'd wait until the night was silent and the bikers were long gone. But smart wasn't something she'd been accused of being too much lately.

"Fuck," she mumbled to herself.

Carefully, she crawled her way backward until she was in between her car and the pickup truck and stood up. She kept low and slow to avoid notice and got back into the driver's seat.

As soon as the last biker passed, she started the car and backed away from the pickup. Leaving the headlights off, she pulled onto the road and turned after the bikers.

"This is a terrible idea." She reached to the center of the console and turned the radio off so she could concentrate more fully. And since it was summer, she opened the windows. The pleasantly warm evening air, ripe with the scent of flowers and trees, mixed with the exhaust of the passing motorcycles and flooded the cabin of the car. The open windows also turned the volume up on the loud engines, which was the real reason she'd opened the windows.

But for now, she didn't need to worry about following them based on sound; the swarm of headlights in front of her were easy enough to follow on the straight road. She had no idea where they might be going.

She didn't know this part of town at all, save for a few delivery trips she'd done over this way. She'd spent most of her life in a different part of Red City. Her main adventures into other neighborhoods and the surrounding environs had been with her friend Cory, when they did their wolf runs and followed them with a trip to some burger joint he'd heard of and wanted to try.

The thought of Cory brought a brief pang of loss. Once he had gotten wrapped up in the chaos her father's gambling debts had caused, his mother forced him to cut off contact with Jamie and moved them out of town. She still hadn't heard from him. Not an email or a text or a phone call. And that hurt even more.

Fighting back a burn in her eyes, she shook her head and took a deep breath. Concentrate. Bikers.

Up ahead, taillights flared to life as the bikers put on their brakes and slowed. A surge of adrenaline zipped through her veins. She hoped they hadn't spotted her tailing them. Maybe she should have turned on the headlights. If they spotted a vehicle following them with the lights off, it would probably look more suspicious than just a random car being on the same road—suspicious enough that they might investigate.

She made a snap decision and flicked on the headlights. In front of her, the bikes began turning at an intersection, splitting into two groups. One group went left while the other turned right.

"Crap, crap, crap…"

She wasn't sure where either road went, and she didn't want to make a choice that would result in her becoming trapped down some dead-end with no escape. Looking first left then right, she decided to follow the group turning right. Left took her farther north toward the edge of town. The roads could be troublesome that way. The right turn led back into town and would provide plenty of side streets to escape down if she needed them. At least that's what she hoped.

She resisted the urge to speed up. Being calm and not attracting attention was the wiser move on a road that originated in bad decisions. But she couldn't trust that this huge group of bikers weren't the ones looking to kill her and her new friends. She might have been cynically naive about a lot of the deepest, darkest parts of Red City, but she was learning fast. This many bikers riding together was probably no coincidence. They likely announced the resumption of hostilities after the last narrow victory.

Bad men rarely gave up when they got their asses kicked. They just rounded up more bad men and tried again. It was only when the good people got complacent that the bad guys stood a chance at victory. And even then...

Once she made her decision and her turn, she felt slightly more confident...for a few minutes. Until the next choice.

Although the bikers didn't split up again, they did move onto smaller roads that led into the really bad part of town. Carjackings weren't common in Red City, but they weren't unheard of. She'd hate to lose the car she'd been entrusted with. If the bikers didn't reach their destination soon, she'd have to cut off her pursuit and let her better-decision-making skills take control again.

She was considering her options when the bikers slowed and turned into a fenced-off compound. Quickly, she grabbed her phone, opened the map app, and pinned her current location. Now she just had to make good her getaway.

She kept her eyes forward, although she did add a bit of an angle to her head so she could keep a watch out of the corner of her eye. Peripheral vision was better than nothing.

As the bikes rolled into the compound, she saw some people walking out of the buildings. A brief flash of white highlighted in the headlights of the bikes drew her attention. Risking a quick look, her jaw dropped, and she inhaled a gasp of air. A large white dot the size of a fist with bent lines radiating from the edge stood out in stark contrast to the black leather vest it was stuck on.

It was the logo of the Black Suns.

They were back, and there were a lot of them.

THREE

DAX

Dax pulled up to the bar in his black 1965 Lincoln Continental and parked along the street in front of Mama Adele's restaurant. He didn't like that he'd been called in to the bar on a rare night off. Sighing, he climbed out of the car and shut the door with a loud *whoomp* that sounded too loud in the quiet night.

It was now after the bar's closing, so he pulled the keys from his pocket and let himself in. A bit of light trickled down the hallway that led to the beer cooler, the office, and the tearoom. He heard the slight murmur of conversation.

"It's me," he called out.

The pocket door into the tearoom slid open. "Hey, Dax. We're back here. Grab a bottle of whiskey," Little Suzie replied.

He wondered who "we" was, but he'd find out soon enough. "There's one behind the bar in there."

Suzie scoffed. "I don't like that one. It tastes like kelpie jizz."

"What?" He wasn't sure he'd heard her correctly.

"You heard me. That Islay stuff tastes like stanky Band-Aids and kelpie jizz. Grab a bourbon."

He wasn't going to argue Suzie's tasting notes. He had no idea what kelpie jizz tasted like nor did he want to find out why Suzie knew, though it was probably something she'd made up for comedic effect. He still didn't always get human humor. Most of the time he lacked a lot of the cultural touchpoints to get the reference or the basis for the jokes, and by the time he dug through the memories trapped inside the brain of the biker body he'd hijacked, even if the reference was there, the moment would have passed, and he still wouldn't have gotten the joke anyway.

He grabbed a decent bourbon from behind the bar and headed to the tearoom. Jamie Rodriguez, a tallish, young Latina woman of eighteen with short black hair, sat on one side of the long, communal table that ran down the center of the tearoom. Suzie, a short, chubby Black woman, sat opposite her. Suzie was in her mid-twenties. He didn't remember her exact age. He hadn't filled her out hire paperwork, Tomi had.

If Jamie was here in his bar at this time of night, it probably wasn't good news. She generally avoided him. No doubt the eighteen-year-old, who'd seen him commit wholesale slaughter many times in his skeletal form, was scared of him, especially since she'd shot him once. He'd forgiven her for it. It hadn't truly been her fault.

Setting the bottle on the table, he went behind the bar along the back wall and picked up three whiskey drams he kept there so he wouldn't always have to fetch them from the front if he or Tomi wanted a whiskey.

"Grab four. Tomi will be here too," Suzie said.

She'd called them both in. He didn't like that. It meant something bad was likely in the wind. Little Suzie had only been working for him for a few months now, but Tomi's cousin was already a fixture in his business life and had done amazing work as a wheel woman to keep Jamie alive during their escape from the bikers at Tallulah's bar. And Suzie was Tomi's family, the daughter of Adele's sister, which made her part of his family since Adele and Tomi had adopted him when he turned up in Red City as a freshly exiled entity.

Without speaking, he set the glasses down and filled them, sliding two toward Jamie and Suzie. A moment later, Tomi slid the door open and closed on his way in. As he moved into the room, heading to the side of the table Jamie sat on, Dax handed him one of the glasses, then sat next to Suzie.

As soon as his butt hit the bench, Dax threw back the shot of whiskey in one go and refilled his glass. "OK. Hit me with the bad news."

Tomi followed Dax's example with his own shot. "I don't know, it could be good news…that called us in here…after closing. Yeah, that could be it."

Dax shook his head slowly at his friend.

Jamie took a quick sip, grimacing a little as she set down her glass, and inhaled deeply. "The Black Suns are back in town."

"Are you sure?" Dax asked.

She nodded and frowned. "And there are a lot of them."

"Well, fuck."

Tomi filled up his glass again. "You said it."

FOUR

DAX

Dax pulled his phone out and began firing off texts. The first went to Boudreaux, warning him to keep an eye out for any bikers. He had a huge network of people he could tap into, plus he'd always been very useful as an ally. The next went to Madame Delphine, inviting her to tea. The gris-gris she'd made him had proven themselves during the last few escapades. Maybe she'd have something interesting to offer in their next round of hostilities with the bikers.

He also fired one off to The Rat—the strange man who controlled at least most of the city's rats along with the weird warren of tunnels under the city where he and the rats lived. They'd had been invaluable allies. The Rat had finally come to trust Dax enough to give him his phone number.

Last, he sent a text to Ragnar. He was no friend to the wolf shifter bikers and had run afoul of them when they'd taken over his friend's roadside dive outside of town. Dax didn't have Tallulah's number, so he asked Ragnar to relay the message to the rest of his band and associates.

Dax'd sent them each a request to meet up so they could all talk over the potential threat to their disparate interests. Compared to where he'd started at the beginning of the year, he'd come across an impressive list of people in his ongoing war with the bikers. Going it alone wasn't an option anymore, not that it had been a very effective one to begin with.

Practically as soon as he hit send on the last message, his phone buzzed in his hand. He nearly dropped it in surprise. It was Ragnar.

Dax answered the call. "Hello?"

"Hey, Dax. Just got your message, obviously."

"You're up late."

"Yeah, just finished a show. Anyway, thanks for the heads up. I won't be able to make a meeting. Me and the band are in Texas right now on a tour."

"I'm sorry to hear that." He paused for a minute. "Sorry, that sounded odd. I hope your tour is going well but was hoping to have you here, if you know what I mean."

Ragnar chuckled. "No worries. I know what you meant. We've seen a few of those Black Suns bastards down here but not many. If we hear anything, I'll be sure to reach out."

"I appreciate it, and take care of yourself. You're all alone way down there with no quick help."

"I know, man. But thanks for the warning."

"Can you relay the message to Tallulah?" He probably could just call the bar's business line and get her, but he had no idea if the police had the all hardlines tapped—his, Tallulah's, and likely Delphine's too.

"You can do it yourself. I'll send you the contact as soon as I hang up."

"Thanks. I appreciate it." Dax hoped he kept the disappointment from his voice. Ragnar and his crew were good to have in a scrap. Dax's list of allies had grown over the last few months, but it was still a small list. "And good luck on the tour."

"Thanks, I'll catch ya later." Ragnar hung up.

A moment later, Dax's phone vibrated with a message announcement. Tallulah's contact had arrived. So, he sent her a message. At the moment, that was the best he could do.

"OK. As soon as I hear from everyone else, I'll let you know if we're going to have a meetup." He sat back down. "Now show me where this compound is."

FIVE

DAX

After Dax sent the others home, he sat in his Lincoln and stared at his phone, scrolling through the map and location Jamie had given him. He thought he had a route that would get him close enough without passing right by it. Word of the car he drove had probably been sent to the rest of the gang, and a classic car like his wasn't exactly common, so he didn't want to be seen driving by the bikers' new hideout.

Starting the car, he pulled onto the street and followed the winding directions to the location he wanted. It didn't take him long; it wasn't too far from the bar compared to their usual haunts on the other side of town. That worried him.

So far they'd largely avoided the north part of town in numbers. He'd hoped they'd keep to their part of Red City. But if they were spreading out, it would make it even more difficult to track them down. Now they had two spots on the north side of Red City.

After he parked, he grabbed a pair of binoculars from the glove compartment and stepped into the night. There was no sidewalk along the unimproved road, but he figured the bikers would avoid riding down this kind of street so it would be a slightly safer option.

The gravel and nasty potholes wouldn't be kind to motorcycles or their riders.

Most of the houses he walked by looked abandoned, with partially boarded-up windows and doors. He counted maybe a handful of windows that hadn't been broken out. As he approached the section of pavement that ran in front of the compound, he took a left to walk parallel to it, putting more weed-choked lots and more abandoned houses between himself and the bikers. Once he drew level with their compound according to his map, he walked through the knee-high weeds and by the side of the ramshackle house into the back yard.

Unfortunately, the fence separating the house from the one behind it—the one that faced the bikers' compound—was in solid shape. Or at least there weren't any slats missing.

He stared at the fence for a moment, then reached into the aether and pulled out his scythe. He'd corroded metal bars before, hastening their death. An old, unmaintained wooden fence should be no problem. In short order, he turned five slats into decayed debris. With the scythe returned to the aether, he ducked under the cross-beam and into the backyard.

Now that he was so close to the compound, he found the shadier side of the house and crept along the wall, ducking low and trying to blend in with the weeds. Once he hit the front corner of the house, he had a clear view. He lowered himself onto his knees and put the binoculars to his eyes as he poked his head above the weed line.

Sweeping his gaze along the front fence of the compound, he found several bikers patrolling it. They didn't appear to be carrying any machine guns, but they no doubt had handguns concealed somewhere on their persons. Concertina wire ran along the top of the fence. There'd be no getting in by climbing over. Even if he avoided slicing his flesh open on the razor wire, he couldn't move fast enough to avoid detection from the patrols.

In the background, there were several smaller buildings surrounding two larger ones. Dozens of motorcycles were neatly lined up in front of the two larger buildings. There were a few unmarked vans as well. If there was a body for every bike, it meant there'd be many more than he'd faced before, even when he'd rousted them out of their own bar. And there was at least one more compound nearby. Jamie had said when they'd split up, this group looked slightly bigger, but not by a lot. That definitely wasn't good.

Shadows moved across the well-lit windows of the two large buildings. A few people milled about outside. The occasional bark of a loud laugh broke the silence, but that was it. He couldn't hear anything they were talking about. Not from across the street.

Well, that wasn't exactly true.

He could detach his spirit from his body and drift across the street to spy on the bikers and see what they were doing. He'd done it before when he'd rescued Jamie and her parents from the biker bar. But he'd had Tomi there to keep an eye on him and make sure nothing bad happened to his unattended body. He'd only done it one other time, but that had only been for a few moments.

He stared at the compound and the bikers, his unoccupied hand sitting on his thigh, his index finger tapping out a steady rhythm as he thought over the options. What was the point of coming all the way out here if he went home empty handed? He already knew there were a bunch of bikers here. He didn't need to see that with his own eyes.

"This is a dumb idea," he mumbled to himself.

Getting up, he crouch-walked backward so he could keep an eye on the fence and ensure he'd gone unnoticed. He didn't want to do what he was planning if they saw something moving about and sent some guys over to investigate.

Once he cleared the house, he stepped through the hole he'd made in the fence and looked around the backyard. There. A scraggly rhododendron bush dominated the back corner of the lot.

By the time he got situated, he had plenty of scrapes and raw spots from crawling under the bush. He should have switched to his skeletal form first, but what was done was done.

Still erring on the side of caution, he sat quietly for ten minutes, though it felt like an hour. Silence ruled the two yards. It was time.

SIX

DAX

Dax took a moment to ensure he'd created a firmly anchored tether to his corporeal form. He didn't want to risk the death of his body or transform into some sort of unhoused being. He didn't know if he'd deteriorate and become like those trapped spirits at the morgue. That was something he'd have to deal with eventually, but right now, survival was at the top of his priority list.

He gave a last tug on the tether. Satisfied it would hold, he slipped his spirit out of his body.

The world, already desaturated by the low light of the night, slipped even more into the realm of the monochromatic. Before heading to the compound, he lifted into the air and surveyed his surroundings. He didn't see another living soul save for the bikers.

A humorous thought flitted across his mind as he looked down at his motionless body. He was essentially a balloon, floating above his own head and attached by a thin thread. He'd have to be more careful than the proverbial kid with a balloon. If he drifted away, the problem wouldn't be as simple to fix as buying another one or simply getting over the ephemeral interaction.

He descended to the ground and floated through the hole in the fence. He waited at the roadside for a car to pass, then crossed over to the compound. Since he was in the aether, he paused to inspect the fence. There appeared to be something more than steel wires woven into the mesh of a chain link fence—something magical.

He couldn't tell what it was, but it extended through the entire fence and into the concertina wire at the top. So to avoid it, he went up instead of through, floating clear of the fence and landing on the other side.

He thought about walking the perimeter to see if he could learn anything from the guards working the fence line, but decided he didn't really have the time to be that thorough. He made his way toward the largest of the buildings—the one that seemed to be getting the most traffic.

Weaving his way through the motorcycles—more out of habit than necessity—he stopped by the door and waited until someone opened the door, then slipped in after them.

The room looked like a communal space with card tables and folding chairs spread about. Mostly, the tables had beer and liquor bottles on them. Bags of fast food rested on a few. Everything about the place looked temporary and hasty.

He couldn't tell if it was just him, or the general feel of the room, but a low level of tension pervaded. Eyes were wary as they flicked around. Shoulders were a bit higher than they should be, and there was a brittle, almost false, quality to the outbursts of laughter.

He examined the men and their clothing, focusing mostly on tattoos, vests, and coats—all the places where their logos or group affiliation might be marked. Everyone in the room wore the white "Black Sun" logo from which the club got its name. But some wore variations of the design he hadn't seen before.

The Black Suns had brought in people from another chapter since they were underpowered after running afoul of Dax the first time they'd made an attempt on his life. It seemed the difference in markings represented other chapters. There were enough commonalities to pick out maybe two or three other chapters, besides the local markings he did recognize.

That explained the tension.

The Black Suns were a Norse, pagan, white supremacist, wolf shifter, outlaw motorcycle gang, which was a whole lot of identity. Ostensibly, they were all part of the same club, but they were explosive, violent men—and the crowd was entirely made up of men—who didn't know each other well, if at all in many cases. A misspoken word or a too-challenging eye could lead to violence and chaos. These men no doubt believed in the false "alpha wolf" narrative and were trying to size each other up in relation to their own positions within their own clubs.

Working his way through the crowd, Dax looked for side rooms or an office where he might find someone in leadership. Though this wasn't something he normally thought, he really wanted to find Sigur or Ivar. They were the two leaders he knew. They'd be the ones to listen in on for the best intelligence. Unfortunately, the few side rooms he found seemed to be unoccupied. He'd have to circulate through the main room and see what he could pick up.

Eavesdropping had never been a hobby of his. He did it a bit at the bar, but mostly because it was a small space and people tended to talk loudly in a bar with loud music, especially after a few drinks.

He wandered from table to table, sifting through the minutiae of small talk as burly bikers got to know people from other chapters. In a lot of ways, it reminded him of some of the first dates he'd witnessed at the bar, until he reached a table near the back of the room next to one of the doors he'd checked earlier.

The three men sitting at the table weren't relaxed or even feigning it, like so many of the others were. They leaned across the table, their heads close together and their drinks largely forgotten except for the occasional quick sip that felt more perfunctory or fidgety, as opposed to a desire to drink.

A white man without a beard drained his glass and filled it from a bottle sitting in the middle of the table. He lifted the glass but didn't take a drink, instead looking around the room. "I'm not sure I've seen this many chapters in one place that wasn't a national rally."

"When will Sigur and Ivar get back?" one of them asked.

A particularly shaggy bearded biker replied, "Same time I said five minutes ago when you asked."

"Fuck you."

"Just relax. They're meeting with a local power broker who can provide us some extra protection."

A third one patted his vest, revealing a hard, straight shape under the leather. "What do we need extra protection for? I have this."

"Not everything can be solved with bullets, even those fancy magic ones they've been handing out. We were told to sit tight and keep everyone in check. That's what I'm going to do. Now why don't you calm down and keep your shirt on. I didn't come here to get dead—either from our target or Ivar and Sigur. They are wound up tight, and it's our jobs as the enforcers to do what we're told and set a good example."

The biker who'd been complaining shut his mouth and ground his teeth, the muscles in his cheeks flexing. The one with the thick beard raised an eyebrow, and that was all it took to quell the moment of near rebellion.

Dax would have to keep an eye on that one if they came up against each other in a direct engagement. Fortunately for him, he didn't rely purely on muscles during physical engagements. Years of reaping Earth's finest warriors—many of whom didn't wish to go quietly—had honed his direct combat skills to a razor's edge nearly as sharp as his scythe. And that was before he brought any of his magic to bear, though his magical power was severely curtailed compared to his glory days.

He reached for his pocket to check for the time. But he had no pocket and nothing in it. Looking around for a clock, he only found blank, beat-up walls. The bikers hadn't added any of the homier touches one might put into a new space. Then again, he doubted this would be their new clubhouse. This was just a gathering spot for the many out of towners coming in to aid the local boys.

Wanting to check the time to see how close dawn was, Dax moved around, looking for an exposed wrist with a watch or a cell phone with the screen facing up. He wasn't sure if he could maintain the tether in daylight, so he thought he'd better make sure he had a plan in case it was near dawn. The only times he'd tried leaving his body had been at night. He shouldn't have an issue in the light, but he'd only been exploring his powers in his human form for a few months. Everything he tried was an attempt to see what power was left and how he could use it to protect himself and his friends without pushing over the unknown line his watchers kept.

Finally, someone flipped their phone over to check something and he was able to see the time. He needed to hang out as long as he could. But despite lacking his mortal flesh, he felt the urge to yawn. The tether holding him to his body also felt like it was getting heavier. With still a couple hours to go until dawn, he wasn't sure if he'd be able to make it until then.

SEVEN

DAX

As Dax was deciding what to do, the issue was solved for him. Ivar, Sigur, and a third, unknown biker walked into the room. Sigur was a bit taller than the other two men, his dirty blond hair freshly cropped on the sides and long on top. His beard was longer than the last time Dax had seen him.

Sigur appeared to have added more tattoos. Dax couldn't see any skin free from them on the muscular biker with the dirty-blond hair. The third looked like a barrel of a man, resembling a professional strongman. He had a long, brown beard that was split in two, with each section braided. The greasy brown hair coming out of the bottom of the black bandana he wore on his head was gathered in a ponytail and tied with several thongs, gathering it into a long rope that ran down to his mid back. His faded black T-shirt was slightly too small, and his stomach hung out of the bottom of it. All in all, he looked like the classic stereotype of a dirtbag, outlaw biker.

All the bikers quieted as they entered, all eyes training onto them as they maneuvered their way through the room toward a door Dax had guessed might be an office. He shot through the tables and waited by the edge of the door. This was too good of an opportunity to waste.

Sigur fished a set of keys from his pocket and unlocked the door, pulling it open. As soon as there was enough space, Dax hustled in and moved to the back corner. Two of these men were likely magical in some way. Ivar was probably the runesmith enchanting the bullets and other mundane weapons Dax had been encountering.

He didn't have a read on what kind of power Sigur had, just that Jamie had felt it and commented on its dark nature. Though it could have been entirely the man's aura. He oozed sinister and malevolent energy. Dax resisted the urge to probe into the man's life thread to discover what kind of power he might possess. If Sigur could work with death or the spirit world, messing around with his essence might tip him off to Dax's presence.

The third man felt almost mundane in comparison. He was certainly a wolf shifter like all the rest of the men, but that was probably all he was. His power derived from his swagger and confidence, and, no doubt, a healthy dose of violent reputation. The eyes looking at him as he passed through the room had held their fair share of fear.

Dax just wished he knew what positions they held within the overall structure of the gang. Ivar was likely the de facto president of the local chapter after Jamie had killed the last president to protect Dax. Sigur had breezed into town with his own gang to help Ivar reestablish the Black Suns in Red City, but Dax didn't know if he was a president in his own right, some sort of general fixer, or something else entirely.

The third man was a complete mystery. Hopefully the trio of bikers were feeling particularly loquacious tonight and would reveal a healthy bit of information Dax needed.

"Do you trust the bitch?" the man with the belly asked, plopping down into a wooden chair at a round table. The chair groaned under the stress of the man's bulk.

Sigur held up a hand. "Let me secure the room."

He pulled out a bag from inside his vest and returned to the door, locking it. Then he dipped his fingers into the bag and pulled out some sparkly dust and sprinkled it along the floor in front of the door and then along the top of the door's frame. He stalked across the room to the room's lone window and placed some more dust along the bottom of the window and the top of frame. After that, he stopped in each of the room's four corners, dropping a pinch of dust into each spot.

Something magical snapped into place, straining the tether anchoring Dax to his body. He didn't like that, but he could deal with a little discomfort in the name of proper espionage.

He pulled his attention away from the magical feeling. It wouldn't do to miss something important because he was distracted by trivialities.

Sigur had his phone pressed to his ear. "Stand by the door and listen. Text if you hear us or not." He hung up. "Hey, fuck you!"

Dax startled at the loud yell. Everyone in the other room should have heard it. This wasn't a soundproof booth. And everyone in the building were wolf shifters. Even if they weren't in their wolf forms, their human forms still had enhanced hearing.

After what felt like forever, Sigur's phone buzzed. He typed a message back, a wicked grin spreading across his lips.

"Well?" the man with the belly asked. Ivar, standing behind a chair with his arms folded across his chest, tilted his head and raised an eyebrow.

"Didn't hear a thing," Sigur replied.

Ivar nodded and sat down. "At least we know the dust works. She might be mildly trustworthy, at least as much as one of her type can be." He said the last with a bit of mild distaste threading through his words.

"What about the other piece?" the third man asked.

Sigur snorted, joining the other two men at the table. "We'll see, though it'll be hard to confirm its effectiveness. Unless we can catch us a ghost to test it on."

"I can go make us one," the third man said, adding a guffaw at his own violent humor.

"I'm not sure any of the boys would volunteer for that," Ivar added, grabbing a bottle of whiskey off a nearby decrepit sideboard. He opened the sideboard and pulled out three glasses, spreading them around the table and filling them.

"We're going to have to trust her. For now," Sigur said, taking a solid drink from his glass. "Mutual self-interest and a recommendation from our paycheck."

"I still don't like it." The third man drained his entire glass in one go, grabbing the bottle for a refill.

"Neither do I, Grinder, but our employer is getting impatient and the national chapter told us to get the fucking job done if we want to keep our heads attached. We've all done shit we don't like before," Ivar said.

Sigur nodded slowly. "Enemy of my enemy."

"Well, before we say anything else, set up the fucking crystal." Grinder rolled his eyes and mumbled, "I can't believe we're using a fucking crystal."

Sigur snorted a half chuckle, one side of his mouth tipping up into the barest of smiles. Reaching into his vest, he pulled out a large chunk of crystal about the size of his fist. It appeared to be clear with milky veins running through it. Cupping it in both hands and holding it up to his lips, he mumbled something Dax couldn't hear.

A pulse of power and a flash of white light emanated from the crystal. As the light hit Dax, he felt momentarily exposed. Sigur carefully set the crystal in the middle of the table. The other two men, their eyes open a little wider, leaned away from the table. All three stared at the crystal as a faint point of red light blossomed in the center of the crystal, growing gradually until it throbbed blood red.

"Fuck…" Grinder said quietly.

"I guess it does work," Ivar said. He picked up his glass of whiskey and emptied it before slamming it down onto the table with a loud *thunk*. The table groaned a little from the violence of the motion. Dax was surprised the glass didn't shatter.

Whatever the crystal did, they seemed impressed by it, but it made Dax nervous.

Sigur stood up and walked to the door, opening it carefully so as not to disturb the line of powder. "Everyone, shut the fuck up and get packed. We're bugging out. This place is compromised. You'll split into three groups of equal numbers. One will follow me, one

Ivar, and one Grinder." No one responded. "Now, you stupid fucks! And remember, don't say anything. Not a word until we're safely in our new spot."

Chairs scraped across the floor, some clattering as they were tipped over in the bikers' haste to execute the order.

"What's going on?" one of the bikers asked. Someone shut him up with a fist to the mouth. Once he picked himself off the ground, he didn't say another word.

Sigur returned to the table and finished his whiskey, setting the glass down and picking the crystal up. He stashed it back in the inside pocket of his vest and exited the room, careful to step over the line of powder at the door.

Whatever the crystal did, it had caused them to abandon their base. The only thing that could have done that was if they'd felt like it was exposed in some manner. And it was. Dax was there.

He wanted to grab the crystal and turn it to powder, but he probably couldn't in his current state. Before the door was closed on him, he moved toward it but ran into an invisible wall. It knocked him back. Stepping forward carefully, he felt along the edges of it. It perfectly covered the door.

He ran to the window. It too was blocked.

The powder caught his eye. Apparently it was more than just a sound blocker, it was also blocking him. He tried to push the powder aside or break its plane, but it was as immovable as the pyramids. He ran back across the room to the door. He tried to push the dust aside with what would have been his foot. Again, nothing.

Getting down onto his stomach, he tried to blow the dust aside, but he had no breath. He wasn't thinking straight. Taking a split second to calm himself, he exhaled mentally and gathered his resolve, along with some power from the aether. Using his power, he formed it into a wedge and pushed it toward the line of powder on the ground. His magic dissipated as soon as it met the line of the powder.

In front of him, Sigur grabbed the doorknob and slowly pulled it shut, leaving the line undisturbed. The bolt clicking home felt heavy and final. He was trapped.

EIGHT

J amie woke earlier than normal, despite the late night waiting for Dax to show up so she could tell him about the bikers. She worked mostly in the afternoon and evenings, delivering tasty soul food from Mama Adele's, so she normally didn't worry about being up bright and early. But today she had her own mission. She was headed to the main campus of Red City Community College to speak with an admissions counselor and find out how much it would cost to enroll, or if they might have scholarships available.

She had good enough grades to get into a fancy four-year school, but she just didn't have the money or the life stability thanks to all the issues her dad's gambling debts had caused her. And her mother would be no help. She was barely surviving on her crappy job, trying to save enough to get an apartment of her own. In the meantime, she was bouncing from long-term motel to long-term motel, but that burned a lot of money. Being poor cost a lot.

Jamie quietly showered and fixed a simple breakfast of cereal and oat milk along with a little peach yogurt. Suzie was still asleep. Jamie split groceries with Suzie, but a lot of the time they ate at Mama Adele's, since they both basically got to eat there for free. The food was fantastic, and the price was right. Although it wasn't a hamburger, Cory would have liked to have had access to the food at a place like that.

The thought of Cory brought a momentary pang of sadness and regret. She missed the big idiot, though the forced separation and his mother's betrayal still stung bitterly. But that sting didn't bite quite so hard as it first did. Suzie had turned out to be not only a willing roommate but a good friend. At least that was the way things seemed to be going. Suzie regularly asked her to hang out, inviting her to house parties or to events at places where people who weren't yet the legal drinking age were welcome. She was building a new life.

Jamie couldn't thank the Chenevert family and Dax enough. She was still scared shitless of Dax, but it turned out that the Grim Reaper, or whatever the hell he was, was alright. From what she'd been able to gather, he'd been another of the strays the Cheneverts had picked up—like Jamie—and given a home and a place in the world. Although, there was something deeper in the relationship than charity leading to friendship. Whatever had brought them together wasn't her business, no matter how curious she was. Digging into Dax's background was likely to lead to nowhere but trouble, of which she'd had too much already.

Her dad's debts had forced her connection to Dax, and she'd somehow survived it and come out on the other end better off, all things considered. She wasn't about to look a gift horse in the mouth. She'd respect the secrets of her tentative new friends. If they wanted to let her in on them, that wasn't for her to decide. She'd be loyal, work hard, and be grateful for their kindness. That was the least she owed them.

It was a nice summer late morning when she emerged from the one-bedroom apartment Suzie graciously shared with her. Jamie had to admit, the couch was pretty comfortable, but she longed to get a tiny place of her own and a bed to go in it.

She rounded the corner of the building, walking briskly down the sidewalk to where she'd parked the Toyota. She had a few extra bucks in her pocket and was going to stop by her favorite new coffee shop for a latte or a cappuccino, if she felt extra fancy. She didn't know what the difference was, but she enjoyed both drinks. After discovering the shop, she'd thought maybe getting a job as a barista would be a good way to get some extra money. Assuming she could make her schedules mesh.

A smile bloomed on her face when she saw the Corolla, but it disappeared a moment later as a bit of fright and confusion replaced the good feelings. A large crow stood on the roof, staring at her. It was the largest crow she'd ever seen, but it didn't quite look like a raven. It lacked the frilly feathers along the beak. At least that what she thought the difference was.

"Shoo!" She flicked her fingers at the crow. "Go away."

The bird just stared at her.

"Fine. You'll fly away when I drive off." She took a step forward, but the crow unfurled its wings, flapping them menacingly, and squawked loudly at her. "Damnit."

She took another step, but the crow hopped forward. A faint red tinge glowed in its eyes. She swallowed as her mouth grew dry. "Please. I have things to do."

She didn't know why she was trying to reason with the animal. She was a wolf shifter and could chase it off, even if it pecked and scratched her. Even in human form, she was faster, stronger, and could heal better than a mundane human. But she'd heard crows held a grudge if people were cruel to them, teaching other crows about the bad human. She had no desire to be the enemy of a murder of crows. And something about this crow seemed extra... menacing.

She took a step back, hoping the crow would deescalate and maybe fly away. Instead, the crow hopped onto the ground between her and the car. She took another step back. The crow hopped forward several steps.

"Come on..." Jamie backed up again, and the crow followed with its hopping gate.

Her day had started out so well, but now it was going downhill and in the oddest way possible. For each step back, the crow took a few hops toward her to keep up with her. Tired of playing this game, she turned around and dashed off, running to the door leading into the apartment building. She thought that would be it. She'd return to Suzie's apartment and wait until the bird got bored and left.

The sound of flapping wings chasing her drew a bit of fear into her annoyance. Why was the crow so fixated on her? She'd thought it was unusually big, but the red eyes and its behavior caused her more than a little anxiety. Could a bird carry rabies?

She jammed her hand into her pocket and pulled out her keys, sliding to a stop in front of the door, and fumbled as she tried to poke the key into the lock. Yanking the door open, she darted in, pulling it shut behind her but not fast enough. The crow dove into the small gap and turned at the last moment to avoid hitting her in the head.

Panting with effort and frustration, she ran by the elevator, hitting the button on her way by. As soon as she reached the door that led to the stairwell, she pulled it open and ran in. The crow, still in pursuit, flew through the door and around her.

Instead of dashing up the stairs, she used her grip on the door handle to stop and reverse her direction, running out of the stairwell and back to the lobby. The elevator door had nearly closed. She squeezed in without hitting the edges and triggering the door's safety reopen mechanism and slammed into the back wall, barely getting her hands out in front of her in time.

Closing her eyes and panting, she turned around and slumped against the wall, letting her back hold her weight against the material covering the wall. She stood still for a moment. The only sound in the elevator was her heart and her breathing calming down. She stood straight and opened her eyes.

"Fuck!" she bit out between clenched teeth.

The crow stood on the floor in front of the door, staring up at her with its head tilted to the side. It was almost a human gesture that seemed to encompass both a curiosity as to why she was running away and mocking laughter, as if a crow could laugh. Sighing, she reached forward and pushed the button for Suzie's floor.

Maybe Suzie could figure out what to do.

NINE

JAMIE

Jamie walked calmly around the crow and exited the elevator, striding purposefully but not frantically to the door. Behind her, the crow's taloned feet clicked on the tile floor as it followed her. This time, she tried patience and unlocked the door then slid in, doing her best to block the narrow opening she created. She shut the door quickly, exhaling a sigh of relief.

"Um, what's going on there, roomie?" Suzie asked.

Jamie squeaked and hopped a little.

Suzie chuckled. "A bit jumpy this morning?"

Before Jamie responded, she looked down at the ground at her feet and saw only her shoes. Maybe she'd finally evaded the crow. "Sorry. Just… The freakiest thing happened. I went to my car, but a giant crow was on top of it. Then it chased me into the building. It even followed me into the elevator…"

A steady tapping at the door sent a new surge of adrenaline through her body. *Tap, tap, tap, tap, tap.* Then a pause followed by another five taps.

"Jamie… What did you bring back to my apartment?" Suzie walked across the open-floor-plan kitchen and living room to stand next to Jamie. Together they stared at the door as the five taps repeated.

"Maybe it will go away if we ignore it."

Suzie, both hands wrapped around a large coffee mug, lifted it to her lips and took a drink. "Maybe. But I don't think you're that naive or hopeful."

Jamie sighed and slumped her shoulders. "No. So what do we do?"

"I don't know. I'm just a bartender. Have you pissed off something else supernatural lately?"

Jamie's brow furrowed, and she took a moment to think her way through the question. "I don't think so. Just the werewolf Nazis."

"Nazi werewolves." Suzie grinned ruefully. "What kind of Norse gods do the whole crow thing?"

"How the fuck should I know? I'm half Mexican and was raised sorta Catholic."

Suzie took another sip from her mug as they stared at the door. The crow continued tapping at the door. "Can it cross the threshold of my apartment?"

"It's a crow, not a vampire."

Tap, tap, tap, tap, tap. The tempo and volume intensified.

"It's starting to get pissed."

"Ya think?" Jamie groused. It wasn't the best idea, but she gripped the door handle and turned to catch Suzie's eye.

Suzie shrugged and took three large steps backward. Jamie pulled the door open, keeping the door in front of herself so it blocked her body. She poked her head around the side of the door.

"What do you want?" She spoke quickly, but the confidence and conviction she'd hoped to push into the words were entirely lacking.

Taking it as an invitation, the crow hopped into the room. Jamie pushed the door shut once the bird cleared the swing space, then slowly backed away from the bird.

"Holy shit!" Suzie scrambled away until the back of her legs hit the couch and she fell onto it, sloshing coffee out of her mug and onto her hands. "Fuck!" She set the mug down and wiped her hands on her shirt.

A short, curly-haired white woman with black hair and very pale skin stood in place of the crow. She wore black leather pants, a black shirt that exposed a lot of cleavage, and a leather jacket. Her eyes glowed with a faint red cast.

"It's you. What are you doing here?" Suzie asked.

"You-you know her?"

"Not really. She came into the bar looking for Dax. Pissed him off something serious." Suzie's eyes drifted wide, realizing she might have said something that could have offended their unanticipated guest.

"I am here about…Dax, as you call him," the woman said. Her voice was luxuriously husky with a hint of the spooky—the kind of spooky that slipped into Dax's voice when he was doing the reaper thing.

"Who-who are you?" Jamie asked, recovering her ability to speak.

"It is none of your concern, wolf mortal. Dax is in need of your assistance. Before this morning's dawn, the ones like you"—she jabbed a finger toward Jamie—"trapped him."

"Like me?" Jamie narrowed her eyes. "Wolf shifters?"

The woman nodded once.

Jamie's brow furrowed. "The bikers? Shit, that's bad. That's really bad."

"Calm yourself. It's not nearly that bad. They don't know he is captured and have abandoned their base and him inside it. But he must be freed before he weakens."

This all could be a trap to capture her and Suzie. They both were probably on the gang's wanted list after the shenanigans they'd both pulled during their last encounter. She didn't know the woman, but Suzie did or at least had met her once.

"Suzie?" She swallowed a mouthful of fear-induced saliva before continuing, "Do you think it's a trap?"

The woman's eyes turned redder. "Do you think I lie, little wolf?" The freaky harmonics in her voice got scarier.

"I don't think she's with the Nazi werewolves," Suzie said to

Jamie, returning her hands to her mug. "Dax didn't treat her like one of them…"

The red in their visitor's eyes dulled and a smirk pulled up one corner of her lips. "Your caution is warranted. I know Dax of old. We have not always…agreed upon things. Heed my warning or not. But he is separated from his mortal flesh, and the tether holding him to it is weakening."

Jamie's eyes flicked back and forth between Suzie and the woman. Suzie's shifted between the woman and Jamie. A decision had to be made, but the older woman didn't seem to be interested in being the one to make it. It was on Jamie's back.

"Where is he? What do we need to do?"

"He is trapped in a compound. Fence. Buildings. Dirt. From here, to the north of the setting sun. He is trapped through means of magic." The woman relaxed almost imperceptibly.

"North of the setting sun?" Jamie mused.

"Northwest of here. He wouldn't go to that compound you found without taking someone, would he?" Suzie absentmindedly took another drink of coffee, grimacing. "Too cold." She stood up and went into the kitchen to refill her mug from the carafe of her coffee maker.

"I guess he did. Are you busy, Suzie?" Jamie pulled out a chair from the small round table that sat in the corner and sat down.

"Yeah, but you and I shouldn't go there by ourselves either. The bikers may have left, but it's possible they could have come back. And I don't think either of us can deal with any magic." She pursed her lips then sighed. "I guess I'm going to have to call the manbo."

Suzie had been avoiding the subject of the voodoo priestess since the manbo had insisted she needed to have a long private conversation with Suzie after the last round of fighting was done. Jamie had asked her friend about it a couple times but had been brushed off.

"I'll let Tomi know about Dax," Jamie volunteered. She had everyone's contacts now. Since they were all so entangled because of the biker gang's violence, Tomi had insisted everyone keep in touch about anything pertinent. And now that she worked for his mom, it made even more sense that she have his number.

"Um, would you like a cup of coffee?" Suzie asked their guest, remembering her manners.

The woman, who stood near the door, relaxed a little more, the last of the red disappearing from her eyes. "Yes. That would be welcome."

Suzie fetched a mug and filled it, setting it on the counter along with a small carton of half and half. "Sugar?"

The woman picked up the carton and opened it, sniffing at the contents. "No, this should suffice." She poured some into the mug and took the offered spoon from Suzie.

Picking up her phone from the counter, Suzie excused herself to the bedroom so she could call the manbo. While the scary woman propped herself against the counter and drank her coffee, Jamie used the quiet to send a quick text to Tomi that was vague enough to not ping anyone who might be monitoring their communication, but clear enough to know something was up. Apparently Dax had been arrested and roughed up by same skeezy detective who'd grossed her out when she'd gone with her mother to identify her father's body at the city morgue. No one knew if the cops were tapping their lines or monitoring their texts, so the order of the day was caution.

Suzie reemerged a minute later. "She says to pick her up at the shop. Said she'll get some supplies ready. Not sure what that means. Did Tomi reply back?"

Jamie checked her phone. He had. "Yes." She relayed the information about the meetup to him.

"I need to go put some clothes on"—Suzie wore a pair of fuzzy pajama pants and a ratty T-shirt—"then I'll be ready to go. Help yourself to the last of the coffee, if you want." She gestured at the coffee maker then disappeared into her room.

Jamie eyed the carafe. It was nearly empty. Her plan to stop and get coffee hadn't worked out so well, and she still hadn't had any. If the woman wanted the last splash of coffee, Jamie wasn't going to get in her way. The woman scared the shit out of her. Coffee could wait.

Once Suzie was ready, they left the apartment building. But as their feet hit the sidewalk, the woman changed into a crow and flew away, squawking noisily.

TEN

DAX

It hadn't taken long for the bikers to evacuate their base. Now silence reigned over the empty building and compound. Occasionally Dax could hear a larger vehicle moving down the road outside, but they never stopped, not that he could yell to catch their attention since his lungs and vocal cords were in an abandoned yard a quarter mile away.

Whatever the powder was, it had effectively blocked him from leaving the room. Even where he found cracks in the poorly constructed walls, he was met with an invisible force that kept him contained. He really wished he had his body, if for no other reason than to be able to vocalize his screams of frustration.

Outside, a crow cawed, sounding almost like a laugh taunting him. Eventually, the bird took off, but not before flying by the window, adding the salt of its freedom to the wound of his captivity.

But the more frustrated he grew, the more difficult it became to focus. Eventually, he'd found a spot in the corner and rested, trying not to stare at the door or window. At one point his mind wandered, his thoughts being about the only thing that could leave the room, at least metaphorically, he noticed a dragging sensation from the tether attaching him to his mortal flesh. He was growing weary. His time was running out.

The longer he focused on that sensation, the more his frustration returned and bordered on something akin to panic. It was as if he were tied to a rope being pulled through a set of bars. He couldn't move no matter how much the rope was tugged. If it was possible for a discorporate spirit—that was the closest he could guess that he was—to become fidgety, he would have been wiggling uncontrollably.

Perhaps it was kind of how the spirits tethered to their dead bodies felt. It had only been a few hours for him; he couldn't imagine how bad it was for them. The days, months, or maybe even years they'd been unable to move on? It must be driving them insane.

He thought his own sanity was slipping when he heard furtive voices in the distance, but when a door banged shut and floorboards creaked nearby, he realized he wasn't alone anymore. He wanted to shout for help, that he was in the backroom, but again—no lungs.

"Careful... Let me open the door. There's something not right here," said a familiar voice.

A moment later, the office door cracked open a few inches. Fingers belonging to a Black person poked through the opening above the line of powder but didn't touch it. A disruption of the powder line was all Dax needed. Just a small break in the magical circuit. Then he'd be able to return to his body.

"OK. Don't touch this powder. Not until I've had time to examine it."

"Is it dangerous?" a man asked. Tomi. It was Tomi's voice.

"Everything could be dangerous. And I think whatever this dust is is being dangerous right now, but I doubt it's harmful to us." That was Manman Delphine.

Somehow, Tomi had found him and had brought the one person they all trusted to help with magical issues. Dax was saved. Relief washed over him, though the tugging sensation didn't recede entirely. It was still a persistent irritation that was almost impossible to ignore.

Delphine opened the door and stepped over the line.

"Is there anyone in there?" Tomi asked.

"The room appears empty—"

"What?" Panic creeped into Tomi's voice.

"I feel something powerful in the room. Something familiar. It might be Dax. It has the right...vibe. But I've never felt this aspect of him before, so I can't be one hundred percent sure." She turned around, still holding the door open. "Can he become invisible?"

"I don't think so," Tomi replied. "He can hide in shadows, but he has to generate the shadows. I mean... Well, one time he... How did he describe it? He left his body behind to scout ahead. Do you think that's what he's done?"

"You know him better than I, but that may be what happened. Then he became trapped."

"Can't he just walk out now that we've opened the door?" Tomi asked.

"I doubt it. This line has something to do with blocking the entrance."

Another voice chimed in. "A line of dust? That seems pretty weak."

It was Jamie. What was she doing here?

"The powder isn't important. It's the magic that was worked with it. It's forming a barrier that'll keep certain kinds of...energies trapped in this room."

"Can we just sweep it away?" Tomi asked.

"I don't know. I want to examine it and the room before we make any rash decisions. I don't want Dax or one of us to get hurt. I'm going to close the door and look around, so give me a few minutes to come up with an educated solution. Also, if anyone can find me a container of some sort, I'd like to take a few samples of this powder home to study." Delphine didn't wait for an affirmative response. She closed the door gently and strolled around the room, her hands clasped behind her back.

The tall Black trans woman was dressed down compared to her normal colorful style of dress. She wore stretchy black workout pants and a flowy black, long-sleeved T-Shirt. Tomi and Jamie must have caught her pre-workout. Or she'd come prepared to run if she had to.

Dax tried to be patient, but the weariness and the constant tug of the tether burned away any patience he had left. He wasn't sure how much more time he could sustain out of his body.

She stopped at each corner and the window, making appreciative noises. When someone knocked diffidently on the door, she returned to it and opened it.

Jamie held a spoon and plastic baggie. "I cleaned these as best as I could."

Suzie, just visible in the background, laughed. "Baggie was full of weed. Smelled like cheap crap, so we just dumped it."

Delphine chuckled indulgently. "It'll do."

She took the items and returned to the window, opening the baggie and holding it just under the bottom of the windowsill. Careful to avoid spilling more than necessary, she scooped as much of the powder into the baggie as she could until she'd cleaned up the windowsill from one end to the other. Some of the tension holding him in the room dissipated. He still wouldn't be able to get out through the window. His tether had come in through the front door and the office door.

She carefully sealed up the baggie and put it in her pocket. Then she called out, "It's OK now. If you find a broom, let's get the threshold cleared off. If he really is trapped in here, removing the powder line will break the magical hold on the room and open the door for him."

"We'll need to open this door and the front one. I think he has to move in reverse, or go out the way he came in." Tomi stepped in and held the office door open as Jamie swept up the line of powder. Suzie held a small dustpan in front of Jamie's sweepings. "I'm not sure, but that was how it seemed when he did it last time. Suzie, can you go hold open the front door?"

As soon as the powder on the floor was cleared and the main door opened, the tugging on the tether yanked him out of the building, though the yard, over the fence, and across the street.

ELEVEN

DAX

Dax reentered his body and started coughing. His mouth was as dry as a desert, and his muscles ached. When his eyes popped open, he was forced to slam them closed. The sun beaming down on his face was too bright for eyes that had gone dormant during the late hours of the night.

He tried to move but yelped when his hamstring cramped. Rolling to his side, he tried to straighten out his leg. Once he got the cramp calmed down, he lay on his side and took slow, deliberate motions to get the blood flowing through his body properly. His neck was going to be a problem spot. A knot had formed thanks to his head being flopped over at an odd angle while he rested.

Thankfully, the rhododendron bush had shaded him and still did. He wasn't ready to crawl out from under the bush quite yet. That might have been more movement than his body could sustain.

In his pocket, his phone buzzed and stopped, then started again. With a groan, he twisted enough that he could pull his cell from his pocket. It was Tomi, so he answered it.

"Are you alive?" Tomi asked anxiously.

He grunted instead of answering and tried to moisten his dry mouth. "Yeah. Mostly. I think. How'd you find me?"

It came out in a dry, raspy, near whisper.

"We all just guessed you came here, and Jamie gave us the directions. Where are you?"

"I'll send location." He hung up and sent a text for Tomi to bring water. Next, he took a screen capture of the map and drew a line showing how to find him. He wished he'd thought to look at the address on the building before venturing into the backyard, but the map would do.

Since they were coming to retrieve him, he continued trying to get his body functioning well enough to get out from under the bush. It was slow going. In the end, he just decided to wait until they arrived. If someone spotted him, he was in no shape to run.

Fifteen or so minutes passed before he heard his friends.

"Damn it, Dax, where are you?" Tomi called, keeping his voice low and his irritation high.

"I'm back here."

"Quiet. I think I can hear him," Tomi said.

"He's near. I can hear him clearly," Jamie replied. "I think he's under that bush."

Tomi squatted and looked through a gap in the bush's limbs. "This wasn't the best idea, Dax."

"Just help me out." Dax crawled forward far enough to stick out his arms.

"Jamie, give me a hand." Tomi took one of Dax's hands in both of his and made room for Jamie, who took his other hand. Between the two of them, they easily dragged him out from under the bush. It was one more indignity stacked on the day's pile.

They pulled him to a sitting position and propped him up against the fence. Tomi had a broad grin playing across his face, though he tried to conceal it. Everyone else looked similarly amused.

"Nice spot," Tomi said.

Dax didn't bother answering, unsure if his mouth and tongue would work well enough to address the comment.

Delphine stepped forward, unscrewed the lid off a metal water bottle, and handed the bottle to him. It was the sweetest nectar he'd had in ages.

He started with a small sip, swishing it around his dusty, dry mouth, and spit it out. He took a long chug after that, the cool water feeling good as it went down his throat. He sighed happily and took another long drink.

"Not to harsh your vibe, but we really should get out of this neighborhood. It's like a demilitarized zone," Suzie said, looking around the yard.

"She's right." Delphine took the bottle back. "Do you need to go to the clinic?"

"No. I'm alright." He was able to speak much easier now that he had some moisture in his mouth. "Just get me home. Tomi, can you drive my car?"

"If it hasn't been stolen," Tomi grumbled.

Dax hadn't even thought of that. He'd been confident it would be reasonably fine sitting for the few minutes he'd allocated for this little adventure. If his car had been stolen, he would be pissed off. He loved his Lincoln.

They helped him to stand, and with Tomi propping up his shoulders, they walked him out of the backyard. Once he emerged onto the sidewalk, he felt like his muscles had loosened up enough to let him walk on his own. He led Tomi to his car and was relieved to find it still there and undamaged. Tossing Tomi the keys, Dax climbed into the passenger side. Delphine, Jamie, and Suzie got into the large backseat, and Tomi dropped them off at Suzie's Honda Civic. Suzie and Jamie were going to drop off the manbo at her shop, then go about their days.

As soon as Dax and Tomi stepped into Dax's living room, Morty came flying out of the back room until he saw Tomi. Then the kitten rotated sideways and hopped along, his back arched, and hissed at them until he reached Tomi. Morty rubbed against Tomi's leg, purring.

"Hey, you little shit," Tomi said, picking the black-and-white tuxedo cat up and flipping him onto his back in his arms.

The smug little kitten seemed to be enjoying all the attention. While Tomi focused on the cat, Dax went to the bathroom to relive the pressure on his bladder. After he washed his hands, he bent over the sink and stared into the mirror.

"Fuck. That's the spot Tomi was talking about," he mumbled.

Apparently the bush hadn't completely shaded him. He had a bright-red patch of skin covering most of his forehead, upper nose, and around one eye onto his cheek. No wonder why his face hurt whenever his expression shifted. He'd gotten sunburned. Considering all the things that could have happened to his unattended body in a neighborhood like that, he'd gotten off lightly. He didn't even want to think about what might have happened to his essence if his friends hadn't found him.

TWELVE

JAMIE

Jamie kind of wished she'd kept her mouth shut during their planning meeting after Dax had taken a day to recover from his adventure. They all had liked her proposed plan. It had been a good idea, and it had worked before.

But because it was her idea and The Rat had volunteered to help her with it since the plan involved him, here she was, hiding in a storm drain and waiting to sneak into one of the bikers' compounds with a pocket full of GPS tags and a backpack full of rats.

The Rat had assured her the rats could help her hide the tags on the bikes. But not all the bikes would have places to easily stow tags. Some of the saddle bags were more secure than others. Some motorcycles didn't have bags. For this plan to work, the GPS tags needed to go unnoticed.

If the bikers found one, they'd likely scour the other bikes and find more, then disseminate the word out to the rest of their gang members. All the work would be for nought. But The Rat had assured her his furry minions understood how to hide things. She struggled to trust humans and other supernaturals at the best of times. She wasn't sure how she'd wound up leading a pack of rats and trusting their whiskered sensibilities.

She took one last look out the storm grate and ducked down again. The route seemed to be clear. She opened her backpack and pulled out a rat, handing it a tag, then set it on the ground just outside the grate. The other small rats in the backpack jostled around, creating a writhing motion that in the low light conjured all kinds of nasty, horror-movie images, which gave her the ick.

Once the first rat disappeared into the shadows, she sent off another until her bag was empty. Steadying herself, she took a deep breath, pushed up the access lid to the storm grate, and pulled herself out quietly. She propped the access panel open with a foot and twisted around to grab the grate, withdrew her foot, and lowered the panel onto a thick stick so she could quickly escape down storm grate if she needed to.

Sticking to the shadows and bushes in the empty lot next to the compound, she darted from cover to cover until she reached the fence blocking the darkest part of the compound, where there were no windows or lights. She pulled out a pair of wire snips and went to work cutting an opening at the bottom of the chain-link fence. Once she cut two parallel vertical lines, she folded the fence up and hooked it into place higher on the fence with a couple of carabiners. The space was barely big enough for her to wiggle through. There'd be no way the bikers could follow her through if she had to escape this way.

After she wriggled through the opening, she squatted and looked around to make sure she'd gone unnoticed. So far, so good. Since she stood in a dark part of the yard, she popped up and walked briskly toward the wall of the building that dominated the bikers' base, pushing her back against wall when she reached it.

The bikers at this compound had stashed their bikes in the back of the lot, which was fortunate for her. It was darker there, with fewer bikers to contend with. Most of the guys on watch were stationed near the front of the compound to guard the gate.

Once she arrived at the building's corner, she poked her head around briefly, saw no one, then pulled it back. Ducking down, she crouch-walked around the corner, making her way to the two line of motorcycles. She opted to go down the avenue between the bikes instead of staying by the wall, which required her to dart out to get to the bikes. This way, she could hide more easily in the dense forest of steel, chrome, and leather.

She had a half-dozen trackers left. Dax and Tomi had more on order, but this was the best they could do on short notice. Finding the first compound had required a bit of sleuth work and luck, but after Dax had spoiled the location of her find, they'd picked up a couple clues from local businesses and found this compound.

Relying on her sharp, supernatural eyes, she tried to focus on bikes that had gang logos on them, selecting ones that appeared to be from different chapters. They'd hoped picking a variety the out-of-towners would get the best dispersal of the GPS tags and yield the best results, since chapters probably would move and stay together, kind of like military units. The goal was to spread a wide net to find as many potential compounds and targets as they could.

She couldn't say she agreed with Dax's plan to go on the offensive. They were horribly outnumbered. But it made sense to try to even the odds before the bikers could gather more of their kind to Red City. He was the one they were targeting after all. She just hoped he remembered that everyone else was more mortal and vulnerable than he was. And even he wasn't impervious to everything. The bullet she'd put in him had nearly killed him, according to Tomi.

"Anybody got a clue when go time is?" A voice drifted on the wind to her sensitive ears.

She ducked next to a large bike, hiding in its shadow.

"No idea. I don't ask questions. I walk the fence cause that's what I'm told to do. When they say we ride, I'll do that too," someone else replied.

"Ain't you the least bit curious?" The voices sounded a little closer.

She risked shifting her position to poke her head above the seat of the motorcycle. Her short, wavy black hair was contained inside a black knit beanie. In her black, stretchy leggings and T-shirt, she felt like a proper burglar. She patted the lump under her T-shirt to remind herself of the gris-gris's presence. She'd maintained it, feeding it regularly, as Manman Delphine had instructed. She'd been so impressed by how well it had worked to disguise her from someone she knew that she didn't want to risk losing any of the magical bag's potent power by being lackadaisical about its treatment.

A flicking lighter helped her identify their exact location as the two men strolled along the fence line. A faint whiff of marijuana smoke drifted toward her. She smirked, glad to see they were going for full alertness.

"Would you roll me one of those?"

"Sure." The two men stopped walking.

A minute later, a lighter flicked again, and they resumed their patrol. Soon they'd pass within twenty feet of where she crouched. She backed up so she was near the front wheel and waited. When they drew almost level with her position, she held her breath. As they moved past, she took a delicate crouched step to move to the other side of the bike.

Her lungs burned from holding her breath, as she waited for them to hit the corner and head down the other fence line…toward her exit hole.

A barely vocalized "fuck" slipped out of her mouth as she slowly exhaled. It would be a miracle if they didn't find the hole she'd cut, even if it wasn't big. The carabiners would likely give it away. Perhaps that hadn't been the best idea. Once the two men disappeared from view, she stashed the last two GPS tags, then crouched in the shadows again, wondering what the fuck to do.

Could she get to another dark spot and cut an exit? The carabiners had been all she'd left behind, so she wouldn't be leaving anything important. She didn't have long to decide. They had to be getting close to the hole.

Nearby, a squeak drew her attention. One of the rats was shimmying its way up the wooden support pole of the patio roof.

"What the fuck?"

"What? Oh, shit. Go get someone. I'll stay here."

"Right…" Heavy footsteps ran toward the front of the building.

They'd found her exit hole. There was no way she'd have time to cut another one. She looked around, her eyes stopping on the shadow of the rat at the top of the pole as it crawled onto the roof. It looked to be about ten feet tall.

Popping up, she ran quickly to the pole, ducking low to avoid any windows. It wouldn't be a quiet enterprise, but she had an idea about what was about to happen. The front door slammed shut. Indistinct yells came from inside. That was her cue. She crouched, then sprang up and grabbed the edge of the roof just as the inside of the building turned into chaos, chairs and tables being noisily shoved around as bikers sprang to their feet. It was good to be a wolf shifter with supernatural abilities. If she'd been a regular human, she'd have never been able to jump that high and pull herself up.

Some of the bikers would get orders to go investigate the fence further, but most would likely flood out to see for themselves anyway. She needed that moment of chaos. She pulled herself up and swung a leg onto the patio roof as it creaked under her. Sticking close to the edge where there was a beam to support her weight, she moved onto the roof of the building itself and stopped. She needed to get away from the edge.

Casting a prayer to whatever god was stupid enough to be watching over her, she took a step forward, hoping she'd guessed the right amount of space between roof beams. Each step raised a bit of noise she couldn't help but cringe at. Fortunately for her, the bikers were providing more than enough noise to cover hers up. Once she felt safely away from the edge, she lowered herself onto her belly and flattened herself out. Now that she was out of sight, she just had to rely on the power of the gris-gris to conceal her scent.

THIRTEEN

JAMIE

Bikers tromped around noisily in the gravel, shouting that they hadn't found anything. Other bikers cursed at their comrades for getting in the way of the people working. Noise came from all parts of the compound. If she were discovered, she'd be in more trouble than she'd ever been in before, and she'd gotten herself into a lot of trouble lately.

She needed to calm her breathing and heart rate, or they'd hear it thundering as soon as they quieted down. She forced herself to control her breaths in and out until they were steady and smooth. As her breath evened out, her heart slowed to more a reasonable pace.

"Anyone find anything?" someone shouted.

"Nothing here."

"Any scents?" the first person asked.

"Nothing definitive," someone else replied. "It feels vaguely shifter."

"Will one of you stupid fuckers shift over to your wolf? Everyone else, back up against the walls and clear the path. We don't need you fouling any stray scents because you're curious."

There were general mumbled assents as gravel crunched all around the building. She was totally surrounded. She reached up and grasped her gris-gris. Bringing it to her lips, she breathed into it and gave it a kiss. So far it had worked to obscure her scent from the other wolf shifters in their human forms, she just needed it to fool them in their much more sensitive wolf forms, with their canine noses.

If she made it out of this, she'd owe Manman Delphine big time.

A rodent squeak not far from her position drew her attention. *No… Stay quiet.*

"You hear that?" someone asked. "It sounded squeaky."

Someone else snorted. "You cut a loud fart and this piece-of-shit building shifts to one side. I'm surprised we can hear anything over it creaking and dying a slow death."

"Will you two shut the fuck up," commanded the voice she'd designated as the leader. It wasn't one of the men she recognized— neither Ivar nor Sigur.

One of the rats—the others must have come up here, too—scurried across the roof, its toenails making tiny little clacks on the hard surface. With increasing dread, she watched the animal move toward the corner they'd both climbed up. No one wanted rats in their building, even if it was only a temporary home. If they saw the rat, they might climb up on the roof and see if there were more.

Please don't…

It poked its head over the roof and squeaked. She closed her eyes and restrained a sigh of resignation. But instead of drawing attention upward, it jumped off the roof. A moment later, someone yelped and squealed. The rat had probably landed on someone's head. She wanted to laugh at the ridiculous thought but stopped herself. Her nervous energy was making her oddly giddy.

More shouts sounded from below.

"Get it off me!"

Other men laughed. Then she heard a squeaking yelp and more laughter.

"Get it!"

People scrabbled noisily over the gravel. One of the bikers in their wolf form growled. A moment later, motorcycles crashed to the ground. She could no longer hear the sounds of the rat squeaking frantically over the crashing metal and shouts that had turned from jocular to angry.

"What the fuck you doing, moron!" The shout was nearly drowned out by the other men yelling.

She had to hand it to the little creature; it had created a whole bunch of chaos and mayhem. It was no doubt helping to churn up the scents and distract everyone.

One of the other rats, perhaps drawn by the noise, moved to the edge of the roof. Then it joined its furry little packmate and became airborne.

"Gods dammit! It's fucking raining rats. I'm not staying in this shithole another night."

"Will you shut up! Someone catch one of these rats."

"Didn't the local boys say something about a rat man with a rat army?"

"Catch those damned rats!"

More shouting ensued. The men absolutely couldn't do anything silently. If Jamie wanted, she could sing the chorus to one of the punk songs Suzie always had playing at the top of her lungs, and they'd probably not hear it down below. She remained silent though.

"Fuck it all! It got away." The man's declaration was punctuated with a growl and yip from one of the men in wolf form.

"I lost the other one," someone else said, sounding embarrassed.

"If you bastards don't shut your fucking yaps, I'm pulling out my pistol, and I'm gonna start shooting."

That seemed to get the men's attention, and silence finally returned to the lot.

"So none of you caught the rats?"

"Nope. Looks like they both got a way."

"Damn it all. If it's the rat man's rats, the base is likely compromised. Pack it up, boys. We're moving out in an hour. Your new destinations will be relayed to you after we've left." Nothing seemed to happen. "Now! Move it! You lot, get those bikes off the ground. The rest of you, tear down the equipment inside and get your personal shit packed. If we're one minute late departing, I'm pistol-whipping every son of a bitch who isn't ready."

That sent everyone scrambling. Jamie hoped they were the most efficient men ever, but if not, she only had one hour to wait. But if she got away clean for the price of an hour on a roof on a warm summer evening, it would be worth the price to plant the GPS tags.

It was one of the longest, most tense hours of her life.

FOURTEEN

DAX

Dax revved the engine of his new motorcycle as he waited at the three-way intersection. Looking down at the map on his cell phone, he watched the dot marking the planted GPS tracker approach from his left. Soon the hunt would begin.

Though it was just after midnight and he didn't see any light from headlights behind him, he cast a quick glance at the little round mirror at the end of his handlebar. Nothing.

Revving the engine again, he reveled in the vigorous purr and vibration of the freshly tuned engine. He'd just gotten it back from Boudreaux. As usual, his friend had cleaned up the bike, repainted it, and made sure its origins weren't traceable back to the outlaw biker gang it had been stolen from.

Dax just wasn't sure about the paint job. The Black Suns logo needed to go, but painting the fuel tank and the rear fender—carrying the theme across the rest of the bike, including a custom leather seat—to resemble a skeletal horse might not have been the most subtle of options. But he had to remind himself, to almost everybody who saw him, he was just another scruffy-looking biker. Eyes passed over him and looked away, avoiding eye contact for fear of drawing unwanted attention.

He didn't like being the object of average people's fear. Intellectually, he knew humans had lived in terror of him from the moment living beings gained enough sentience to be scared of death. But it was different to be a human who scared people in a city ruled by the corrupt and violent, especially if he was assumed to be one of the brokers of the structure.

However, there was a bonus to the situation. Being feared did come in handy when you needed to move about in plain sight. He regretted the fear he caused the people trying to go about their lives, but he'd use it nonetheless. But right now, he planned to intentionally inspire terror in those who deserved to experience it.

"Almost…" Dax could hear the roar of the motorcycle approaching. He tipped his ear toward the sound. No. Motorcycles.

Stuffing the phone into his pocket, he drew a bit of the darkness in and pushed it out in a weak veil of shadow—enough for him to blend into the dark road and surrounding bushes while allowing him to see through the cloak of shadows.

Several headlights burst onto the cross street as they came around the corner. Ahead of him in a nearby neighborhood, a few fireworks burst into the air. Even if there was no occasion, people like to light off illegal fireworks in the summer since they were so available thanks to Independence day.

Patting the long, hard lump inside his jacket, he smiled, reassured. The sawed-off shotgun had been Boudreaux's idea. It would do good work in close situations and add another tool to Dax's arsenal. And on a night filled with illegal fireworks, it would be easy to hide a few extra gun shots. Not that anyone gave a shit about gunshots in Red City, not if they didn't want to get mixed up in something deadly.

He quickly counted five headlights moving on the two-lane road, often crossing over the center line as they pleased. After they passed, Dax waited for a moment, then slowly pulled out onto the road behind them. The veil of darkness came with him.

He gave the bikers time to notice that something had pulled onto the road behind them, but when they didn't, a feral grin spread across his face. He let the veil disappear and accelerated.

The cool summer night air whipped through his shoulder-length black hair and brought with it the scent of gunpowder and burnt metal from spent fireworks. The bike handled beautifully as it ate up the distance between himself and the five wolf-shifter bikers.

He didn't know if they were from the local chapter of the Black Suns or if they were out-of-towners who'd come in to reinforce the local chapter and help them exact vengeance for the destruction of their bar and headquarters. The one Dax had burned down.

He reached toward his slightly open black leather jacket and the handle of the sawed-off but stopped halfway. Tonight, the first night of Dax and his friends' counter-offensive, demanded something different. Something more personal. Something more Dax.

He reached into the aether and found his skeletal form. Tattered black robes flapped out behind him, though the hood stayed in place, covering the bleached white bones of his skull. The otherworldly blue light of the flames in his eyes cast a faint glow into the night. Extending his bone hand out to the side, he brought forth his scythe. The dull metal gleamed with the light of a partial moon, occasionally reflecting the bright sparks of another explosion of fireworks.

He laughed and the sound, tainted with its hollow disharmonics, blew back into his face. Accelerating, he readied his scythe to strike. So far, they hadn't noticed... One of the bikers looked back, his eyes opening and revealing the whites of his eyes like two small moons glowing back at Dax.

Dax left the headlight off, instead pushing out and letting the blue flames of perdition sweep up the shaft of the scythe and onto the wicked hooked blade. He tossed back his head and laughed.

Up ahead, the biker who'd spotted him and couldn't return his eyes forward shivered involuntarily and violently. His hands wobbled on his handlebars, sending the bike swerving back and forth. If the biker wasn't careful, he'd lose control.

Having nearly caught up with them, Dax had to glide into the oncoming lane to get next to the wobbling biker. As Dax swerved by the biker, he lowered his scythe. The biker screamed and tumbled off his bike, rolling along the pavement and under the blade of the scythe. Dax had missed him. But with a quick shift in his wrist, he dragged the blade through the motorcycle as it spit sparks and pavement pebbles into the air. The hot blue flames of death cut through the metal of the motorcycle, leaving a rusty gash in its wake.

After experiencing the drag created by the thick frame, the fuel tank felt like tin foil. The tank split, spewing gasoline into the air to turn into vapor and mix with the air. The sparks joined the party, and the vapor exploded into a bright fireball.

Dax yanked his scythe free and sped away from the explosion, swerving back into the lane behind the bikers. They'd discovered him when their friend had fallen. They cast furtive looks over their shoulders, though none of them let themselves become beguiled by the presence of what by all appearances was the Grim Reaper.

He didn't know if the bikers had been a few who had escaped from either of the fights he'd had with their gang. They might not know who their enemy was or believed those who'd told them. But they did now.

They rode as if Death himself was on their tails.

Dax continued to gain on them. Boudreaux's guys had done a great job adding more muscle to his bike. And perhaps the fact that a skeleton rode it meant it had a lighter load than the bikes carrying their beefy, wolf-shifter riders. Dax wasn't actually sure about his mass in this form. He snorted, chuckling to himself. Maybe he'd have to test it on a bathroom scale. If he owned one.

Stupid thoughts to have while hunting Nazi bikers…

FIFTEEN

DAX

The cluster of four bikers spread out, either by plan or circumstances. The formation would work better for him this way, so he didn't care why they'd done it. As he gained on the biker last in line, the gleam of moonlight glinted off the dark steel of a handgun in a biker's hand.

Dax started slaloming side to side to make aiming harder. Though it would likely miss him in this form, he didn't want to risk it. If a bullet hit bone, it would still hurt like the fires of hell. And if it was one of the magic bullets they'd been using, it might fuck with his form, perhaps forcing him back into his mortal shell. Then the real pain would begin.

He didn't want to risk either possibility.

The biker repeatedly returned his gaze forward to make sure he wasn't going to crash. Crack and a flash of muzzle fire. The biker missed. Dax had nearly caught him. Swerving to the left into the oncoming lane, Dax readied his scythe to strike. The biker, with his gun in his right hand, couldn't twist around enough to keep his pursuer in his gunsights. He righted himself and tried to swap the gun to his left hand. But it was too late.

Dax held the scythe level as he passed the biker, and the dark blade bit into the biker's flesh and sliced through his torso like a hot knife through soft butter. The biker's lower half slipped backwards and tumbled off the motorbike as the death grip of his hands kept his upper half clinging to the handlebars. The bike swerved left, just passing behind Dax.

The remaining three riders, using the time Dax had spent in the oncoming lane, had adjusted their grips on their guns to their left hands. Two shots flashed at him. Swerving hard, Dax corrected at the last moment as he bounded over the rumble strip on the shoulder on the right side.

Unlike the bikers, he didn't have to clumsily juggle his scythe as he balanced a speeding motorcycle. He threw the scythe into the aether, returned his right hand to the handlebars, and pulled the scythe back into this plane with his left hand.

With an angled downward arc, Dax claimed his next prize, splitting the biker in half down the left side, from where his neck joined his torso to just above his right hip. Blood and guts splattered out into the wind. A haunting, blood-hungry roar of a laugh erupted from Dax's skeletal jaw.

He was tired of playing. Tired of being their punching bag. Tired of visiting the hospital for nearly mortal wounds. It felt good to be on the hunt.

The two remaining riders gave up on shooting at him and focused on speed and evasion, swerving wildly and making sure neither moved near the other. He didn't know if it was a coordinated attempt to force him to split his attention or the dirtbags just trying not to be the one chosen next.

He chose to split the difference and ride the center line, his robe flapping behind him. He wondered if he looked as cool as Batman on his weird tank-wheel motorcycle. As he gained slow feet on the trailing biker, he smiled at being a vigilante going after the corrupt scum of Red City.

The Black Sun Motorcycle Club had made a huge mistake when they took a contract to kill Dax. The club had been the enforcers for the city's most corrupt power brokers—and the cops when they wanted the violence strictly off the books.

He'd had enough of being on someone else's books, under the table or above. It was time to find out who was pulling the strings. But first, he needed to work his way through the trash to get to the one collecting it.

In annoyance, he clenched his teeth and tried to get more speed from his bike as they approached a three-way intersection. The bikers, seeing their chance, split up. In a brief second, Dax went after the one taking a right. He'd lagged behind his fellow biker. Sure enough, he wobbled as he cut the corner too shallowly and nearly went into the ditch on the far side of the road.

His mistake cost him his life, and Dax's scythe sheered through the bike and the dirtbag riding it. Waiting until he was past the rolling wreck he'd just created, Dax stopped when the sparking heap slid off the pavement and into the ditch next to the road.

The biker who'd taken the left was already making good his fortune, shooting away into the distance. Dax soon lost him as he took another turn into a tree-shrouded lane.

"Fuck." Dax thought about attempting to track him down but decided against it. Let him tell the tale to his brothers.

As he turned his head to see if anyone was coming down the dark road he'd just been on, he saw a shadow running along the blacktop. The biker who'd fallen from his bike, the one he'd missed, was sprinting down the road away from him.

Kicking his bike into motion, Dax turned left and gunned it. Once the biker realized he hadn't gone unnoticed, he sped up. Why he didn't try to go through the fields or find a dark hiding place, Dax didn't know. Hell, the biker could have stripped off his clothes and gone wolf and disappeared in the field where Dax couldn't chase on bike or foot. The shifter picked up his speed, such as it was. Motorcycle boots were not renowned for their versatility as running shoes.

As Dax neared the man, he checked ahead and found no cars coming, so he whipped around the biker and slid to a stop, blocking the road. The biker skidded to a halt, losing his footing on the bits of broken pavement and loose pebbles and gravel that accumulated on poorly maintained roads.

Casually stepping off his bike, Dax forced more flames into his eyes and slowly advanced on the biker as he tried to regain his footing—the click and clack of Dax's bones on asphalt staccato notes marking the biker's impending doom.

The biker abandoned his attempt to rise to his feet and turned and tried to crawl off. Reaching out through the aether, Dax grabbed a hold of the biker's life thread and tugged on it, halting him in place. The man flipped over and tried to crab walk backward but found he couldn't move. With a whimper, he flopped onto his butt, his eyes wide with terror.

"Where is Ivar?" Dax asked, disharmonics filling his voice.

The biker's teeth chattered as he panted and looked away.

"I. Want. Ivar." He gave a little tug on the life thread and raised his scythe.

"I-I-I d-don't know." The man shook his head vigorously. "I'm new to town. P-p-please."

"Give me Sigur's location."

He shook his head again, his mouth working open and closed like beached carp.

"Sigur! Now!"

"I don't know…"

Dax took a step forward, flushing more flames into his eyes and onto the blade of his scythe.

"I swear! I'm not from their chapters. We just got to town a couple days ago. Please."

Dax raised his scythe to strike, debating whether to claim the biker's life or let him scurry away to report what had happened. The one who'd already escaped could only witness the events. This pile of trash could carry a message.

"You've seen my work. Witnessed my power. This will be the only warning. Red City belongs to me now. The Black Suns—ALL OF THEM," he roared, "must leave town immediately. You have twenty-four hours. After tomorrow night, I'm coming for you. Each and every one of you. And I won't stop until you're wiped from the face of the earth." Dax bent over, pushing his face near the biker's bearded mug. "Do you understand me?"

The biker cringed and whimpered but nodded aggressively. He

couldn't seem to get his tongue to work as his mouth flapped open and closed. The scent of fresh urine filled the air. Standing up, Dax turned and walked back to his motorcycle, mounting it. Without a look back, he fired it to life and rode away. After he disappeared around the corner, he released the biker's life thread. He laughed. There wasn't much length remaining.

SIXTEEN

DAX

Dax left the biker behind and rounded a wide curve, where he pulled his skin back out of the aether and headed for the rendezvous. After the adrenaline of the hunt wore off, he enjoyed the brisk feel of the cool evening wind whipping through his sweaty hair. Off to his right, the neons, windows, and streetlamps of Red City puked their light pollution into the sky as he skirted the line between the suburban and rural landscape.

Nearing a main highway into town, he pulled into a truck stop and aimed his bike toward the gas pumps. Though he was probably fine, he wasn't sure how much gas the new bike used, especially after all the upgrades Boudreaux's crew had added. He was glad he'd stopped when the dials kept rolling on the gas pump. A buzz in his pocket reminded him he needed to check in.

He rode into a less-populated part of the parking area and found a patch of darkness missed by the tall-poled lights illuminating the lot.

Tomi had texted. *"No luck here. You?"*

"A handful of apparent newer recruits. Or maybe better to say, members from another chapter who hasn't been in town before," Dax replied.

"Fuck. Another chapter? How many Nazi werewolf bikers are there?"
"A few less than there used to be."
"Meet at objective 2?"

Dax sent back a thumbs-up emoji, then stuffed his phone in his pocket and fired up his bike to roar into the night.

Since they broke Dax out of the bikers' compound, they'd taken Jamie's idea and expanded it, using The Rat's furry minions to plant trackers on the bikers' bikes. They'd done a few spot checks to observe the results but had kept in the background to go undetected.

Until tonight, they hadn't attacked any gang members, merely using the data to look for patterns and lairs. They hoped by sneaking around and being smart, they could track down where Ivar or Sigur were hiding. Dax wanted to cut the snake's head off. Those two men were the dangerous ones. They wielded real power and had the brains and ambition to use it. Without the heads, Dax could mop up the lesser elements more easily.

Dax shook his head and smirked as he enjoyed the night ride. A few months ago, he'd been doing his best to lead a meek life of hiding and being less than. He still wasn't sure what his boundaries were, but meekness hadn't worked. Now his pendulum was swinging the other way.

His enjoyment of the ride soon ended when he pulled off the highway and into one of the rougher neighborhoods of Red City, which was saying a lot in a city that was more rough than smooth. The rank odor of trash cans too full thanks to service which was too infrequent, returned the normal, brooding almost-frown to his face. After a few blocks of the stench, he gave up and just grimaced.

He pulled up the bandana that had been draped around his neck and maneuvered it into place with one hand, so his nose and mouth were covered. It helped a little, but not enough. Maybe next time, he'd try a gas mask... Though that might be a bit too much, at least in the scare-anyone-who-saw-it sense.

He slowed down to avoid hitting any of the numerous potholes and kept his eyes peeled, sweeping them from side to side as he watched for any unwanted attention. If someone noticed his lack of logos on either his jacket or bike, they might think he was some unaffiliated biker too stupid to know he'd wandered into the wrong neighborhood and try to rob him and jack his bike.

It would be the last mistake they ever made, but Dax didn't have time to deal with crooks and idiots. Nor did he want to risk any incidental injuries in some random skirmish.

He didn't recognize any of the landmarks he'd noted on the map view when he'd surveyed it earlier from the safety of his laptop's screen. Finding a patch of darkness to slip into, he pulled a shroud of shadows around himself and took out his phone. He checked his map app, determining he was a couple blocks off.

"Status update. I'm nearby." Since he was stopped, he figured it might be a good idea to get some more information before blundering in.

"Come in quiet. Surveilling."

He laughed to himself—Tomi seemed to be enjoying the covert mission—then fired up the bike. Leaving the headlight off since there was enough light from the sparsely spaced streetlights, he pulled back onto the road and cruised quietly toward where Tomi and Boudreaux were waiting for him. He was careful to accelerate slowly since the bike's big motor made a lot of noise when it revved up.

Once he figured he was close enough, he pulled the bike off the road and parked in between a couple of tall vehicles—a pickup and a work van—so his ride would be blocked from view well enough. With one last glance at his phone to see if any new messages had come in, he headed to Tomi on foot. As soon as he turned a corner, he brought up the same thin veil he'd woven earlier, which kept him nearly invisible in the darkness without being too thick too see through.

When he passed through the dim pools of light cast by the underpowered and overworked streetlights, he imagined he looked like a ghost or wraith out for an evening stroll.

He saw Boudreaux's unmarked black Sprinter van parked across the street. He crossed over and checked the vehicle. Empty. He took a moment and looked back the way he'd come before inspecting the way forward. It was nervous work, but better to be cautious. He wasn't fast enough to win a running contest, and he was a long way from his motorcycle if he needed to get out of there in a hurry.

Fortunately, he didn't see anything except for a brief flit of a shadow that might be a figment of his nerves or a cat darting from hiding place to hiding place in pursuit of a snack or mischief. When he could delay no more, he took a deep breath and stepped out of the shadow of the van, walking quietly to avoid jangling the chains on his boots. Perhaps he'd have to get a pair of sneakers and see if their name indicated its superior stealth.

"Psst. Dax."

He nearly jumped out of his skin but stifled the yell he'd almost let free.

"Over here."

He followed the voice to a set of tall, unkempt bushes. A hand waved at him from the shadows. Using the excuse of checking out the tall grass for obstructions to catch his breath and get his heart rate under control, he inhaled deeply and licked his lips before stepping off the rough sidewalk. Once he was sure the bushes blocked him from view from the street and the site they were there to check out, he slowed down. He might have been the personification of death, but that didn't mean he wanted to twist his ankle in a gopher hole.

Tomi waited for him, his arms crossed and a broad grin on his face. "Took you long enough," he whispered. The heavy-set Black man wore black jeans, a black T-shirt, and a black knit beanie on the top of his head.

"I'm not wearing hiking boots."

"Ah." Tomi chucked his chin toward the bush and the place they were surveilling on the other side of the foliage. "Not much activity. A few bikes in and out."

"They could be bedded down for the night." It was quite late, even by hard-drinking-biker standards.

"Maybe." But the tone told Dax that Tomi didn't really believe it.

"What do you think?"

"I don't know. Could be that they're out for the night. Could also be that they're spreading out their resources so it's harder to take them out in one fell swoop. Hell, could even be a decoy." Tomi shrugged. "But I'm not an expert in this kind of thing."

Boudreaux's timing was impeccable as he pushed up from the ground and stood up. He was dressed similarly to Tomi, though he wore black cargo pants that looked like they might have been military issued. The tall, muscular Black man had served in the army as a medic.

"Tomi summed it up pretty well. I can't add much." He lifted a pair of binoculars he'd been holding by his side. "You can check for yourself if you want."

Dax held up a hand, palm facing the two men. "No, I trust your assessment."

"So what's the play?" Tomi asked quietly. They'd all been whispering, though the compound they were watching was far enough away it was unlikely anyone would hear them, even talking, save for the fact the compound might be occupied by dozens of wolf-shifter bikers with supernaturally enhanced hearing.

Dax shifted his eyes back and forth from the two men as they waited for his answer. Boudreaux would have been the better one to come up with a plan since he had military training. Other than his ability to fight, Dax wasn't a strategist.

He took the binoculars from Boudreaux and walked back to the sidewalk. He didn't feel like crawling in the dirt through branches. He swept his optics-enhanced gaze over the compound they'd tracked their GPS tags to.

A tall chain-link fence topped with razor wire blocked the compound from the road. Beyond it stood several buildings. A few of them of had light shining through their windows. Focusing in on a glint of metallic reflection, he spotted a handful of motorcycles, but not the dozens he'd expected. It was entirely possible they were parked out of sight.

He had to weigh his options. It all depended on if they were expecting him or not. Closing his eyes, he tried to focus in on the general life force a bunch of bikers might be casting into the aether. Unfortunately, there were too many people in the houses in the surrounding neighborhood for him to pick up on anything.

Tomi and Boudreaux had followed him. Dax stepped behind the bush and returned the binoculars to Boudreaux.

"See anything?" Tomi asked.

"No. Not anything more than you described. It's all quiet over there."

"Do you think it's an ambush?" Boudreaux asked.

"Could be. I just don't know. I can't tell how many lives are over there. Hell, their rune workers—whoever created the magic bullets and knives—might have come up with a way to block their vital signs from being found in the aether." That thought had been gnawing at him for a while, though he doubted its plausibility. But he wasn't as powerful as he once was, not by many orders of power, and perhaps someone particularly powerful could come up with a way to fool his magical senses.

He'd hoped taking a look and talking over the possibilities with his friends would have helped him form a plan, but so far he had nothing more than he did when he'd arrived.

"Our options are to observe some more, try to sneak in to get better information, bust our way in and see what happens, or go home and start fresh tomorrow night."

"Yup," Boudreaux replied.

They weren't going to make it any easier on him.

"Well, shit. We can't accomplish anything by going home. I'm not sure we have enough time to find a weak point for sneaking in. And staring into the darkness won't accomplish much more than we already have." Dax tapped his foot nervously on the dirt of the weed-choked empty lot. "I'll go in hot through the main gate. You have your boys follow me in if I need help or extraction."

Boudreaux narrowed his eyes. "Do you want the van? It can punch through the gate."

To Dax's ear, Boudreaux didn't seem too eager to have his van used as a battering ram. "No, I can take care of the gate. Get your people ready. It'll take me five minutes, maybe a couple more, to get back to my bike."

He didn't allow time for anyone to object, instead turning around and walking briskly back to where the van was parked then his motorcycle a block away. He also didn't allow himself any time to second guess his decision.

He'd spent years stagnating as a human in his tiny corner of the world, trying to avoid thinking about his circumstances. Now that he'd overcome his own inertia, he didn't want to give himself a chance return to that state. It was time for action.

SEVENTEEN

DAX

Dax grabbed the helmet off the back of the bike's seat and put it on, pulling his phone out for a quick check to see that Tomi and Boudreaux were now in place and ready. Kicking the bike to life, he glided out from between the two vehicles and drifted slowly down the street. Once he reached the intersection with the road leading to the front of the biker's compound, he reached into the aether and retrieved his scythe.

Before taking off, he took a moment to adjust its shape, lengthening the shaft and changing the angle of the blade so it pointed out straight from the end of the shaft like a halberd or some other polearm. He drove off, turned the corner slowly, and aligned himself with the gate to the compound, then poured on the power.

The bike roared, surging forward. As he approached the gate, he gradually lowered the tip of his modified scythe and shifted into his full skeletal Grim Reaper form. He forced power into the blade and ignited it with the same spooky blue flames that glowed in his eyes and haunted his enemies.

He expected the gates to pop open and fly back as if they were being hit by a normal car. Instead, they exploded into blue sparks and shards of glowing metal. The force shot him forward, throwing up dust in the bike's wake.

Then Dax's world exploded.

Flames burst into the sky, throwing dirt and rocks. He felt small flecks of pain dotting his body. The explosions preceded him and spread out in a semi-circle away from him. His bike bounced violently as he hit the potholes created by the detonations. Everything was happening too quickly. He couldn't get the bike to a full stop as he ricocheted around the yard of the compound.

Then all he knew was air as his bike bucked, and he flew over the handlebars.

He slammed into the ground, dirt grinding into the bones of his skull. If he'd still been in his human flesh, his face, hands, and chest would have been hamburger. As it was, he still hurt as he tried to figure out what was going on.

He'd stopped moving. Dust surrounded him. The explosions had ceased, though his ears screamed, even in the aetherial plane. As he lay groaning, he thought he heard shouts, but he couldn't tell if they were coming from behind him or in front of him. Hell, he couldn't tell where his front and behind were oriented.

He tried to push himself off the ground, but his bony hands slipped in the loose gravel, and he fell on his face, knocking some of the dirt free from his skull. He coughed on the dust even though he had no lungs to affect, but the autonomic responses of his human body sometimes intruded on his skeletal form.

The shouts grew louder. An automatic weapon rattled nearby, sounding odd and distorted through his ringing ears. He couldn't decide whether he should get up or stay down as his mind ground to a halt. He'd hit the dirt hard.

Before he could make up his mind, rough hands grabbed him by the shoulders and dragged him upright. Someone screamed and let go of his right shoulder, and he fell quicker than he could get his hands under him to stop his face from smacking into the ground for the third time in only a few minutes.

"Get him up, you stupid cowards," someone barked.

"But—"

"If you don't get him up, you'll be joining him on the ground. Permanently."

Dax was yanked up again, the hands gripping his robe-shrouded upper arms tightly.

"Let go of our friend." Through the distortion of his messed-up ears, it sounded like Tomi.

"You'll get one chance to walk away, but we're keeping your race-traitor pal here," spat out the one who'd been giving the orders.

Dax couldn't quite see what was going on. Everything looked blurry and obscured.

"Don't come any closer, or we'll open fire."

"I think you misunderstand the situation." Boudreaux's voice, closer than Tomi's had been a moment ago, held a deadly edge Dax rarely heard from the normally jovial man.

A split second later, a distant shot pierced the night, and a body thudded to the earth nearby. Dax tried to shake his head to clear some more of the dirt from his skull. The hands holding his shoulders trembled. A moment later, another shot rang out, then Dax was falling again. But this time, instead of landing in the dirt he fell on something softer and leather covered.

"Dax, stay down!" Tomi yelled.

Then guns opened up. At first the shots came from where Dax'd heard the voices of his friends. Bodies thudded to the ground. One of the bikers finally recovered his wits enough to shoot back, though the shots were few and far between, seeming anemic compared to the robust outburst from his friends' weapons. Soon, the nearer shots stopped, followed by the others a few seconds later.

Once his ears cleared from the ringing the gunfire had added, he could hear some faint groaning. He tried to push himself off the body of the biker whose freshly dead body had cushioned his fall. The padding of running feet approached.

"Dax, don't move. You could be seriously hurt." Tomi, coming in too hot, pushed him back onto the body more aggressively than perhaps he'd meant to.

Dax groaned. "Fuck"—cough—"dude. Easy."

"Sorry. Let me help you."

With Tomi's help, Dax rolled over, resting his back on the corpse. Tomi squeaked and fell back on his butt. "Next time, warn me."

If Dax had had eyes, he'd have rolled them. He was in his reaper robes, that should've been warning enough. His skeletal from still frightened Tomi, no matter how many times he'd seen it lately. But Dax guessed it made sense. Except for right after they'd met over five years ago, he'd never showed Tomi the form, since there was little need for the owner of an on-the-edge-of-going-out-of-business dive bar to slip into the robes and bones of the Grim Reaper. But lately, there'd been too many reasons for him to take the form.

"Can you change back?" Tomi asked.

Dax shook his head. "Water. A bucket. Or a hose."

Boudreaux chuckled. "You heard the scary fucker, get some water."

"Dreaux, that ain't right, man. What the fuck is he?" someone said.

"Thirsty. Now hurry with the water before you find out why everyone's so scared of him."

"Shit, man, I'm on it. No need to be so pissy about it. That's just some weird shit, that's all."

Boudreaux sighed. "Sorry, man. I'm just really fucking tired of these dirtbag Nazi bikers. Someone go keep an ear out for cops. I'm going to inspect this building."

"Careful, Boudreaux. There might be more booby traps," Tomi said.

"The bikers came out of the building, it's probably clean, though I'll be careful. My guess is Dax detonated all the landmines in the yard out here." Boudreaux didn't wait for a response and headed away from them.

"You got lucky, Dax," Tomi said. "You almost got blown the fuck up."

Tomi wasn't wrong. If Dax hadn't pushed so much power into his scythe when he hit the gate, he'd have rolled right into the middle of the minefield and taken the full brunt of the explosions. The wave of power and the pieces of exploded gate had done a good job of clearing the field. Otherwise, his friends would have been assembling a Dax-shaped jigsaw puzzle.

"Here, Tomi." Water sloshed nearby.

"I'm going to need some help," Dax said, trying to keep the scary harmonics out of his voice.

"Damn…" Someone muttered an invocation against evil.

Tomi gently picked up Dax's hand and guided it to the edge of a plastic bucket. Groaning, he rolled over so he was on his hands and knees. He groped around until he found the bucket again and adjusted himself until his head was over it. He plunged his skull into the water and shook it vigorously.

Lifting it free, he looked around but still couldn't see clearly. He dunked his head again and stuck his hand in as well, using it to pry around the orbital bones of his eyes and his nostril holes. When he thought he'd cleaned himself up enough, he sat up.

"How do I look?" he asked Tomi.

"Wet. A bit muddy, but OK, I guess."

He nodded, then mentally braced himself. He needed to shift back to his mortal form. He hoped he wasn't in too bad of shape. As soon as his flesh emerged from the aether, he grimaced in pain.

"You OK, Dax?"

Grumbling, he wiggled his whole body some to test its limits. "I don't know. Now how do I look?"

"Sorta scraped up. Muddy. Wet."

"Help me up."

Tomi set a hand on Dax's shoulder. "Stay down until Boudreaux can look you over."

"Fine." Dax didn't want to get up, but their time in the compound was probably nearing an end. They'd made a lot of noise between the explosions from the landmines and all the gunfire. But then again, the bikers had probably let the cops know to avoid the location, since the bikers and the cops were two different arms of the same violent, corrupt power structure of Red City.

One of Boudreaux's vans pulled into the yard and backed up to the building, and a couple guys began loading up the biker's motorcycles. Dax hadn't inspected the area to see how many bikers Boudreaux and his boys had dropped. He didn't care.

Since he was stuck there for a few more moments, he pushed into the aether and looked for the life threads around him. Skipping over the strong lines of his friends, he found two life threads frayed nearly in two.

He wasn't sure what had happened to his scythe, but it didn't matter. He reached out for it in the aether, and it appeared in his hand. He took it and sliced through the two threads, putting the bikers out of their misery. "Good riddance," he muttered to himself.

"Hey, Tomi, can you ask someone to check on my bike? It hit that pothole pretty hard."

Tomi chuckled, a note of relief in his voice. "Yeah, you can say that again. It launched your ass like a catapult."

Dax tried adjusting to get into a more comfortable seated position, but his sore muscles protested. "Don't remind me."

"Don't worry. I won't let you forget."

He sighed. "That's-that's not what I asked for."

Now that Tomi had proof his friend was OK, he apparently thought it was a good time to make fun of him. Dax didn't mind, not really. It was Tomi's way of relieving stress and worry. Tomi reached over and patted his knee. Dax hissed in pain.

"Oh, sorry about that." He stood up and looked around. "Where is it?"

"Looking for his bike?" one of Boudreaux's men asked. "We loaded it up. If it needs any work, we'll take care…" He perked up his ears. "Shit, sirens."

EIGHTEEN

DAX

Boudreaux's guy took off, running toward the building Boudreaux had disappeared into. They both reappeared a moment later.

"Everyone load up! We need to roll." Boudreaux twirled his hand above his head.

"There's not going to be room for everyone in the vans," Tomi said. "Not with them stuffed with motorcycles."

"I'm not going to be able to move that fast." Dax held up his hand to Tomi, who pulled him to his feet. He tried to restrain the groan of pain the effort caused "Boudreaux, get Tomi and your people out of here. Drop Tomi off at his car. I can hide myself. Then when the police leave, if they're actually coming at all, he can pick me up."

"There ain't going to be room for me either," Tomi said. "And I'm not leaving you here on your own. Not when you're injured. Can you hide both of us? Like you did when you hid me and The Rat?"

Dax thought about arguing so he could get his friend to safety but knew it would be a waste of time. Tomi was nothing if not loyal. "Fine. Help me to the path." A row of rocks cordoned off a pea-gravel path running along the side of the building toward the back of the compound.

"Tomi, throw me your keys. I'll drop someone off by your car. They'll come grab you when it's safe." Boudreaux jogged over to Tomi, who was fishing in his pocket for the keys.

After Tomi handed them over, he slipped his arm under Dax's to support some of his weight. Together, they shuffled to the pea-gravel path. Dax nodded in the direction he wanted to go, and they headed around the building. A moment later, the vans peeled out, spraying dirt and gravel around. Hopefully it would obscure everyone's footprints some.

Even this much movement was tiring. By the time they turned toward the back of the building, Dax was already panting, and a sheen of sweat had formed on his forehead.

"I'm going to prop you up here." Tomi laid him against the wall at a nook of where a brick chimney stuck out the back of the building about half way down the back wall. "I'll be right back."

"Stay on the gravel so you don't leave footprints in the dirt." Dax wiped the sweat off his forehead, then dried his hand on his pants.

Tomi rolled his eyes. "Yeah, I know. I'm not completely incompetent."

"Sorry. My brain is a bit rattled from the crash."

"You got to work on that. Your head is not landing gear. You're lucky you didn't have a face to scrape off, or you'd be even uglier."

"Ha-ha." He flipped off his friend.

Tomi returned the gesture and disappeared around the corner.

Sirens drew closer. Dax hoped he had enough strength to build a proper shield. Even with some supernatural healing, he could already feel the soreness setting in. He was going to need a lot of rest to recover. That was time he couldn't afford, with the bikers back in town. Especially since he and his friends didn't know what the bikers were up to.

Tomi jogged back around the corner. "Looks like the cops coming to check out the commotion. Only a couple of cruisers though. Not a whole SWAT team."

"That's a bit of luck, I guess." He straightened up and braced his back against the wall. "I'm going to have to shift over, so no squealing."

"I don't squeal, dude."

Dax gave a half a chuckle then let his mortal flesh disappear into the aether. The pain and soreness receded slightly. That was one benefit, at least.

He pulled in the surrounding darkness and pushed it out around him and Tomi, creating a cocoon of shadow to block them. It was just in time, too. A car or two pulled into the lot, tires crunching on gravel and sirens blaring. The cops switched off the sirens a moment later.

"You two, fan out and check behind the building. Watch out for windows. We'll hold down the front," one of the cops barked out.

Next to him, Tomi tensed up, his breathing shallow. Footsteps approached from both sides of the building. Dax pushed himself back into the wall, trying to reduce his profile as much as possible. Tomi followed his example.

"You see anything?" one of the cops asked.

"No. All clear back here," the other one called out.

"Alright, come up front. We'll check out the inside."

The footsteps receded, and Tomi exhaled slowly and quietly, sagging next to Dax.

One of the cops kicked in the door, making a loud racket as they did so. "Go, go, go!"

Feet stomped quickly into the building, then voices dulled by the walls shouted out what were probably orders. The shouts were loud but lacked the urgency of finding something or someone. After a couple of minutes, feet crunched on the gravel leading to the back of the building. Tomi tensed up again. Reaching over, Dax patted his friend's forearm to reassure him, then looked to the shroud of darkness to check for any weak points or thinning of the walls. Everything appeared to be OK.

"Who do you think killed them?" one of the cops asked, his voice seeming almost bored.

"No idea."

"Better them than us," replied a third cop.

The group chuckled. Dax could distinguish four male voices. Redemption City Police Department had only sent out a couple cars, despite all the explosions and the automatic gunfire. Most civilians in Red City minded their own business out of self-preservation, but explosions from landmines and automatic gunfire usually warranted a more robust response. The police and their proxies, such as the bikers, liked to keep their monopoly on violence.

"I don't know, man. These fucking bikers have been dropping like flies lately. Eventually, someone is going to get pissed enough that we might have to step in. And I don't want to tangle with whoever the fuck is mean enough to kill those bastards."

General grunts of agreement followed.

"What are we supposed to do about the bodies? We can't just leave them here."

"I'll call it in. Word will get back to the bikers, and they'll come clean it up."

"Why can't we just have the ME take them? Get them off the ground fast. It's not like anything will get done with the bodies. They'll just stack up like the rest of the dead bodies that go to the morgue."

Dax felt his anger growing. It was one thing to know he lived in an utterly corrupt city, not that cops in any city were any better. But to hear it spoken so plainly?

"Beats me. Ain't my job to ask questions like that. I just follow orders."

One of the cops scoffed. "Yeah. Asking those kinds of questions is a good way to end up a victim of a 'training accident.' But hey, free body bag!"

"Bullshit. They'll charge your next of kin for the pleasure."

Tomi, his body rigid with tension, trembled—probably from fury. He'd grown up in New Orleans, where the cops were some of the dirtiest. But Red City cops made them look like Boy Scouts and proper civil servants.

Just to be on the safe side, Dax reached out into the aether and brushed a brief thought across the nearest cop's lifeline. Mortal. Human. Mundane. He worked through the other three briefly, also coming back with the same results. Once he determined that, he pulled back into himself.

They might be mundane, but that didn't mean they didn't have someone magical looking in on them who might be savvy enough to detect a firmer touch. The bikers had at least two powerful magicians of sorts. Dax didn't know what exactly Sigur or Ivar were. At least one of them could work powerful runes, maybe both of them could.

He hadn't been able to interact with either of them enough to be able to recognize their magical fingerprints in their work. Although he guessed the runes were likely the work of Ivar, since Sigur was a newer arrival in Red City. But that didn't mean he couldn't also work the magic that had been popping up on bullets and other weapons.

None of the other bikers he'd encountered had shown a grasp of magical powers beyond those of their innate selves as wolf shifters. Just the two men who led their rabble had additional skills. Dax, when he had a moment, needed to reach out to Ragnar and see if he'd provide a bit more information on the subject of wolf shifters and magic.

One of the cops made a quick phone call. "OK. Let's go block off the entrance. Once the Black Suns show up, we're out of here."

Tomi jerked slightly. If the cops blocked the entrance, the two of them were trapped inside the compound with more bikers on the way. If the bikers decided to thoroughly inspect the scene, their enhanced senses might uncover the two lurkers. Dax still hadn't asked the wolf shifters he knew to help him do a sniff test on his shield to see if it also blocked scent, though he doubted it did since it didn't really block out sound.

The cops launched into some other unrelated conversation, laughing and guffawing like braying idiots as they stomped off.

This long night was going to get even longer and more tense.

NINETEEN
DAX

Once the conversation disappeared into the distance and the crackle of tires on gravel receded, Dax let down the shield. He was healing, but his energy levels were very low after crashing on his bike. If he was going to need his abilities when the bikers came, he didn't want to burn his reserves when it wasn't necessary.

"What are we going to do?" Tomi hissed quietly.

"I don't know at the moment. Keep hiding, I guess," Dax replied.

"Then why'd you drop the shield?" Tomi looked around nervously.

"I don't know how long we'll be here. I need to preserve what energy I have. Shit. You better text Boudreaux's man and let him know what's up. He could be waiting with your car for a while."

Tomi pulled his phone from his pocket, checked around again to make sure no one was around, and fired off quick text. His phone vibrated a moment later, and he squashed a brief *squawk* and juggled his phone before dropping it. It thudded into the gravel. He and Dax both hissed inhaled breaths through their teeth, staring down at the lump of plastic.

Tomi craned his neck out from behind the little nook they hid in, then squatted quickly and picked up the phone. Checking the message, he held a thumb up before setting the phone to do not disturb mode. Dax grabbed his phone and did likewise. They didn't need something silly like a noisy vibration giving them away.

"You stay here. I'm going to check out the cops." Before Tomi could argue, Dax stepped away and shrouded himself in shadows.

Taking careful, quiet footsteps, he made his way to the other corner of the building and peered around it. He saw nothing but darkness, so he thinned out a small strip in front of his face and checked again. All he could see was dulled red and blue lights flashing somewhere near the road. He knew Tomi would scold him, but he had to proceed farther anyway.

Sticking close to the wall and ducking under windowsills, he crept along the path toward the front corner of the building. Even in his skeleton form, his body, after standing still for so long in the cool evening, was stiff and unhappy about the sudden exertion. He wanted to groan in complaint but clamped his teeth together and gritted his way through the pain.

He could feel the exertion of keeping up the shield, so he dropped it, trusting to his dark clothes and the deep darkness where he stood. Once he stopped at the corner, a cool breeze that had been blocked by the wall danced across his damp forehead. He almost sighed in relief at the sensation.

The cops had pulled up to the gates and taken station on either side, leaving only enough space for motorcycles to ride through in single file. It appeared that both sets of cops were inside their vehicles, waiting. Dax joined them in waiting.

He wasn't sure how long he stood there, but he could practically feel his sore muscles petrifying. If he had to move quickly, he doubted he could without his bones creaking like an abandoned shack in a gale.

The distant sound of motorcycles alerted him to the end of his wait.

He couldn't tell how many approached, but it sounded like more than had been stationed here in the first place.

"Dax… Dax. You there?"

Shit. Tomi had moved. Dax turned and saw Tomi's head poking out from the back corner. He took a step away from the front corner. Holding a hand up to Tomi, he took one last look toward where the rising thunder of steel and gasoline was approaching from. He'd have liked to stay at the corner and count how many bikers were entering the compound, but he had to protect his best friend.

Somewhere nearby, a crow squawked several times, the noise too similar to a laugh for Dax's comfort. Taking one last glance at the approaching bikers now visible on the road, he turned and walked to Tomi, though it felt more like a hobble. He was going to need to soak in an ice bath, quite possibly forever. Not for the first time, he thought about how much it sucked to be stuck in a human body.

Tomi didn't say a word, but his reproving look spoke loud enough. They returned to the nook by the chimney they'd hidden in earlier, though Dax didn't raise the shadow shield yet. He wanted to hold off as long possible. Once he heard the crunch of motorcycle wheels in the gravel and the first motorcycle engine turn off, he reached into the aether and plunged himself and his friend into darkness.

Either the bikers didn't trust the cops, or the cops hadn't told them much, because a pair of bikers swung around the back of the building, stomping loudly with guns and flashlights out.

A beam fell on their hiding spot but swept over them. Then it returned. It looked like the biker was squinting at them, then he shook his head and wandered off after his compatriot. After the biker scouts swept through the rest of the back portion of the lot, they returned to the front, loudly declaring everything looked clear.

"Good. Help Vidar and Helg load the bodies into the van. We need to report in to Ivar."

Leaning over, Dax whispered into Tomi's ear. "I'm going to try something. Stay here and don't move."

"What? No!" Tomi hissed.

"Trust me. This is too good of an opportunity." Dax didn't wait for his friend to respond.

He dropped the shield and stepped away but raised it around Tomi again before his friend could protest. It wasn't as easy to hold it when he wasn't in the middle of it, but it held. He held it for about thirty seconds to make sure he could, then pulled another piece of shadow from the aether to wrap around himself. Though shadows shouldn't have had any weight, it pressed down on him and stooped his back, raising a sweat over his body.

He hoped he'd be able to hold both shields in place. As silently as he could, he returned to his earlier vantage point and counted a dozen bikers, ten motorcycles, and one unmarked, windowless black cargo van. Its back doors were open, and the bodies were being stacked in like pieces of lumber.

"Where did their bikes go?" one of the bikers asked, looking around.

"They took them. They always take them. Dirty fuckers. Now you out-of-town boys can see why the bosses want this target handled."

"Well, your boy Ivar doesn't seem to be doing too good of a job of it."

The work stopped and several of the bikers stared at the one who'd made the comment.

A particularly large biker took a step toward the commenter, flexing his shoulders. "You'd better shut your fuckin' mouth if you don't want to end up in the back of the van with the rest of the meat."

The two men stared at each other until the one who'd made the comment took a half step back and raised his hands in supplication. "OK. I get it. But I'm not the one in charge, and fair warning to a new friend… There are rumblings from those who are running things that he's on his last shot. Loyalty is good, but don't go down for someone else's failures."

The bigger man didn't say anything but just stared at the smaller man for a moment until some of the tension left his shoulders, and he reduced the aggression in his stance. "You're probably right. Just watch who you say what to; some ears belong to flapping gums and there's little intelligence between them."

The commenter chuckled and nodded. "Understood."

The crow squawked again, and this time it seemed much nearer. The bikers looked up at the roof of the building.

"Fucking crows." One of them pulled a handgun out of a holster under his vest and took aim.

Another biker stepped up and placed his hand on the gun. "Knock it off." He chucked his chin toward the flashing lights of the cop cars. "Let's not cause any issues with our little friends over there. They always get antsy when guns go off near them. Besides, it's just a fucking crow, and there are dead bodies here." He laughed roughly. "It thinks it's dinner time."

The biker with the gun lowered his weapon and shivered. "I don't care. I still don't want no fuckin' carrion bird peckin' out my eyes if I get clipped."

The big guy pointed at a dead man on the ground. "Get the last body in the van, then we can get out of here and you won't have to worry about it." He turned and stalked off to the cop cars.

"Man, he's sensitive," mumbled the biker who'd just been rebuked once he figured the bigger man was out of hearing range.

"You and your chapter are new to town. You haven't been watching your brothers die in droves. Just be careful what you say around the locals," another biker said.

"Yeah, I hear ya."

The doors to the van slammed shut after the last body had been placed with the others. Off near the gates, the cop cars turned their red and blue lights off and drove away. That signaled the bikers to mount up. Above Dax, the crow squawked a couple times then took off, its wings flapping noisily as it gained altitude.

Dax wanted to follow the bikers, but he had no access to a vehicle. If he'd been thinking earlier, he'd have told Boudreaux to leave one of the bikes just in case. But the bikers probably would have loaded it up with the bodies.

The man who'd been complaining about the crow stared up at the bird as it circled around the lot, leaving him as the last biker not mounted up. Dax wondered if he could kill the biker after the others rode away without them noticing and catch up and follow them.

"Let's go!" the lead biker called out and rolled forward.

The rest of his brothers followed as the straggler jogged toward his own bike. The others weren't keen on waiting around for him and rolled out the gate, just as the crow dove at the last biker. He let out a scream and covered his head with his arms while trying to swat at the crow.

But before the crow could either hit him with its outstretched claws or swerve off, it transformed into a short, curvy woman with wildly curly black hair—The Morrigan. From out of the folds of a billowy, diaphanous black dress, she withdrew a short, bronze sword and plunged it into the biker's chest. Their combined opposing forward momentums pushed the sword clean through the biker, only stopping when his rib cage ran into the narrow, curved hilt guard.

She faced Dax, shrouded in darkness. "Go, you fool, before you lose them." Her voice was husky and filled with dark harmonics, her eyes glowing with a slight blood-red tinge.

He didn't wait for a second command. He dropped his shadow cloak and turned his head to call over his shoulder. "Wait a few minutes, then get out of here, Tomi."

Digging deep, he grunted through the pain of his sore body and dashed to the unattended motorcycle. He snatched the helmet, which resembled a World War II German military helmet, and slapped it on his head a little too hard for his sensitive and roughed-up skin.

"Morrigan. Keep my friend safe." A moment later, he fired up the bike and took off, sending up a rooster tail of dirt and gravel.

TWENTY

DAX

Fortunately, the bikers weren't riding hard and fast, nor had they turned off the road that ran in front of the compound. He was able to catch up without doing anything stupid. He hung back far enough that his face, especially with the helmet obscuring some of it, wouldn't be immediately recognizable. And to be extra cautious, he pulled out a scrap of shadow from the aether and placed it in front of the lower half of his face. It would further hide his appearance while hopefully resembling the biker's beard well enough to pass a glancing inspection if the other riders looked back at him.

He'd briefly thought about detaching his spirit from this form and taking the biker's body like he had over five years ago. But he'd grown used to this body. Also, he wasn't sure if the vessel would survive the removal of his spirit.

In the past, he'd been able to slip his spirit free and leave the vessel behind, but he'd always left a tether connecting the two. He should have had Tomi check to see if his body had a pulse after he slipped out of it. But that might have been too much for his friend, who still found Dax's abilities and essence disturbing when it moved beyond the mundane world of his flesh. Besides, he didn't want to leave his body in the care of The Morrigan.

They maintained their southerly course for a few minutes. Off to the east, the first rays of the morning's sun peeked over the horizon. It had been a long night, and he was beyond exhausted, but he kept going anyway. If the bikers led him back to Ivar or Sigur, or hopefully both of them, he might be able to take care of this war against the bikers in one fell swoop.

He wasn't foolish enough to believe that if he killed the two leaders the whole regional or national gang would leave him alone, but it would definitely buy some time and eliminate two powerful, magical enemies. But they were both slippery bastards and had already escaped from him on a few occasions. This time, he'd have to set aside his normal timidity about dancing around the line of violating his agreement with the gods who'd exiled him. Those were consequences for future Dax. Present Dax needed to survive to worry about tomorrow.

There were too many people relying on him these days. He couldn't afford to be conservative. Not if he wanted to keep his friends and found family alive and protect their livelihoods.

Then there was The Morrigan.

What was her interest in him lately? He hadn't seen her for years. Not since she'd betrayed him to his enemies, resulting in the compromise that forced him to survive in a much-weakened state as a mortal-ish human. He really didn't know if he'd live forever, but he hadn't aged much since he'd detached the biker's spirit from his current body and taken it over.

Why had she helped him? And how had she known what he needed or had been thinking? He didn't want to think about the possibility that she'd been keeping an eye on him, spying on him. For his enemies. Or her own nefarious reasons. He sighed.

The two of them had been close, very close.

They'd spent a lot of time together. Reaped together. Explored the beauty and mysteries of the world together. He knew all the death gods and psychopomps of earth. All of them—from the first one birthed from the minds of the earliest humans, to the more modern iterations. He'd even been friendly with some of them. As friendly as a being like him could be. But The Morrigan…

Then she'd betrayed him.

He had to back off the bike's throttle, or he'd overtake the bikers. He couldn't risk them discovering the cuckoo in their midst, not if he wanted to find their real base of operations. Checking his shadow mask, he found it mostly gone, thanks to his wandering mind. He reapplied it, struggling to get it situated correctly. He hoped they wouldn't be on the road much longer. His energy was flagging, and he didn't know how long he could keep dipping into the well until he came up empty. And there was still the possibility he might need to fight.

Chasing off after the bikers alone might not have been the best decision he'd made lately.

At the first flash of brake lights ahead, he slowed down and followed as the bikers and van turned to the east. A slight lightening of the dark night into the deep blues of predawn, with a few hints of deeper oranges over the eastern hills surrounding Red City, made for a nice tableau.

He hoped there would be a new dawn for him and his friends, one free of dirtbag Nazi bikers, but there would no doubt be a lot of darkness along the way.

TWENTY-ONE

DAX

After another fifteen minutes or so of riding, they approached a fenced compound on the southeastern side of town that could have been a clone of the one they'd come from. Two men clad in leather stood watch at the gates. When they saw the approaching bikes and van, each of them grabbed their section of the gate and walked backward, opening the way for their brothers.

Unsure of what to do next, Dax let off the throttle and faded back from the bikers. Inhaling a deep, fortifying breath, he reached into the aether, pulled out a thick shroud of shadows, and wrapped it around himself until he almost disappeared from the world, leaving him a mere smudge of darkness barely perceivable.

He drifted around the corner of the last street before the street running in front of the compound and cut the engine as he coasted to a stop under a shaggy weeping willow. Ducking down, he pushed the bike deeper into the safety of the falling branches and dismounted.

He hoped the bikers wouldn't be too concerned about the disappearance of the biker the Morrigan had killed. Likely they'd think he'd rolled off to join his own chapter in whichever compound they were stationed.

He left the shroud in place, listening for approaching motorcycles, but all he heard was engines in the distance being silenced. When the last rumble died out, he pulled out his phone to check the time. Just seeing the number made him yawn.

As tired and sore as he was, he couldn't let the opportunity to find out more pass him by. He'd dig deeper.

He let his mortal flesh disappear into the aether, embracing the form more closely aligned with the magic of the world, and soaked in the power. The tiredness and soreness receded into the background, becoming a dull but manageable ache in the back of his mind.

He stepped off the motorcycle and walked into the lot, free of the concealing limbs of the willow. The willow dominated the lot, but it wasn't the only tree there. Many scraggly bushes partially blocked the compound, but he could see glimpses of the chain link fence through their foliage.

Aiming for a particularly thick and tall bush, he kept it between himself and the compound, leaving his shadowy shroud behind to cloak the motorcycle. Once he was close enough to the shrub, he found a spot that blocked him from the view the bikers. He reached inside the bush and shifted a branch down so he could see the gate.

The compound appeared to have gone quiet. The same two men stood station at the entrance, but the van had been parked inside one of the buildings. He could only see one structure with a large rollup door, though there might be more doors that he couldn't see.

Counting the parked motorcycles, he thought their number matched the quantity he'd been following. They'd apparently given the missing biker no more thought, which worked for Dax. He let go of the cloak hiding the motorcycle, deciding to rely on the weeping willow to obscure the bike from any casual interest. He needed the energy for himself.

He pulled the cloak around himself, though left it thin to save some power in reserve. It was still dark enough that he'd be able to blend into the shadows easily enough.

He headed away from the road leading into the compound, walking parallel with the fence. There was an abandoned or undeveloped lot next to the compound. Like the one he stood in, it had several bushes and tall grass and weeds.

Once the two men at the gates appeared distracted by the conversation they were having, he jogged across the street and ducked behind a bush and waited to see if he'd gone unnoticed. They didn't even spare a glance in his direction. One of them laughed loudly.

Dax drifted from hiding spot to hiding spot until he reached the back corner of the compound, which backed up to a freight rail line. After looking to make sure he was blocked from view from the front of the compound, he felt safe enough to let his cloak return to the aether, though he stayed in his skeletal from and took a moment to let the aether flow through him. It didn't quite mask his fading energy as well as it had earlier. He was truly reaching the end of his reserves. He had to work fast.

Withdrawing his scythe from the place in between magic and reality, he pushed a bit of blue fire into the blade and quickly made two slices in the fence, creating a spot he could move through.

He pushed the fence in and slipped through the opening, carefully letting the fence go so it didn't make any noise. Aiming for the back of the nearest building, he tried to avoid being in the direct line of sight of any of the windows. Once he had his back to the corroded, corrugated tin wall, he slipped silently along it, ducking under a window and finally reaching the corner of the structure. Fortunately, these buildings were cheap and industrial, so a lot of expense hadn't been wasted on luxuries like windows.

Not wanting to poke his bone-white face around the corner, he pulled a bit of shadow into a mask, then peered around the corner. The two men at the gates were leaning up against the thick poles where the gates were hinged. One of them yawned and checked a wristwatch.

Dax pulled back and leaned against the wall. Now that he was here, he wasn't sure what his plan was. There didn't appear to be much street traffic out this way. They were on the outskirts of town, and it was still quite early as the sun rose slowly in the east.

Reaching into the aether, he looked for the nearby life threads.

The two at the gate burned strongly. The larger cluster of threads belonging to the rest of the bikers felt more dull and less vibrant. They were asleep. A ghastly plan began to form in his mind. Tomi would never approve, but he wasn't here.

Dax reminded himself that he couldn't be timid or make safe decisions, not against these unrelenting odds. It was time to make the bikers truly afraid of who they were dealing with. If he had his mortal lips on, they'd have split into a feral and predatory grin.

TWENTY-TWO

DAX

Opting for a mundane option, Dax picked up a medium-sized stone and chucked it in the direction of the two men standing at the gate. It landed and clacked as it rolled over the gravel, coming to a stop near one of the biker's boots. Their lazy conversation halted, and they pushed themselves off the fence. One of them reached inside his leather vest but didn't withdraw his hand. No doubt it rested on the butt of a holstered pistol.

They looked around, eyes narrowed and alert.

Dax, still shrouded in a bit of shadow, tossed another stone their way. This time, their sharp wolf shifter eyes tracked the stone as it arced through the air toward them.

Dax pulled away from the corner and backed up about fifteen feet to give himself room to work.

"Go check out it," one of the bikers said.

Dax thickened the cloak of shadows around himself and pulled out the scythe but left the blade untouched by flames, afraid they'd be seen through the shadows. He'd never tested the cloak to see if it would obscure the scythe doused in the blue flames of his power.

The tip of a gun poked around the corner of the building followed by a burly bearded white man in leather and flannel. He swept the gun around the space, looking for the source of the stones. After a minute, he lowered his gun and looked back to his friend.

"Find anything?" the other biker called.

"No."

"Well, rocks just don't fly on their own."

"No shit."

Dax let his shadows drop and pumped power and blue flames into the blade of his scythe. The man turned around, his eyes wide and his mouth open. Before he could call out for help, Dax brought the scythe around and removed the biker's head. The angle of the man's body tipped him in Dax's direction. When his body hit the ground, his head popped off and rolled toward Dax. Blood pumped from the stump of the man's neck, turning the gravel a dark, sticky-looking red.

Cooling the flames on his scythe's blade and stepping into a fresh shadow cloak, Dax backed up and waited.

"Well, what the fuck did you find?" the alive biker called. "Quit fuckin' around, asshole." He sighed loudly, and his feet crunched in the gravel as he stalked closer to Dax's hiding spot.

He turned the corner, gun out and down at his side. His jaw dropped when he saw his friend, and a gurgling noise emerged from his mouth. The gun snapped up, shaking in a trembling hand as he pointed it around, looking for something to shoot.

Dax needed him to hurry up and move closer. Maintaining the cloak was becoming increasingly difficult as he burned through his limited energy reserves. The biker took a couple shaky steps forward, still sweeping his gun around, until he drew level with the body of his dead friend. Squatting, he lowered the gun and looked at the severed neck of his friend while seemingly avoiding looking at the head a couple feet away.

Lowering the shadows, Dax took the man's head like he had his companion's. His body slumped onto the headless corpse of the other biker.

Two down.

TWENTY-THREE

DAX

Dax worked quickly and quietly, grateful the bikers hadn't locked the van or the building they'd stashed it in. Neither had they locked the door on the building where they slept spread out in hastily erected bunkbeds.

Liquor bottles were strewn about the floor, the air stinking of cheap whiskey and unwashed bodies. He was glad his mundane senses were always dulled by being in his skeletal form. He had to be careful as he moved through the room not to bump into anything or kick one of the empties.

In a small back room of the main one where everyone else slept, he found the large biker who'd seemed to be in charge when they were at the other compound, snoring in a small bed of his own—the perks of leadership. In his hand, he had a mostly empty bottle of whiskey so cheap and rotgut, Dax wouldn't even have touched it when he wanted to punish himself. The big man snorted and shifted, rolling over.

His hand holding the jug of whiskey flopped to the side and let go of the bottle. Dax tensed, waiting for the sound of cheap glass breaking, but the bottle bounced. He chuckled to himself. Plastic.

Dax turned and slipped away from the small room, stopping in the middle of the large open one. Instead of taking the personal approach like he had with the first two bikers, he simply reached into the aether and severed each of the sleeping bikers' life threads. He was working for effect and didn't want the surprise spoiled.

After the last of the bikers exhaled his final breath, Dax moved through the room and removed each biker's head, setting it on the owner's chest and facing the door to the small room where their leader slept.

The heads he'd taken from the bodies in the van and the two men watching the gate, he arranged in a semicircle around the small room's door.

Bending over, he snatched up an empty bottle off the floor, glad it was glass, and hurled it at the door where the man slept. The snoring stopped briefly before resuming.

Annoyed, Dax found the man's life thread and yanked it. He woke with a scream. A moment later, springs squeaked. A shadow moved across the glass window at the top of the door a moment before it swung open.

"What the fuck do you think…" The big biker stumbled out, his head down. Rubbing his eyes, he stopped and yawned. "What the…"

He shook his head, and his eyes drifted down to the ground, a semicircle of severed heads staring back at him. His mouth hung open as he looked up and noticed the heads of all his companions all facing him, accusing him. He stumbled backward, his heel caught on the doorjamb, and he tumbled back onto his ass.

Dax stepped out of the shadows, igniting the blade and his eyes with the cold, hard blue flames of death, and stalked forward, raising his other hand, which held a head. The biker crab-walked backward, jabbering senselessly as he stared at the head in Dax's hand staring back at him.

Dax stopped just behind the semicircle of heads and tossed the one in his hand at the biker, who'd run out of space as he'd pushed up against the back corner of the small room. The head tumbled through the air toward the biker. Out of instinct, the biker caught the head.

It had been the last one Dax had harvested and was still warm.

The biker screamed once and sagged in on himself, fainting. The head plopped into his lap.

Dax hated when they fainted. Now he'd have to revive the man to ask his questions. On the positive side, he'd certainly put the fear of death into the biker. The questioning would probably go well, as long as he stayed conscious.

About to reach into the aether for the man's life thread so he could give it a nudge and wake him, Dax paused. Lives were approaching, lots of them. Along with them came the deep rumble of motorcycles.

Shit. He thought he'd have enough time to conduct his questioning then depart, leaving the biker with his life so he could relay word of what had happened to his brothers to Ivar and Sigur. Growling, he let the aether go and jogged back to one of the doors at the front of the building. He kicked a glass bottle, and it bounced off his foot, skittering across the floor.

It was full light outside now, the morning in full effect. Motorcycles pulled into the compound. He didn't even bother counting them. There were too many to deal with in his current state. The rumbling of their big engines seemed to keep coming, becoming louder and louder as more dirtbag white supremacist wolf shifters arrived. If he didn't hurry, he'd be drowning in bikers.

Stepping away from the window on the door, he quickly swept his eyes around the building to orient himself. Hoping he was right, he ducked under the window and ran to the back corner of the building. He took out his scythe, fired up the flames, and sliced four quick lines into the warehouse wall.

He didn't have time to deal with the wall quietly, instead pushing it out to thud loudly on the ground. Tucking away his scythe, he reached for shadows but found almost none left. He'd truly reached the bottom of his tank.

TWENTY-FOUR

DAX

Dax didn't wait to see if the clatter he'd made had gone unnoticed with all the noise of so many motorcycles. He darted through the hole and slid to a stop behind the nearest building. With a deep breath to prepare himself, he poked his head back out and looked to the open gates.

Six bikers were slowly making their way to him, guns out and pointed at the ground. They looked intent but not focused. They'd probably just seen motion and something about person-sized moving in a suspicious manner. If they knew it was him, they'd be sending a whole lot more manpower, and the rest of the gang would be on full alert, fanning out to cover the whole compound. They certainly had enough bodies to do it.

He walked briskly to the other end of the building and stopped. He could see the cut he'd made in the fence, but it was a bit of a stretch between the corner of this building and his escape. There was another building closer, but he'd have to angle away from the cut some. And it would put him out in the open between buildings for anyone who happened to be looking between the ramshackle structures.

He settled on the most direct route and sprinted to the fence.

Even in his skeletal form, he could feel the strain of a body pushed nearly past its breaking point.

"Stop!" someone shouted. A moment later, a gun cracked.

A bullet whistled past his ear. It was accompanied by more shouting as engines were killed and commands relayed. Another few feet…

He pushed out with his arm and shoved the cut section of the fence out of his way. It snagged in his tattered robes and dragged along the bones of his forearm. Gritting his teeth through the pain, he yanked his robe free as he ran and turned to the nearest cluster of bushes. He needed to get across the street and into the other lot before they could get out the gate and cut him off. But if he ran completely in the open, he'd make too easy of a target, even with some shadow to obscure his form. At least he hoped there was still some shadow left.

If he'd been in his human form, he'd have been huffing and puffing raggedly. A quick glance to his right inspired him to reach for a new level of speed as people ran out the gate and down the road toward him. He had to beat them to his motorcycle. Shit.

His keys were in his mundane pockets. He grunted as his bony feet hit the hard asphalt of the road. More gunshots rang out. Bits of pavement exploded as bullets hit the road around him. He felt one nearly graze his back.

As soon as he reached the lot, he cast away his shadow and brought out his human flesh. The transition didn't go as smoothly as he'd wanted it to.

His motorcycle boot slipped on dry weeds and loose dirt, and he tumbled forward, landing on his stomach in a heap as bullets whizzed overhead and thudded into a nearby tree. He pushed himself up, trying to dig in with his feet, but the boots wouldn't give him any traction. Finally, he made it back to his feet.

He shoved his right hand into the pocket of his jeans. His palm stung as it brushed over the rough fabric. Ignoring his newest injury, he fished out the keys to the motorcycle and made sure a finger looped through the key ring so that if he tripped again, they wouldn't go flying away. If that happened, he'd be truly fucked when dozens of vengeful wolf shifters caught up to him. And he'd have no energy left to put up any kind of real fight, not without potentially crossing too many lines and bringing down the wrath of his divine enemies.

He risked a glance of his shoulder. Bodies dashed between trees, making their way to him. He adjusted his course toward the weeping willow. Its thin, dangling branches whipped at his face as he tore through them, not risking using his hand with the keys in it to shield himself.

As soon as he made it through the outer layer, he saw the bike sitting at the edge of the street inside the curtain of willow branches. It was the best thing he'd ever seen. If he was a praying man, and the gods he knew weren't dicks, he'd have cast one their way. The bike had to start on the first try. The biker he'd taken it from better have been more consistent with his motorcycle maintenance than his own hygiene, or Dax would be truly good and fucked.

He threw a leg over the bike and slammed the key into the ignition. It slid home on the first time, and a small modicum of relief washed through him. The bike roared to life, and he laughed.

Gunning the throttle, he spun the rear tire, sending up smoke. More guns cracked out into the morning. The tire finally bit and launched the bike forward, the branches of the willow whipping at this face as he tore through them.

In front of him, a car honked and swerved out of his way, narrowly missing him. The bike shook, or rather his trembling body shook it as it wobbled slightly. Taking ragged breaths, he stabilized his arms and aimed the bike down the street to make sure he didn't lose control of the powerful machine.

Too many adrenaline dumps in a very short time were starting to wear on him. Bending low over the bike's fuel tank to lower his profile, he risked a look into the small circular mirror near the left end of the handlebars. A few bikers still chased him on foot. They'd never catch him that way, even if he had to stop at a stop sign. But the more who tried it, the fewer who'd be available to run back and get their motorcycles.

Ahead, he had a choice to make. Left and he'd loop to the road running in front of the bikers' compound. He could try it and charge them from the rear. But he wasn't sure he wanted to risk a rolling battle in broad daylight. Also, he didn't think he had the energy to carry it off.

Left could also be a gambit, doubling back and then heading away on the main road. But all it would take is one set of eyes looking down the road at the wrong time. And the broad street appeared to be flat and straight, so he'd be in the open for a while.

Right it was.

He swung wide into the oncoming lane and slowed down enough to make the turn to the right safely in a big sweeping arc. A quick glance over his right shoulder, and his stomach dropped. At least a few of the bikers had stayed on their motorcycles and guessed which direction he was going. There was nothing to do for it now. Time for a chase.

TWENTY-FIVE

DAX

Dax straightened out into his lane and hit the throttle. The bike surged forward, the front wheel popping off the pavement about a foot into the air before it slammed back down, jolting him. He grunted in pain. The slam hadn't been that aggressive, but his body was beat up and spent. He just needed it to hold together long enough to get away from his pursuers.

The road before him stretched out toward the horizon. A few houses and more industrial lots lined it. He was tempted to stay on it and use the power and speed of the bike to see how much distance he could put between him and the bikers. But they weren't that far behind him, and they'd see him as soon as they turned the corner.

Making a snap decision, he drifted into the middle of the road, then into the oncoming lane and kept his eye peeled. There. Just ahead. On his right, a street met up with the one he was on. It would send him back the way he'd just come, but if he could make a few strategic turns, he could maybe ditch his pursuers and disappear into the city.

He leaned into the curve on the big bike, his knee nearly touching the pavement. Another fraction of an inch and the bike might have toppled over. It wasn't meant to turn that aggressively. It wasn't a sport bike. Once he got back upright and straightened out, he looked for his next turn, but didn't see one. Soon he'd intersect with the road leading directly to the compound. There was nothing to do about it now. Everything was a gamble at this point.

As he approached the intersection, his stomach dropped. A handful of motorcycles crossed in front of him. He'd jumped from the frying pan into the fire, and now into a potential inferno. He completed his turn and merged into the middle of a group of about a dozen bikers.

Keeping his head forward, he looked around out of the corners of his eyes. So far no one seemed to realize he wasn't one of them. He was dressed like a biker in boots, jeans, and a leather jacket. But he lacked the identifying tattoos and club patches.

Around him, the bikers moved along the street, taking up both lanes. They shifted positions relative to each other like a flock of birds. Blending into the chaos, he drifted toward the right edge. Perhaps he could slip down a side road and disappear.

As he passed behind a biker, he caught a glimpse of the man in his mirror in time to watch the biker's eyes go wide. The biker reached into his vest and pulled out a gun. Twisting on his motorcycle, he tried to draw a bead on Dax.

"Fuck. So much for that."

So far, no one in front of the biker had noticed anything, but no doubt the ones behind Dax would quickly catch on to what was about to happen. The slight shift in the hand around the gun alerted Dax, and he swerved back behind the biker as a shot rang out. He was now behind the biker who was trying to get back into a shooting position.

A quick peek in his mirrors told Dax he was in deep shit. The bikers behind him were whipping out guns of their own. He was going to have to do something profoundly stupid.

Dax reached into the aether and pulled out his scythe, forcing what flames he could into the blade, and gunned the throttle. At the last moment, he whipped over and dragged the scythe through the back wheel and motor of the motorcycle, and through the leg of the biker who'd just tried to shoot him.

A faint scream followed by shrieks of metal on road greeted him as he swerved away from the tumbling pieces of the motorcycle. He twisted enough to look over his shoulder. Several bikers behind him had gone down, the bikes sliding on the road on their sides, sending up sparks and chunks of gouged-out pavement. Other bikers dodged their fallen brothers. One or two more went down, but it was hard to tell for sure in all the chaos.

There was no sneaking now.

He looked forward and accelerated. The bikes in front of him still hadn't noticed the chaos behind them. Lining up directly to the rear of the next motorcycle ahead of him, he prepared himself for the next slice. He was barely able to finish the cut. His power was nearly gone, and the flames licking over the blade were pathetically small and weak.

At the last moment, he pulled to the right and dragged the blade of his scythe through the biker's back. Normally, it would be like running a hot knife through soft butter. He couldn't even complete the slice. He used what power he had to shift the angle of the blade so the partially bisected body slipped off it.

The change in balance sent the dead man's bike swerving. Its front wheel jerked perpendicular to the bike and turned it into a catapult, launching the body over the handlebars. Dax cringed, remembering his similar crash hours ago. The bike hit the body and flipped into the air, tumbling chaotically and throwing bike and body parts in all direction.

With only one hand to guide the bike, Dax barely managed to keep it upright without hitting anything. Yet another dump of adrenaline surged through his veins. This time, he didn't have it in him to check out the results of the crashes to his rear. By now, the bikers in front of him had noticed something was going on or at least the last few had.

He didn't think he had the energy to light up the blade anymore, nor did he think he could finish a proper cut with a blade that was now functioning more like a mundane weapon. He left the blade poking straight out from the shaft and aimed for the next biker.

As he drew behind the next biker, he lowered the scythe like a lance and angled it to the side, thrusting at the last moment. The biker didn't expect it and fell over, his bike going down on top of him. Dax grimaced. The biker appeared to be trapped or stuck to his bike somehow and was being dragged along.

There were only three bikers in front of him now, but they'd all clocked that he was behind them. They split up and spread out.

A gun shot exploded the mirror on his left handlebar, spraying him with glass and metal. Several small points of pain joined his litany of complaints. Another shot rang out behind him.

He wasn't sure how much more power his bike had, but he tried to coax more speed out of it. He slowly gained on the bike in front of him. Clenching his jaw, he took a deep, shaking breath and dumped his skin, hoping he'd be a bit lighter in his other form. It seemed to work as he came up on the tail of the middle bike ahead of him. If he closed on the group, perhaps their brothers would be more reluctant to take shots at him for fear of hitting one of their own. It wasn't often he hoped they had the special magic bullets loaded up. Using those would likely inspire even more of a desire to avoid hitting their shifter brothers.

He took aim with his scythe-lance and thrust out. But the closest biker swerved away, barely avoiding Dax's attack. The maneuver had cost the biker some speed. Dax adjusted as he and his target pulled even. Instead of trying to knock the biker off his seat, Dax shifted his aim and hurled his scythe into the front wheel of the motorcycle to delightfully predicable results.

The biker achieved flight, and his bike cartwheeled down the street toward the biker on the far-left side of the road. Swerving, the biker dodged the tumbling motorcycle but drifted too far to the left and went down on the edge of the pavement before sliding into a ditch. Out of the corner of his eye, Dax saw the biker bounce a couple times on the edge of the road until he slid to a stop using his face for brakes.

That left only the one bike on his right. Hoping he had enough energy to call his weapon, he reached out with his right hand into the aether, his skeletal hand shaking from exertion. He slumped and sighed in relief as he felt the rough wood of the handle against the bones of his fingers.

The last biker near him kept looking over his shoulder, his eyes wide and teeth bared. Dax was maxed out on speed and wasn't gaining, so he lined up straight behind the one out front. Dax tried to keep a bit of a slalom up to add an extra layer of difficulty to anyone behind him who wanted to open fire.

Judging his distance, Dax stabilized his bike and took aim. With every last bit of strength, he threw the scythe like a spear. It didn't have to travel far, but it still barely hit its target. It plunged into the rear tire of the motorcycle. He'd been hoping to put it through the biker's back, but he'd have to accept the small victory.

The bike fishtailed around as the biker tried to keep control of his wounded machine. Dax, now with both hands free, grasped both his handlebars and pulled into the middle of the road, riding the alternating stripes that separated the two sides of the street.

A quick mental check into the aether told him his scythe would be ready and waiting when he needed it next. He left it there and concentrated on escape. When he glanced to his left to peek the mirror, he found only the busted stem remained. The mirror on the right side of his handlebars showed no motorcycles pursuing. Unless he turned around and made a charge, he had no one left to fight and no energy to do it with.

TWENTY-SIX

DAX

Dax sat on the wooden dining table chair, carefully cleaning the blood from his leather jacket. Snorting, he shook his head, then yawned. He was thoroughly exhausted. But there was still more to do if he didn't want to spread biker blood all through his apartment before he retired for the evening…day. The sun was well up in the sky. It was probably closer to midmorning. He'd barely had enough energy left to take a circuitous route home in case he was followed. But he'd managed it by taking brief sips from the aether. It wasn't a sustainable practice for long periods, but it kept him topped up with enough energy to make it home before he totally burned himself out.

One unanticipated side effect of his unwanted war against the bikers was that he'd gotten very good at getting blood out of his clothing. Maybe he and Tomi could open up a laundry, though he wasn't sure he wanted to find out what kind of repeat customers he'd get.

Once the jacket was suitably clean, he draped it across the back of the chair next to the one he sat in, then stood and stripped down to his underwear. Tossing shirt and jeans into the kitchen sink, he filled it with water and poured in some of the enzymatic cleaner he'd found that worked best. It did a great job of removing the blood. Whatever residue might be left was hidden in the dark fabric. Another unanticipated side effect—discovering the benefits of a monochromatic wardrobe.

He hung up the hand towel next to the kitchen sink after washing his hands. As if he'd been waiting for his friend to finish, Morty meowed loudly and pawed at the cabinet door which hid his food.

"Sorry for the late dinner, buddy. Thanks for being patient." Dax bent over and scratched the kitten's ears as the cat wound his way through his person's legs, purring loudly. Dax dragged the scoop through food in the resealable container and dropped the breakfast into Morty's bowl with the clatter of kibble on stainless steel.

Now to remove the blood from his face and hair. He'd wiped himself down before entering the building in case one of his neighbors in the apartment building was a busy-body and poked their heads out into the hall as he walked by. It was an unlikely scenario. People in Red City kept their noses out of others' business because such things often led to bad results for the nosy one. But he was a cautious fellow anyway.

Dropping his undies, he tossed them into the hamper in his bedroom on his way to the bathroom. He turned on the water and shut the shower door to let the water warm up. A brief inspection in the mirror revealed hair glistening with dark, dried blood.

"Ughck." He stopped himself before he started to run his hands through his hair. He didn't need to leave blood prints everywhere. The easiest mess to clean up was the one not made.

As steam kissed the edges of the mirror, Dax decided the water was warm enough. Sighing, he let the water cascade over his head. Opening his eyes at that moment had been a mistake. He looked like he belonged in some gory horror flick. Water-diluted blood ran down his body in rivulets.

The sound of music entered his awareness. He hadn't turned any on before heading to the bathroom. Perhaps Tomi had stopped by to check on him. Then the song became clear—"Still Loving You" by the Scorpions. He thought he'd made his feelings for that song clear to Tomi.

"You always looked good covered in blood," a husky feminine voice said.

Startled, Dax screamed, and his foot slipped on wet tile. He flailed, trying to keep from falling in the tiny shower. With some luck, he braced himself and got his feet under himself. The voice laughed.

His hands shot down, covering his privates. With the blood-tainted water running out of his hair and over his face, he was reluctant to open his eyes. Removing one hand, he reached up and nudged the shower head to the side, then dragged his hand over his hair from front to back to push the water away from his face. He stuck his face into the stream, wiped the hopefully clean water off his face, and risked opening his eyes.

A giant crow sat perched on the shiny metallic top of the shower door. It tilted its head to the side and focused an eye on him. A glint of red passed over the dark orb of its eye.

"Not bad. Nicely formed. A bit skinny." The crow chuckled. "Have you taken your human body out for spin? Tested all the pleasures the form has to offer?"

Heat flooded his cheeks. He hoped his face was already red from lingering blood or that the heat of the water hid his blush.

"What the fuck are you doing in my house, Morrigan?" He sneered at the crow.

"Can't an old friend just stop in to make sure you got home safely?" There was an oddly friendly lilt to the question.

"We stopped being friends when you betrayed me. You're the reason I'm stuck in this 'a bit skinny' husk, washing my enemies' blood from my body."

"It's not the first time you've been covered in blood. We used to wade in it together when the job required it."

He snorted. "Aetherial fabric cleans easier than denim and skin." Before he'd been exiled to live as a human, he could simply will his own cleanliness into existence and the blood would be gone. Now, even if he shifted over to the Grim Reaper form, his human clothes retained whatever was on them. If he could shift away the blood and dirt, he'd save a fortune on laundry.

He stood awkwardly in silence, one side of his body hot from the streaming water and the other cool. The crow moved her head about in a crow-like fashion, keeping one eye keenly on him.

"You've been a busy boy lately."

"Have you had enough enjoyment at my expense? Did you come to get another dose of my humiliation to satisfy whatever cruel need you have?" Dax asked, heat in his voice.

She didn't answer immediately. He thought she was ignoring the question. When she finally spoke, her dark, husky voice startled him. "Do you really hate me so?"

He opened his mouth but let it hang open, words unspoken. Hate was a strong word. He'd seen the wages of hate. He'd explored the memories of the body he'd stolen from the biker who'd threatened Tomi and Adele all those years ago. Besides the tattoos he'd burned off the body, he'd found a mind rotted and corrupted with vile hate.

"No. I don't hate you. But you hurt me. Badly."

"And it hasn't healed yet? I thought mortals were good at healing their hurts?"

"Wounds may heal, but they leave scars. Especially in the mind and on the spirit. I was closer to you than any being attached to this world. And you used that closeness to betray me."

She sighed wearily. "I know you don't believe me, but not all appears as it seems. To you, it was betrayal. To me, it was all I could do to save you."

"Whatever."

She croaked at him, her eyes flashing red, and shivers and goose bumps rose on his skin despite the steam of the water. Even though he'd seen those eyes and the anger in them before, the base instincts of the human's reptilian mind still reacted to fear, and The Morrigan could be one of the scariest of divine beings when she desired.

Ruffling her feathers, she settled down with an exasperated sigh. "Someday you'll give me an opportunity to explain…" She trailed off and shook her head.

He didn't know what to say to that. Pursing his lips, his mind wandered to how she'd gotten into his warded and protected home. Even though the manbo had said her protection gris-gris would work, they wouldn't be able to block someone truly powerful. If Morrigan had forced her way in, he'd have felt the power—even in his diminished capacity.

"How did you get into my home?"

"Mortholomew let me in."

"That cat? You're blaming the fucking cat?" He removed his hands from over his privates and moved them to his hips so he could properly scoff at the suggestion, then hurriedly covered himself again once he realized what he was doing.

The crow squawked with laughter, turned around, and launched herself into the air. But instead of flapping around the closed bathroom, she disappeared through the wall, leaving her fading laughter in her wake.

"Just be careful and mind your power."

He almost didn't hear it, but instead of going through his ears, she'd said it directly into his mind.

"Always has to get the fucking last word." He angled the water so it streamed over his whole body. It felt noticeably cooler than it had a few minutes ago. "And you've ruined my hot shower."

TWENTY-SEVEN

DAX

Dax bolted awake. Something hard and pointy had startled him out of a dream which was already quickly fading into nothing. He squeezed his eyes shut and inhaled deeply, holding it for a few moments. Nearby, a raspy, oddly disharmonic purr grew in volume. Maybe the kitten had been kneading him and got through the blankets with his claws. He'd have to give them a trim in the morning when he woke up again. Or rather that evening, since it had been midmorning before he had finally made his way to bed.

Reaching down toward the sound of the purr, he drew his hand back when he felt something oddly textured and hard. Pushing himself up onto his elbows, he looked for whatever weird thing the kitten had dragged into bed.

He blinked his eyes rapidly as he tried to get them to adjust to the darkness. "What the fuck?"

Scrambling back with his hands and his feet, something white tumbled to the floor with a startled cat yowl. A moment later it jumped back onto the bed.

It was a skeleton cat—a small one.

It looked around, its bone jaw opening wide as it yawned, and started purring again. It stalked toward him, the tiny white bones of its tail clicking a bit as the cat wagged it slightly.

Dax swallowed and narrowed his eyes at the skeletal kitten. "Morty?"

The kitten spun a couple donuts before plopping down in his lap. Dax rubbed a finger over the kitten's skull between where the ears would normally be. The fleshy pad of his finger dragged along the slightly rough texture of the bare bone.

"What are you, little buddy?"

In response, Morty purred louder, butting his skull into Dax's hand. He'd thought Morrigan's instance on blaming the cat for letting her in had been purely bullshit. But...

"Mortholomew, did you let in a big crow?" He didn't expect an answer. But at least the kitten acknowledged his voice by rolling over and exposing the ends of his ribs. "You know being soft and fluffy is one of the draws of petting a cat, right?"

The kitten just nudged him with a bony paw.

"Fine." Dax rubbed the kitten's rib bones gently.

Maybe The Morrigan hadn't lied. He looked down at the skeleton he'd thought had been just a normal kitten. She'd called him Mortholomew. He'd never spoken that nickname out loud in front of anyone but the kitten. Perhaps she'd plucked it out of his head and used the information to blame Morty and obfuscate the hole in his defenses she'd exploited to peep on him while he showered.

A pang of regret and longing for old memories washed over him. She'd been his confidant and friend. They'd roamed the planet reaping souls together, sharing in the small joys of the mortal world, such as tea. But she'd betrayed him, and now after nearly six years of ignoring him, she wouldn't leave him alone. If she'd stood by him, even if the result had still been the same—his exile to Red City to live as a human—it might have been a bit more bearable if he could've talked with someone who truly understood at least a piece of who he was and where'd he'd come from.

Tomi did his best to be a friend and not judge his weirdness and lack of experience as a human, but he'd never understand what Dax really had been or his true power. At first, Tomi had only felt comfortable with their relationship being that of boss and employee, though at times it felt more like Tomi was the boss, since he had years of experience working in bars. But proximity and familiarity had bred friendliness which had turned into a real and deep friendship.

Dax trusted Tomi and had witnessed the kind person he was firsthand. Tomi was someone who was loyal to his community and family, and Dax had been welcomed into both.

Sighing, he reached over and grabbed his phone to check the time. It was just after nine p.m. He still felt tired, but the bone weariness of being overexerted both physically and magically had receded to a dull throbbing in the background. And though he didn't want to, he needed to get into the bar and relieve Suzie, who'd pulled a double shift to make up for his unavailability due to his exhaustion.

Running a business in Red City was hard enough. But trying to do it while fighting a guerrilla war with Nazi werewolf bikers? That was just plain asinine.

He picked up the skeletal kitten and set him on the floor. "You need to be careful not to show this side of yourself to anyone but me. OK?"

He wasn't sure if Morty understood or not, but the kitten mewed in those odd creepy harmonics that Dax had when he was in his skeletal form. It made him shiver, and it was just from a kitten. He couldn't imagine what his voice, especially when he was angry, must do to his friends…let alone his enemies.

Morty hissed at something, the noise sounding more normal. Then the kitten bounded away, once again a little black and white bundle of fur. After Dax dressed, he called in an order to Mama Adele's. He might as well fortify his tired body with whatever today's special was.

TWENTY-EIGHT

JAMIE

Jamie inhaled deeply as she got back into her car after making her latest delivery. The lingering aroma of cornbread and spicy sausage was way better than new-car smell, but it did have the deleterious effect of making her way too hungry.

For the first time in ages, she felt properly full most of the time. During the stress and added poverty of hotel hopping to avoid being tracked, she'd dropped a bunch of weight, until she was nearly skin and bones. She'd been running on fumes, anger, and whatever food she could scrounge with what little spare cash she had, or whatever her mom left in the fridge. Mama Adele had taken it as a personal mission to put "some meat on her bones."

Whenever she got her free shift meal, there was always an extra helping of cornbread and whatever the protein was. When she'd commented that it must be adding extra expenses, she was told to mind her own business. It was a management decision. Of course, Mama Adele had said it with her characteristic warm smile. So, Jamie ate all the extra food she was given and enjoyed every bite. Now that she was being regularly fed and had a welcoming place to sleep, her mood had improved a lot. It was amazing what consistent nutrition could do for a person.

By the time she returned to the restaurant, she was practically drooling in anticipation. The closed sign had been turned on, but the interior lights still shone brightly. No one dined this late in the evening, but they served a few simpler platings for orders at Dax's bar as a not-quite-late-night menu.

"Just in time, girl," Berta said, stuffing some food boxes into a bag. "One last delivery for you."

"Oh…"

Berta chuckled. "Don't worry. It's just dinner for Dax, Tomi, and Suzie. Take it over to the bar, then you're done. Want me to plate your food?"

Jamie hadn't talked to Suzie much since their little adventure rescuing Dax. With all the activity related to tracking down the bikers, Suzie had been covering a lot of extra hours at the bar. It would be nice to catch up with her friend. "Actually, can you add it to the bag? I'll eat with Suzie."

"You got it. It'll just be a minute."

"I heard," Mama Adele called from the kitchen. "I'll box it up."

The phone rang, but it was the ring that indicated it was a call from the bar. Berta picked it up, jotting down notes on an order pad. When she was done, she tore it off and attached to the wheel where the tickets were placed. She rang the bell on the passthrough window into the kitchen. "Order up for the bar."

A moment later, Mama Adele set some boxes on the window and rang the bell. "Order up for Jamie. I'll dish up the bar order right now."

"Mind running it over with your stuff, Jamie?" Berta asked.

"Not at all."

A couple minutes later, she had a large bag filled with their food in one hand and a box with the bar order in the other. Berta let her out the door and locked it behind her. Jamie walked briskly, the box making her hand hot. When she arrived, she backed into the door, pushing it open into the bar.

"I've got an order for Geoffrey," she called out.

Suzie, who stood behind the bar, waved her over. "At the bar, Jamie."

She wove her way through the crowd at the bar and handed Suzie the box. "I've got food for you in the bag."

"Right on. Go feed Dax first, then I'm done for the night. He's in the tearoom." She turned to a white man in a gray suit, a glass of whiskey and a napkin with silverware sitting in front of him. "Want me to put it on a plate for you?"

"Nah. No sense making you wash a dish. The box will do," he replied.

"You got it."

Jamie smiled at her friend and proceeded down the hallway to the tearoom. As soon as she passed the restroom, she realized she had to use it. So, she quickly dropped off the bag with a quick hello to Dax and Tomi, then took care of her needs before returning.

Tomi had retrieved another plate from behind the tearoom's bar and was busy plating their four dinners, dropping a piece of aluminum foil over one—Suzie's. Jamie sat quietly and waited, her stomach growling in anticipation.

Dax looked...tired. That was the only way she could describe it. He had dark bags under his eyes and looked paler than normal, which was a trick since the guy looked like skim milk at the best of times. She hadn't heard what had happened last night with their raids. She'd helped Dax, Tomi, and Boudreaux plan them, but had been forbidden to participate.

They had been the first planned attacks using the GPS data she and The Rat had generated. After nearly being captured by the bikers and escaping through a mix of sheer luck, voodoo magic, and a couple of brave rats, she had been relieved when Dax and Tomi had asked her to sit this one out. Dax was a force of nature when he wanted to kill people in hand-to-hand combat, and Boudreaux and his crew were trained ex-military.

She was eighteen with a vicious survival streak that could turn either toward fight or flight, depending on the situation. And though she'd taken a few martial arts classes, she was in no way a badass with fists of fury. She'd do her part to protect her newly found friends, but she was glad they'd chosen to use her in ways that worked more to her skills and strengths—stealth, tracking, and being clever.

"Please, eat. I have a few questions for you, Jamie, but they can wait. I'm not sure I could pay attention with your stomach growling like an angry wolf." Dax attempted a friendly smile, but it exaggerated his tired appearance. After barely letting his lips tip up, he gave up and picked up his fork.

Only slightly curious about what he wanted to know, she chose to indulge her stomach and dug in. It was a struggle to slow down and not make constant noises of appreciation at the food. Soul food really did nourish the spirit and the body. When they all finished, she cleared the table, setting everything in an easy stack that could be moved up to the dishwasher later.

"So," Dax started, "a weird thing happened earlier today." He looked up from his hands clasped in front him on the table and made eye contact with her. "You stayed in my place for a while. Did Morty ever do anything…strange?"

That was certainly not the question she thought he'd ask. "Strange? I'm not sure what you mean. He's a bit odd, but not really out of bounds for a cat. Not that I have a lot of personal experience." She'd always wanted a cat, but her parents had never allowed it. So, she'd had to content herself by making friends with a few of the neighborhood strays.

"Nothing…out of the ordinary, even for a weird cat?"

Tomi looked just as clueless as she felt. She shook her head slowly. "Sorry, Dax. Just cat stuff."

"Dax, buddy, what's going on?" Tomi asked, leaning closer to his friend.

Dax took a sip of his tea, staring into nowhere for a moment. "Well, I don't think he's a normal, mundane kitten. At least not anymore. Assuming he ever was."

"Can you be more specific?"

Dax filled them in on his uninvited visitor and how she'd blamed the cat for letting her in. Morty seemed to be a smart cat but not unlock-that-many-locks smart. Jamie had to clamp her teeth together when he told them the name of his visitor. Morrigan had sworn Jamie and Suzie to secrecy as the source of his location, not that it would change his attitude about her. There was an invective in his voice when talking about her that Jamie had never heard before. Morrigan had done something serious to wrong him in the past, though Tomi seemed to know more of the story than Jamie did, which only made sense. Tomi was his best friend.

"And then," Dax continued, "I wake up and there's a skeletal kitten in my bed. Startled the crap out of me."

She wasn't quite sure she'd heard that last part right.

Tomi's eyes narrowed in confusion. "Like animated, living skeleton, without fleshy bits? Like you in your make-things-dead mode?"

Dax nodded, a worried expression on his face. "Yeah. Pretty much."

"Little tattered robe and scythe?" Tomi asked, one eyebrow rising.

Jamie clamped her jaw tightly to avoid laughing at the image of a little Grim Reaper kitten. She was going to see if she could get him a little Morty-sized robe. The scythe seemed silly though.

Dax chuckled. "No. Just a skeleton cat. But his purr and meow were…off."

Tomi shivered, and Jamie couldn't help joining him.

"Yeah. I know that voice," Tomi said.

"So…what happened to him?" Jamie asked. "Morty, I mean."

"I have no idea." Dax shrugged. "Hell, this could just be his nature."

Tomi rested his elbows on the table, cupping his chin in his hands. "I might… Mind you, I don't know jack shit about this kind of stuff. But that time you got"—his eyes flicked to Jamie briefly—"shot, you were bleeding in your bathtub for a long time. That kitten was covered in your blood by the time I found you. I know you're a human on the outside, but you're not really. You know what I mean?"

He seemed to be struggling with analyzing the nature of his friend. Jamie couldn't blame him. She had even less of an idea of who or what Dax really was, other than someone very supernatural who could do Grim Reaper shit. But why would *the* Grim Reaper be stuck owning a shitty dive bar?

"I mean that was right after you found him, and he was a scrawny little thing. He probably"—Tomi grimaced—"groomed himself after that too. I don't think anything can be in contact with that much of your blood, especially considering he's so small, and not come out changed. Your blood is bound to be full of…magic."

Dax, his eyes drooping to half mast, smiled warmly at his friend. "You always struggle with my world. You grew up with voodoo."

"I grew up with it, but that doesn't mean I paid any attention. Not until I met you." He chuckled ruefully. "Meeting you kind of opened up that world to me. And it's still weird as fuck in a world that only believes in the mundane."

"I guess so."

She'd always known about magic. She was a supernatural being. Her world had always included the world of the magic and the mundane. But she'd grown up in Red City, where corruption tainted it all.

"Huh. So you have a magical cat now." Tomi shook his head, a smirk on his face.

"Looks like it." Dax sighed wearily. "I should probably have the manbo take a look at him. Not sure the vet is the right place to go for this. Anyway, I better go send Suzie back to eat, or her food will go cold."

Jamie wasn't sure how she felt about a magical cat, especially one soaked in death magic. Part of the attraction of a cat was the fur and the cute ears, both of which weren't made of bone. She still wanted to see Morty. She'd made friends, of a sort, with a grim reaper dude, why not a grim reaper kitty?

TWENTY-NINE

DAX

Dax finally felt rested and back at full energy. It had a been a few days since his exhausting night and morning. Other than working and checking on the movement of their tracker tags, he'd pretty much spent every spare moment getting caught up on sleep and eating way more food than he was used to. His body needed it all to get back to base level.

Geoffrey bellied up to the bar in one of his standard gray business suits and rested his elbows on the counter's edge as he surveyed the shelves of whiskey. "I'm feeling a bit Irish today. Anything new?"

Suzie turned around and ran her eyes over the shelves of bottles containing liquid of various shades of amber. "Nothing new and Irish, I don't think. Dax?"

"Nope. A couple new Scotches, a new Bourbon, a Japanese—if you're feeling a bit flush."

"I love Japanese whiskey, but my paycheck can't handle that love affair. I'll go with the Red Breast."

Suzie nodded, faced the backbar, grabbed the stepladder, and unfolded it so she could retrieve the whiskey from one of the high shelves she was too short to reach. After she filled a dram glass, she set it in front of Geoffrey and moved on to the next customer at the bar.

Despite the summer heat outside and the anemic air conditioning inside, the crowd sitting around the bar was pretty good sized. Especially after all the chaos that had happened around the bar thanks to the assassination attempts the Nazi bikers had made on his life.

But life in Red City was never quiet. Violence was all too common, and people had grown used to it, though bombings were rare. But even that hadn't kept the regulars away for long.

Dax had to attribute their loyalty to the crew Tomi, and now Suzie, had helped him put together. Beckie and Fred had turned out to be excellent fits for the bar's customer base and kept people happy and coming back to spend more. For the first time in a long time, business was looking up, and if things stayed this way, they'd be set once the busier rainy season started and people migrated to bars with patios in the summer returned. Though they were planning to add an outdoor space, he doubted they'd be able to get the permits and finish the work before the fall and winter rains set in.

Once she finished serving the waiting customers, Suzie leaned against the bar and chatted with Geoffrey, though Dax paid no attention as he focused on his plans for fixing up the alley to turn it into a patio. The conversation and the normal noise of the bar blurred into background noise. The only thing that pulled him out of his brain was the sound of low, deep rumbling.

He spun around on his stool as the sound of lots of loud motors vibrated the glass of the front windows. It sounded like a bunch of motorcycles…

"Shit," Dax mumbled.

"What's going on, Dax?" Suzie asked, moving down the bar so she stood across from him.

"If you've got Boudreaux's number, give him a call and tell him to get his crew down here. If not, get ahold of Tomi and have him do it."

"I'll call Tomi." She pulled out her phone and opened it.

"Hey, man, what's going on?" Geoffrey had swung around on his stool and now faced Dax.

"Trouble."

The motors stopped, and the resulting silence felt deafening and made the jukebox sound twice as loud.

Screams erupted in the bar as a brick shattered a window and thudded onto a tabletop. Fortunately, the drawn curtains had kept the glass from spraying very far into the bar. Though the couple sitting at the window table scrambled away, spilling their pints of beers in the process.

Suzie bustled through the crowd and stopped at the table. "There's a note tied to it."

A moment later, another brick flew through the other front window, sending the people sitting near it scattering. Chairs scraped and fell, and somewhere a breaking glass announced a dropped drink.

Dax unfolded his legs from the stool and stood up. "Everyone get away from the windows. Suzie, unlock the tearoom. That's the safest spot. And call Adele and warn her."

Suzie, leaving the brick alone, spun on her heel and stormed through the bar to the hallway leading to the tearoom. On the way, she stopped behind the bar and grabbed the Judge—a two-thirds sized wooden baseball bat. "Right. Everyone with me."

Geoffrey stood up but didn't move to join the crowd heading to the back.

"You too, Geoffrey," Dax said, waiting for the path to open up so he could check out the note on the brick.

Suzie reemerged, fighting her way through the crowd like a salmon swimming upstream and using the Judge stuck out in front of her to part the people. "Tomi just called back. He's on his way, so is Boudreaux."

"Thanks, Suzie. You're in charge in here, and if you need to, get everyone out the side door." Dax stopped in front of the table with the brick that had the note on it.

"Hey, fucksticks! Come out here," a rough call came from outside.

"Come on, Geoffrey, into the back," Suzie said.

"No way." He grabbed his glass of whiskey and tossed it back before setting it onto the bar with a hard clunk of glass on wood. He quickly removed his jacket and draped it over the barstool he'd been sitting on. Reaching into the pockets of his suit jacket, his hands reemerged with a set of brass knuckles on each one. With a practiced hand, he rolled up his sleeves, revealing full sleeve tattoos on both forearms.

"Holy crap," Suzie said quietly.

Geoffrey clanged his metal-covered knuckles together, and a wicked grin spread across his face. "No one suspects a Geoffrey."

Dax smirked and shook his head as he unfolded the note.

You have 5 minutes to clear out the civilians, or they go down with you.

"Suzie, change of plans. Get everyone out the front door and take them around the side. They're offering safe passage for customers. I want you to go with them."

Suzie stood up to her full height, which wasn't that intimidating, even in her thick-soled Docs. "I can handle myself, Dax." She brandished the bat as evidence.

"I know, but we need to get the customers out, and I need someone to coordinate communication."

"Oh, nah! You're not turning the Black woman into the phone operator."

"Look, if Beckie or Fred were here, one of them could do it. I need you to be Uhura right now, and if the opportunity crops up, you can set your Docs to their Nazi-stomping setting. But I'd prefer it if you hung back, since these aren't your average biker assholes. These are wolf shifters and way stronger."

"The fuck you say?" Geoffrey asked, his eyebrows pinched together in confusion.

"Shit." Dax stared between Geoffrey and Suzie, trying to figure out how he was going to handle that slip of information. "Um, it's a long story. Just trust me, they're super strong and probably faster than you're used to. If you insist on throwing down, you need to know what you're facing."

"Right, right, right." Suzie looked around, then turned toward the people in the hallway and tearoom. "Alright, everyone grab your stuff and head out the front door. Swing around right and then another right and past the restaurant. If you parked out front, you're shit out of luck, and you shouldn't have been driving to a bar anyway."

The crowd stared at her, a few people slack jawed, but most of them looking scared.

"Move it!" She bopped the floor loudly with the Judge a few times. "Go, go, go!"

At first, one person took a hesitant step, then another less hesitant step, until the crowd finally broke and they shoved their way back through the bar, knocking tables and chairs out of the way. But surprisingly, they didn't shove each other, instead guiding and helping each other to the door. When someone went down, a couple people blocked them off until someone else could help them up.

Suzie watched them for a half a minute before darting into the back. The pocket door into the tearoom thudded in its frame as she must have flung it open. A minute later she reemerged with a cardboard box that rattled with ceramics, the Judge tucked under one arm.

A sense of relief washed over him. Suzie had grabbed some of his teapots and cups while she'd checked the backroom. Once she rattled out the door, it only left Dax and Geoffrey standing in the abandoned bar.

"What now, Dax?" Geoffrey asked.

"I guess we step out front. But I want you to give a good thought to not joining in." Not waiting for an answer, Dax strode purposefully toward the front door. In the back of his head, he reached out into the aether to make sure his scythe and skeleton form were ready to go, if he needed them—not that he should be breaking either out in the middle of a public street. He hoped the bikers left their wolf forms packed away as well. A populated city street wasn't the kind of place supernaturals liked to use to resolve differences of opinion.

Death and magical mayhem were better left for more private environs.

THIRTY

JAMIE

Jamie yawned. Tonight had been a busy night of deliveries, including one to a large party that had nearly filled her car with steaming hot food. She'd also had another larger order that was out of their normal delivery range, but they'd decided to send her anyway. At least they'd tipped well for the inconvenience.

She wanted to check in for any last deliveries, but when her tired eyes flashed over the clock in the dash, she realized there wouldn't be any. The last delivery had taken a little longer than she'd anticipated, and it was past the window where they'd accept any more. If she'd been paying attention, she could have made a quick call to confirm and gone straight home. But it was too late now. She was almost back to the restaurant.

As she drove by, she noticed a small crowd hustling in front of the restaurant, glancing anxiously over their shoulders toward the street in front of the bar. They looked like the normal crowd that hung out at the bar at night—dark clothes, band Ts, and hipster haircuts.

She brought her eyes forward just in time to slow and stop at the corner stop sign. "Holy shit…"

The street was clogged with motorcycles and bikers. Normally, she'd take a left and park or head home. But that way was out. Her fingers tapped nervously on the steering wheel. She wondered if she'd stayed stopped at the corner too long?

Putting the blinker on for a right turn, she followed it by immediately making the right. She didn't want them to stop her or worse, recognize her. She took the first left she could and drove back into the neighborhood, pulling over when she felt far enough away.

As soon as she put the car in park, she started panting, the adrenaline dump of seeing so many bikers hitting her hard. There were a lot of bikers. And they'd nearly killed or captured her too many times. Dax could handle this. He'd ripped through a bunch of them before.

And she wasn't a fighter.

But that excuse didn't sit right with her. She had been fighting. Maybe it wasn't in hand-to-hand combat like a warrior, but she'd been doing loads to fight the bikers. A wave of disgust at herself pushed a frown onto her face.

She caught a glimpse of her eyes in the rearview mirror. "Coward," she mumbled, shaking her head.

Slapping the steering wheel with both hands, she checked the mirror to make sure the way was clear and pulled back onto the road. Just because they weren't directly assaulting her didn't mean she should try to play it safe.

Her new friends had taken a chance on her and given her a job, a car, and a place to sleep. They'd welcoming her with companionship and a sense of belonging. They'd placed their trust in her. She couldn't betray all that by hiding until the bad guys ran away, and she was assigned a specific task to perform.

She'd hung out on a roof, surrounded by bikers who'd do bad things to her if they caught her, for fuck's sake. She'd kept her cool and gotten out of that situation. It was time to step up.

Pausing at a stop sign, she brought up the image of the street in front of the bar. If she went down two more blocks, she could cross the street far enough away from the bikers that she could set up.

Luckily, there was an empty parking spot on the corner. If she leaned forward, she could even see a few of the bikers. While she waited for her next move, she reached over and grabbed the knit beanie off the passenger seat and pulled it over her short hair. Before, her hair had been long and thick. It would have made for a large, messy bun that would barely fit under the hat. It was another benefit of the short haircut Suzie had helped her with. Though she wished she had some other way to disguise her appearance than a knit hat. She couldn't drive with the mask pulled down, and it didn't make for much of a disguise with it just covering her hair.

She smirked. If she had a fake mustache, she'd look just like some random dude driving if anyone looked in their rearview mirror. She'd have to find a novelty shop or order some online. Picturing herself with a stick-on handlebar mustache brought out a small chuckle. It would look ridiculous.

THIRTY-ONE

DAX

The bikers were arrayed in a semicircle in front of the bar, their backs to Thuc and his daughter Minh's convenience store. A quick scan told Dax there were around twenty dirtbag bikers.

"I hear you've been looking for me." A tall muscular man with medium-long blond hair—the sides were shaved—and a well-trimmed beard stepped out from the center back. He wore the club's leather vest over a tight black T-shirt, along with jeans and motorcycle boots. If it wasn't for the burning hatred in his eyes, he might have been considered handsome.

The clicking of metal drew Dax's attention down to the biker's hand. He was playing with a butterfly knife, flicking it open and closed with a practiced motion. Narrowing his eyes, Dax couldn't help but wonder what sinister enchantments had been placed on it. The bikers seemed to find new and exciting ways to create nasty weapons that would hurt in more ways than their mundane purpose.

Putting his hand in his pocket, Dax grunted in dissatisfaction at the emptiness. He'd stopped carrying the switchblade he'd taken off the bikers a while ago, afraid the cops would find it in one of their random stops during their harassment campaign.

Dax lowered his eyelids and let the corner of one side of his mouth quirk up in hopes that it made him look more sinister. It worked on a few of the bikers, and they took a half step back. "How about you and I take this somewhere private, Ivar. There's no need to involve everyone here. Certainly not in a public street where someone might call the cops…"

The biker scoffed. "Do you think they'd actually show up here and now?"

The rumor that the cops and the bikers cooperated had been confirmed when the cops had called the bikers to pick up their dead buddies at the compound, but the comment was one more piece of evidence that pushed it toward the side of cold, hard fact. It also probably explained why the bikers had allowed the non-combatants inside the bar to flee. If they killed too many innocents, it might cause the cops problems which required them to do something about the bikers, when they'd rather keep the relationship clandestine and convenient.

He gave a nonchalant shrug. "If this is where you want to meet your end, fine by me. But are you sure you've brought enough thugs? I tend to chew through them pretty fast…if you'll recall."

A dark wave passed over Ivar's face. "You're stalling. We know your bag of tricks by now. You can come with us quietly, chained up, or we can deal with this here in the street." He looked at the pavement in front of Dax. "You'd make a splendid chalk outline."

"I don't intend to go with you quietly. You can take me by force, or you can fuck off."

"All bluster." Ivar shook his head. "You can talk a big game all you want, but it's finally time to pay the piper."

"Music? I always preferred Nazi stomping to music." Geoffrey clanged his brass knuckles together.

Ivar gave the man, in his button-down shirt with the sleeves rolled up and gray suit pants, a quick glance, then dismissed him.

"Your little friend has a big mouth, but he's not equipped for this kind of fight." Ivar fixed his cold gaze on Geoffrey. "Run away, little man. This fight doesn't concern your type."

The biker was right—this wasn't a fight the human should have been involved in. He was also right about the fact Dax was stalling for time, hoping Tomi or Boudreaux would show up with reinforcements.

"I hope you have a plan," Geoffrey said quietly, leaning toward Dax. "I can handle my own, but I'm not sure I can take this many."

Dax almost wished the man wasn't so enthusiastic about punching white supremacist bikers. If he had to, Dax could handle this crowd much like he had at the bikers' bar. A well-wielded meteor hammer could clear a lot of space…if he didn't have to account for a fragile human.

Ivar looked down at his watch. "Time's up. Anyone left in the bar is toast."

All things considered, Dax's meteor hammer was still his best option. Sticking out his left hand, he grabbed his scythe from out of the aether, transforming it into a heavy, skull-shaped ball attached to a long chain, itself affixed to a short-handled scythe.

Ivar raised a hand and casually brought it down again. A biker emerged from each side of the crowd, their lighters flicking as they held them to cloths sticking out of bottles of liquor.

"Fuck," Dax mumbled. Molotov cocktails.

Unfortunately, a meteor hammer wasn't a "cold start" weapon. Dropping the skull hammer and spooling out reasonable length of chain, he started twirling it. He forced himself to be patient. The laws of physics couldn't be hot-wired. He needed to build up momentum. As his eyes flicked back and forth between the two bikers, he settled on the one who seemed to be having trouble getting his bottle lit.

"Geoffrey. Back up to the wall."

"What?"

"Trust me." Dax increased the circle of his twirling as the human backed away from him.

"Where'd he get that?" Geoffrey mumbled.

Once Dax felt he had enough speed, he spun around and unleashed the meteor hammer at the biker who'd finally lit his cocktail. The bottle shattered, spilling its lit contents all over the biker. He screamed and dropped to the ground. Ignoring the flaming biker,

Dax took several calculated steps and retracted his hammer while keeping the momentum. With a quick shift, he sent it flying toward the other biker.

But this one had been prepared and rolled out of the way. He came up in a crouch and flicked his lighter. This time the rag caught. Before Dax could adjust, the biker flung the bottle.

Dax watched with his jaw hanging open, as bottle arced through the air toward the front of his bar. He forgot about his weapon. The skull-shaped hammer thudded to the ground and rolled along the ground until it ran out chain. Cringing, Dax spun around as the bottle flew through the already broken window into the building he'd just purchased a few months ago.

The bikers laughed and guffawed as the flames licked at the curtains and the window frame. Frustration gnawed at Dax's guts as he clenched his jaw, grinding his teeth. He wanted to unleash himself and reap every last bastard. Not only did he want to cut their life threads, he wanted to destroy their souls and negate their existence from the universe.

THIRTY-TWO

DAX

"D-dax? What…" The words, though coming from someplace close, filtered through his mind as if they were far away.

He wasn't sure if he was maintaining his human facade. The heat building inside his bar felt distant, as if his flesh were hidden away and all that faced the flames was black-robe-covered bleached bones.

Flames were beyond his province. They were neither alive nor dead.

Off in the distance, the rumble of obnoxious motorcycle engines grew louder. He sighed. More fucking bikers.

Drawing in a deep breath along with the last scraps of his will, he forced his mortal flesh to cling tightly to his bones. He took a shaky step backward and turned around to face the bikers, stopping once he caught Ivar's gaze.

The blue flames lighting Dax's eyes intensified, putting the mundane fire behind him to shame. With a twitch of his wrist, he started the metal skull spinning. He moved toward Ivar, who trembled where he stood, seemingly locked in place by Dax's gaze. The leader of the bikers gave his head a shake and took a hesitant step backward followed by a more sure one.

153

The meteor hammer whistled through the air ominously, the nooks and crannies of the metal skull tearing at the wind as it whirled. Snapping into action, Dax sent the hammer whizzing toward the biker who'd been tormenting him for months.

Ivar, seemingly recovered, staggered back but grabbed one of his brothers and shoved him in the way to receive the punishment of the skull. A split second later, the biker's head exploded into bone fragments and goo.

"Get him!" Ivar shouted.

The bikers shifted nervously on their feet, looking back and forth between Dax and their boss.

"You fucking pansies! This is your chance. Avenge your brothers." Ivar shouldered his way back through the last line of bikers, ensuring he had a shield of flesh armor between himself and Dax's weapon.

"I suggest you rethink that last command." A familiar deep voice emerged from behind him. Boudreaux, holding a pipe—likely scavenged from the bins behind the building holding the scraps from the apartment remodel—stepped up next to Dax.

An occasional scrape of a boot on the pavement could be heard through the roar of the building fire. If they didn't do something soon, he'd loose the entire building.

Boudreaux and his crew fanned out around Dax. Most of them were similarly armed with whatever they'd been able to scrounge. He wondered why they weren't better armed.

"No, you can't go in there!" The frantic voice of Tomi joined the general assault of sounds. "Minh, no!"

"Tomi, I know what I'm doing. You have to trust me. Please," Minh replied, adding weight to the last word.

Dax wanted to see what the fuck was going on with his friend and the daughter of the convenience store's owner, but he had to keep his eye on the bikers and maintain control of his weapon as he set it twirling in a tight circle at his side.

"Damn it, Tomi, if you don't let me go, it'll be too late, and I won't be able to save what's left."

"OK." The words sounded scared.

"Thank you. Now get that fire hydrant open." Minh's order was followed by feet slapping on the sidewalk as she ran behind him.

The fire, now a blazing, crackling inferno, dulled for a moment then roared back to its previous intensity.

"Minh…" Tomi said, his voice filled with anguish.

Dax returned his focus entirely to the bikers. The two sides—the bikers, and Dax along with, Geoffrey, Boudreaux and his crew—stared at each other. The stillness was fragile and potent with potential.

Dax had had enough. He sent the meteor hammer sailing toward the nearest target, taking off the side of the biker's skull, and pulled the hammer back, returning it to its deadly spin. The bikers stared at their fallen brother. Next to Dax, Boudreaux lifted his pipe into the air, then charged forward with a mighty yell.

Joining him, his crew surged forward, letting their own yells mingle with their leaders.

The charge caught the bikers off balance, since they'd been focused on the biker Dax had just killed. It was probably a good thing Boudreaux and his friends took the initiative. Most of his crew, the ones Dax had met, were human. Although they were mostly ex-military and had superior training, they were at a physical disadvantage when it came to dealing with the bikers, who were all wolf shifters.

Careful to avoid hitting any of his allies, Dax moved forward, flicking out his hammer on a shorter leash to keep it tightly under his control.

A grunt as ribs shattered greeted him. A biker had tried to jump out of the way, which had saved his life, at least momentarily. Seeing the wounded man, one of Boudreaux's crew brought a pipe down, onto the top of the biker's head, bashing it in.

Now that the bikers had finally woken up, they were giving as good as they got. They still outnumbered Dax and his friends. For the moment, Dax was caught in a pocket of inactivity with no easy targets as he spun his hammer, so he surveyed the action to figure out what to do next.

Off to one side, Geoffrey was juking and punching like he had experience in a boxing ring. The brass knuckles were creating mayhem in their wake. If he didn't outright drop a biker, the punches slowed them down and made them easy targets for whoever jumped in next.

Despite the early success, the bikers used their superior physicality and were turning the odds back in their favor. They still had a greater numbers despite those brothers who'd already gone down.

If things went on much longer, Dax's human friends would be in serious danger. It was time to cheat.

THIRTY-THREE

JAMIE

As Jamie leaned forward, she gasped. The fighting had begun. Narrowing her eyes and staring at the bar, she brought a hand up in shock and covered her mouth. Flames licked at the window from the inside. Either something had caught fire, or the bikers had started one.

Panic filled her gut. If someone didn't put out the fire soon, the whole building would burn down, including Mama Adele's. The whole building would be destroyed, and she'd be out of a job. And if the fire department was as corrupt as the cops, the fire might spread to the other buildings in the neighborhood.

She didn't know if Dax and Tomi all had savings or good insurance, but it probably wouldn't matter. This city was corrupt to the bone. They were just small business owners and not members of the city's privileged elite. They'd get screwed over and some shitty developer would buy the building, turning it into some shitty generic condo that stripped the character out of the neighborhood and started the process of gentrification.

She wondered if that might actually be the reason this was all happening. Maybe developers had paid the bikers to go after the local businesses. She snorted. It all seemed too far-fetched and mundane. There were plenty of other empty lots and derelict buildings to take down. But if it did turn out to be unscrupulous developers, she'd be pissed. She'd almost been turned into a cold-blooded murderer for the sake of a few thousand square feet of dirt and building.

A motorcycle engine revving up pulled her out of her musings about the possible Scooby-Doo of it all. Leaning forward, she saw one biker pull away from the crowd and head her way. Her eyes went wide, and she ducked sideways. She recognized the biker. It was Ivar.

Lying across the front seats to avoid being seen, she hooked her foot on the brake pedal and pushed it down, then reached over and turned the key, starting the car. As soon as the bike passed her position, she sat up and put the car in drive, pulling away from the curb and behind the bike.

She should have waited a few more seconds. She was too close. A quick glance in his mirror would tell him he was being followed. And he'd recognize her. They'd had several close encounters, none of which she had relished. He was a bad, bad man. Far scarier than the bald-headed, pony-tailed president of the club he'd replaced.

And now she was following him. She backed off the gas pedal, letting him open some more distance between them. Reaching up, she tugged the beanie down a bit lower on her forehead, so it came down to her eyebrows. It would be cool if she could shift shapes to a slightly different-looking human, but she could only change to a wolf and back.

That assassin, though—she'd been a shape shifter in the true sense of the word. She'd even taken on Jamie's appearance and tried to kill Dax. She'd never heard of such a being before, but true shape shifting was the conclusion they'd all come to after they did the post-mortem on that whole episode.

She wondered why Ivar had left the rest of his goons behind. But she reminded herself it wouldn't be the first time he'd bailed when the odds had changed. He'd boogied out of their clubhouse in a hurry when Dax got scary and started tearing through his packmates and biker buddies.

Was Ivar that big of a coward?

That thought nearly knocked her frightening image of Ivar askew. He'd loomed so large in her world since she'd taken a gun from him with the order to kill Dax. He'd been terrorizing her and her new friends for months. Was he just a bigger version of Travis? A petty bully who was only tough when the odds were in his favor?

She shook her head and turned the radio off. She needed to concentrate. She'd didn't have a lot of experience tailing people. The one time she'd tried it with Cory, the person they were chasing, Dax, had figured it out pretty fast and ditched them. But her last attempt had led her to one of the biker's compound. A fifty percent success rate didn't exactly inspire a lot of confidence.

Ahead, Ivar sped up, and she matched his speed, keeping what she thought was a safe distance behind him. If she could follow him back to his base, she could relay the location to Dax and let him sort out the leader of the biker gang. A cruel grin spread across her face. She could guess how Dax would deal with the biker gang's leader. When he was done, the world would be a slightly better place, down one scumbag Nazi biker. And it would be a biggie too, taking out one of their main leaders.

She wasn't a terribly vengeful person, but some people just didn't need to be in the world, polluting it with their intentional cruelty. Ivar actively made the world a worse place, spreading violence and racism like the diseases they were. She wasn't so naive as to think the loss of one leader would clean up Red City. This city was rotten to the core. Removing one worm wouldn't do anything to change the base problem, but it would make her life and the lives of several other good people better.

Brake lights alerted her to a stop, but almost too late. She'd let her mind wander again. Perhaps she was too tired to be doing something as reckless as following a dangerous biker. And while he may have been a cowardly bully, he wouldn't feel cowed by her. He'd take out his revenge on her for all her crimes against the biker gang. He'd had her father killed; he wouldn't hesitate to kill her. Her father had just owed the gang money. But she'd sided with the gang's enemies and helped those enemies inflict a lot of damage.

That thought brought another smile to her face. If this went well, she'd add another negative mark against herself in the column the bikers kept.

Ivar turned right. She pulled up to the stop sign and waited an appropriate few seconds before following him. They were headed toward the southeast part of town. That seemed to be where she and her friends had found some of the biker's rotating mix of compounds.

When she came to the next stoplight, she wondered if she could take a different turn and still catch up to him to throw him off. But she pushed the idea aside. She wasn't a super spy who knew the city's streets inside and out. She was a delivery driver who'd only been at it for a couple weeks. She had a map app that told her where to go.

Speaking of which, she grabbed her phone while she was at the stoplight and sent a screenshot of her location to Suzie. Better safe than sorry. The light changed to green, and they continued through it.

She wished there was more traffic, but it was late, and this wasn't the busiest part of town at this time of the night. Oh well, it was dark, and she was driving a generic-looking car. So far, everything was going pretty smoothly.

THIRTY-FOUR

DAX

Dax, still keeping the hammer spinning, reached into the aether and found the nearest life thread of a wolf shifter. With a quick mental twitch of his scythe, he severed it. A biker in the middle of the crowd dropped like a sack of flour. Grabbing another thread, Dax took out another biker. Then another. And another. Their advantage of being wolf shifters was being turned against them. By ignoring the threads of the humans around him, Dax could efficiently decimate his enemy's numbers.

Soon the bikers began to retreat as they lost their numerical superiority. "Fuck this," one of them said as they turned and made a run for it.

That was all it took. The rest of them shoved their way free and darted away to their motorcycles. A few of Boudreaux's crew started to chase after them.

"Let them go," Boudreaux called out between heavy breaths.

Dax spun around as water splashed and gushed over the sidewalk and into the street. Tomi, who'd grabbed a large wrench from somewhere, stood over the fire hydrant, opening the valve.

"Shit," Dax mumbled.

Mihn had gone into the bar. The fire was still burning hot,

though it didn't seem to be spreading. He had no idea what kind of supernatural she was, only that she wasn't purely human, based off when he'd found her in a cage in The Collector's menagerie of supernaturals. Respecting her privacy, Dax hadn't looked at her lifeline. He hoped she knew what she was doing…

The remaining unbroken window exploded outward, and everyone ducked as shards of glass showered them. Dax's cheek stung. A brief touch revealed blood.

"Minh…" Tomi groaned. He shook his head and cupped his hands around his mouth. "Water!"

The yell drew Dax's eye to the gushing water spewing from the open fire hydrant. Blinking rapidly, he leaned closer. The water was moving upstream, collecting around the curb in front of the bar. Waves crested the curb and ran toward the bar, seeping under the door.

A moment later, the water rose as if it were sentient, as if seeking an easier ingress, and flooded up the wall and through the broken windows. Steam billowed and hissed out the windows as water met flame. Squinting against the expelled steam, Dax brought an arm up to his face but was forced to take a couple steps back to get out of the hot blast of smoke and superheated water.

Once the smoke cleared a bit, he could see water circling around the inside of the bar like a tornado made of a swirling wall of liquid.

"What the—" Tomi had moved to stand next to Dax. "What is she?"

"No idea, but she's going to save the building."

Tomi nodded weakly.

Dax could no longer see any flames or even smoke, only water and steam. Just when he thought it would go on forever, the water pulled away from the windows and contracted inward toward wherever the eye—Minh, likely—of the storm was. The vortex tightened and swirled faster until it exploded outward, and water poured through the windows and pushed the door open.

Dax and Tomi had no time to duck or move. A torrent of water and debris drenched and covered them. Tomi sputtered and shook, trying to dislodge the water and bits of charred junk that had landed on him.

After the initial explosion of water, it slowed as it drained out the broken windows until nothing was left but a small trickle running out from under the door. Dax was surprised the automatic door closer hadn't been ripped from the door and still worked. A moment later, the door pushed open, and Mihn emerged from the bar. Like them, she was soaked, her T-shirt and jeans clinging to her slim form.

It might have been a trick of the light and water, but Dax thought she had lines—no, scales—on her arms. Her shiny black hair looked almost blue and feathery. Bringing her hands up, she ran them through her hair, pulling it back and squeezing as much water out as she could. When she stepped out of the shadow of the bar and into the light of a streetlamp, she looked like her normal self except very wet.

She stopped in front of Dax and shuffled her feet awkwardly. "I did the best I could, but by the time I got enough water, the fire had already set in pretty effectively."

"I got the hydrant open as fast as I could," Tomi said, a bit of hurt in his voice.

Reaching out, she laid a hand on his forearm and smiled at him warmly. "I know. You did the best you could. It's just that fire is fast and insatiable." She returned her gaze to Dax. "I think I saved the building, but you'll need to get it properly inspected."

Unable to find words, Dax just nodded.

"Is it safe to go in?" Tomi asked.

"I think so." She looked down at the ground and lifted one foot then the other from the pool of water growing as the fire hydrant continued to gush. "We better turn the hydrant off."

Tomi nodded. "Right, right." He ran to the hydrant, splashing through the deep flood. When he walked into the full spray, it blasted him in the legs, nearly knocking him off his feet.

"Damn it, Tomi." Suzie emerged from around the side of the building, the Judge in her hands, cocked and ready for action. "Walk around the stream." She shook her head and covered her face with her hand.

Dax thought he heard her mumble, "Moron," under her breath. He would have normally laughed at Tomi, and Suzie's rightful observation, but he was feeling similarly brain-dead at the moment, considering everything that had just happened.

Tomi swung around the spray and grabbed the wrench from the ground next to the hydrant. In a few seconds, he turned the water off.

"I'll be right back," Minh said, jogging across the street to her family's convenience store.

Dax just stared at the shell of his precious bar. It was only a dive bar, but it was his. And now he had to start over from scratch. Maybe even farther back. It had been a rough, derelict building when he'd leased the space over five years ago, but it hadn't been half charred and drenched in water.

He didn't know how long he stood in the middle of the street staring, but Minh running by carrying a giant bundle finally brought him back to the present. She dropped the bundle in front of the fire hydrant, then hooked up one end to the hydrant, unspooling the rest. It was a fire hose.

"Tomi, turn the water on just a little so it wets the inside of the hose and expands it."

Nodding, he turned the wrench carefully until the hose puffed up a bit. Dax watched as the water wound its way through the hose and trickled out the end.

Once the entire hose had expanded and the trickle was now a steady stream, Minh nodded and looked up. "That's enough. Turn it off."

A car honked. Dax stood in a pool of light from a car's headlights. Everyone else had cleared the street after the bikers had fled and Minh had put out the fire. He was the only one still standing in the middle of the two-lane road. He strode over to join Tomi and Minh. As soon as he was out of the way, the car zoomed by, spraying water everywhere and re-drenching his lower legs.

"Fucking asshole." Tomi flipped the car off as it sped away.

"At least they were in too big of a hurry to see the bodies. You have a fire hose?" Dax asked Minh.

"Yeah. Most of the businesses around here do. And a wrench big enough for a hydrant." She nudged the hose with her foot.

"We're lucky the construction guys left a big crescent wrench upstairs." Tomi reached down and squeezed Minh's hand affectionately.

"Why do you have a hose?" Dax asked.

She gestured down the street. "This is why. Do you see the fire department? We're not in a rich neighborhood. And it's likely those thugs or their bosses tipped off the local fire house to take their time."

As if on cue, the faint sound of sirens drifted toward them.

"Shit, Dax. I never thought of that. I guess we better get a hose and big-ass wrench. For next time."

Dax snorted and grimaced. "Next time? I sure as hell hope there's not a next time, but you're right. We should be more prepared. We might want to think about what other kinds of supplies we'll need for other situations that might arise now that the bikers have decided to escalate their war to property crimes."

Boudreaux jogged across the street and joined them. "I've got the crew moving the bodies out of the way. We'll have a van here in a minute." He looked down at the fire hose. "You might want to use that conveniently hooked up hose to blast the blood off the pavement."

"Shit, that's a good idea." Tomi grabbed the hose and dragged it toward the blood puddles. "Someone turn me on. But not full power."

Suzie, who'd been standing near the corner of the building, stepped forward and cranked the wrench around with a labored grunt. "Water incoming!"

Minh walked over and watched him clean the pavement. "Looks good."

"And just in time," Boudreaux added.

As if to punctuate his point, the sound of ambulance sirens came from the other direction than the fire sirens. In twos, several of Boudreaux's crew had wrapped the bikers in tarps and picked them up by the feet and shoulders and were moving them to the back of the building.

Boudreaux surveyed his crew for a moment until a Black woman jogged up and handed him a flashlight, which he passed onto Dax. "You should probably get a look inside before the fire department shows up. Maybe take some photos in case they decide to contribute to the damage." A few more of his crew ran up, panting, and gave them a couple more flashlights.

"No one's ever written a song called 'Fuck the Fire Department,' but I think I'm going to start working on it." Tomi grabbed a flashlight and headed to the door, pulling it open.

THIRTY-FIVE

JAMIE

Jamie checked her gas gauge. She was still OK, though she wished she'd filled up today instead of pushing it until tomorrow. Maybe she'd use this opportunity to learn a lesson about procrastination.

Ivar had to be getting near his destination. They were on the outskirts of town, and it was pretty isolated. Way too isolated for her comfort. She double-checked the gas gauge.

It was a Corolla. It got great gas mileage. If she needed to flee, she'd be fine on gas. If the chase lasted long enough for her to run low, she'd have bigger issues to deal with.

A headlight reflecting off the rearview mirror drew her attention. Flicking her eyes up to it, she hoped it was a car with one headlight burned out and not a motorcycle. One motorcycle in front of her was already too much, too nerve-wracking. But another one behind her meant bad news. Especially if it wasn't just some random motorcyclist out after midnight in a sketchy part of town where white supremacist, wolf-shifter biker gangs liked to hang out.

When a second headlight joined the first one in her rearview, she breathed a sigh of relief. They'd been driving around a curve. It probably had obscured the other headlight until they got to a straight part of the road.

Did cars have three headlights? The momentary sense of relief vanished like a bribe envelope full of cash in front of a cop. A minute later, she couldn't easily count the lights in her rearview mirror, especially through her squint. Once she returned her eyes forward, she realized why she'd been squinting so much.

A steady line of lights blocked the road in front of her. She jammed on the brakes and came to a screeching halt. Looking around desperately, she tried to find an escape route.

There were no places to turn of any sort. No driveways, side streets, or service roads. A fence and a ditch blocked each side of the road. She could try to go through the bikers, hoping they'd move. But if they didn't, there was no way her little Toyota Corolla could survive being used as a battering ram.

As she sat still, the bikes behind her closed in while the ones in front of her slowly rolled forward. Maybe a threat would work... She slipped her left foot onto the brake pedal, holding it down stiffly, and depressed the gas pedal a few times, revving the engine. The small engine's higher-pitched sound did not sound intimidating.

A flash accompanied by a *pop* exploded in front of her. She shrieked as a bullet tore through the middle of the windshield. Removing her foot from the gas pedal, she threw her arms into the air but cringed when her hands slammed into the roof. There was no place to run.

Several bikers from the group in front had dismounted and were approaching cautiously. When one flashed across her headlights, she saw a handgun pointed in her direction. She wondered if she had time to send a quick message, but she couldn't risk lowering her arms and inviting another bullet; the next one would be aimed to kill.

"Hey phone, send text to Suzie—" She screamed as something hard knocked against her driver's side window.

The knock came hard again. Turning her head, she saw a dark figure standing outside her window. He rapped on the window again with the butt of his gun. Two other men stood by him, one on each side. Both had their guns pointed directly at her.

Tired of waiting, the man pulled something from his pocket, and the driver's window exploded, sending shards of glass everywhere. Small stings along her face and arms spoke of several cuts.

"Get out of the car, or I'll paint the inside of it with your brains, assuming you even have any," he barked out.

She froze, unsure of what to do. He didn't give her much time. Reaching down, he tried to open the door, but the car was in drive and locked.

"Turn the car off and get out. Slowly." He emphasized his point by poking the barrel of his gun into her forehead.

Her hand shook as she slowly reached to the side to put the car into park and turn it off. Tired of waiting, he stuck his hand through the window, hit the unlock button, yanked the door open, and dragged her out by her shirt.

Once she caught her balance, she put her hands up, hoping she wouldn't give the three men pointing guns at her any excuse to execute her right there. Wolf shifters could heal quickly and from wounds that might kill a normal human, but a bullet to the brain tended to be a universal kill option.

Her eyes flicked around from face to face, then into the darkness, cataloging everything and everyone around her. She didn't recognize the three men closest. She thought one or two of the men a bit farther back might look familiar, but she hadn't seen every biker who'd passed through town. And Dax had eliminated so many of them, she wasn't sure who had survived.

"Anyone know who she is?" called an all-too-familiar voice from the shadows behind the line of bikes.

"No, but I'm new to town. All I can tell is she's probably a wolf shifter," said the man who'd broken her window.

"Anyone who was here last month recognize her?"

A couple men stepped closer, looking her over. One of them shook his head. The other took a moment or two longer. "No. There's something odd about her, but I don't think I know her."

"Hmm." Ivar stepped into the light, stalking slowly toward her. "You're right. There is something"—he sniffed the air a few times—"odd about her."

He waved the three men pointing their guns at her back a couple steps, then moved in closer until he was uncomfortably close. He snatched the black knit beanie off her head and threw it onto the ground. Bumping into her, he gave her hair a deep sniff that made her cringe. When he backed up, he had a creepy smile on his face. "Hello, little wolf."

Fear sliced through her, and she did everything she could to keep her knees from buckling.

"What do you have there in your shirt? A third titty?" He grabbed the leather thong from her neck and slowly pulled the gris-gris out from under the collar of her shirt. He sniffed the bag deeply.

He was so close his hair tickled her nose. His odor was a powerful mix of cigarettes, stale booze, sweat, and sadism. She wanted to vomit.

Stepping back, he yanked hard. The leather thong had been a good one and it took a lot of force to break it from her neck. She staggered forward with a yelp of pain.

Ivar sneered, leaning in close so his lips nearly touched her left ear. "Well, well, well. We meet again, Ms. Rodriguez."

Like lightning, he reared back and smashed his fist into the side of her head. The world exploded into stars, then they were all eclipsed as everything went black.

THIRTY-SIX

DAX

The back of the door was well charred. As soon as it had been pulled open, a punch of burnt wood and plastic chemicals combined with water hit them. Flicking on the flashlight, Dax took a moment to let his eyes adjust, sweeping the beam across the floor to reveal any obstacles. There were more than plenty.

Scraps of burnt wood attached to steel bases that had formed tables were all tipped over. Not a one stood, no doubt testament to whatever Minh had done with her water tornado. The chairs, with their vinyl and foam cushions, had fared even worse, leaving black, sopping foam and curls of melted vinyl.

"I did the best I could to protect the back of the building and the back bar, though a couple bottles of whiskey got knocked down. I think I saved the tearoom."

A gush of air rushed out of Dax's lungs as his shoulders sagged in relief. Now that his eyes had adjusted enough, he picked his way through the carnage of his business and made it back to the hallway. The damage was considerably less there, with only a bit of debris littering the puddle-covered floor. A sheen of water glistened on the sliding pocket door leading into the tearoom.

Cautious in case it was hot, Dax held his hand over the metal handle but felt nothing. He slid the door open carefully.

Water had seeped under the door and around it to puddle just inside the entrance, but it stopped before it reached the long communal table in the middle of the room. Holding his breath and closing his eyes, he turned to face the wall where he kept his teas and special teapots. Once his lungs felt like they'd burst, he exhaled and opened his eyes at the same time.

The wall of tea looked undisturbed, though there were a few blank cubbies where Suzie had pulled down some of the pots and carted them away when they'd evacuated the bar before the biker scum set it on fire. He'd have to do something nice for her to thank her for her quick thinking.

Outside, the sound of ambulance sirens grew loud. A vehicle screeched to a stop.

"The bus is here," Boudreaux shouted through the bar. "We'll take care of the refuse."

Another bit of angst unwound itself from the tight muscles of his back. There'd be a few motorcycles abandoned by the bikers since Dax had relieved the owners of their miserable, hateful lives. Boudreaux could sell them. Dax liked to make sure the man was well compensated for all the help he provided, though at this point they might consider each other friends. He'd have to send a thank you to Manman Delphine for introducing them.

"Thank you, Minh. For saving what you could. This is the important stuff. At least to me."

"No problem. You can perform a tea ceremony for me when you're back up and running."

"If we ever are…" Tomi mumbled. He grunted as Minh elbowed him in the ribs.

"Hey, teddy bear. Be nice."

A smirk spread across Dax's face. "Teddy bear?"

"Shut it, dude." Tomi didn't put much vitriol in his command. He couldn't, with a smile spreading across his lips.

His best friend had a crush on Minh. She'd been over to the bar a few times to have drinks with him. But apparently, the crush had become a relationship. One warranting a term of endearment.

"Alright, *teddy bear.* Oof." Dax rubbed his shoulder after Tomi punched it playfully, but a touch hard.

Debris being kicked around in the front of the bar drew Dax's attention away from his tea and his friends, and he turned to face the door. Boudreaux poked his head in. "We're all good here. Just in time too, the fire department is here. And it looks like a detective followed them."

"Fire inspector?" Tomi asked.

Boudreaux shook his head.

All the good feelings and thankfulness evaporated. Only one detective would be so Johnny-on-the-spot when Dax was involved. A moment later, his suspicious were confirmed when the cop stepped into view — Detective Randall Ryan.

As was his standard uniform, the cop wore a wrinkled suit. Dax suspected if the color were light enough, he'd be able to spot a few stains on it, or at least on his tie. His hair was greasy, and it looked like he hadn't shaved in a few days.

Dax snorted quietly, not wanting to get off on the wrong foot with the detective, though he doubted the cop even had a "good foot." He hadn't ever seen Ryan with a freshly shaved face, leading him to wonder if the man existed in a permanent state of a few days' rumple.

"So you finally decided to set your own bar on fire to try to collect the insurance." The detective tsked and shook his head. "You know that's insurance fraud, right?" The detective pulled his hand out of his pocket, and a set of handcuffs dangled from his fingers.

A motion out of the corner of his eye caught Dax's attention. Tomi had his cellphone open and was pointing it at the detective, no doubt recording, since Dax had an ongoing lawsuit against Redemption City Police Department and Detective Ryan.

"Tomi, turn off the video and put your phone away." Dax folded his arms. "I don't think I'm going to let the detective arrest me today."

"You sure about that, Dax? The lawyer told me to record anytime Ryan showed up."

After the initial shock of the news, a feral grin spread across Ryan's face. He dropped the cuffs into his pocket and pulled something metal from his other pocket. With a flick of his wrist, he extended a metal baton. "So I get to add resisting arrest and assaulting an officer to the list of charges against you?"

Dax backed away, drawing the detective farther into the room. "Tomi, leave the room. And keep the fire department out."

"O...OK, boss." It had been a while since Tomi had called him "boss." He must be nervous. "Minh, let's go."

The pair carefully slipped around the advancing detective and shut the door behind themselves. When Dax's butt bumped up against the solid weight of the giant wooden table, he stopped and leaned against it, folding his arms across his chest.

He'd had enough of the constant harassment from the cop. He'd been dealing with him ever since he opened the bar, back when the detective had just been a uniformed beat cop, patrolling the neighborhood and shaking down businesses for his protection racket.

As the cop slowly advanced, unsureness leaching into his expression, Dax reached into the aether and found the detective's lifeline and roughly seized it. Randall Ryan froze.

Ryan jerked a few times but couldn't get his body to respond beyond a few weak twitches.

A pleasant smile spread across Dax's lips as he straightened up and let his mortal flesh slowly fade from his frame. He enjoyed every exquisite nuance of the fear and dread that spread across Ryan's face as Dax transformed from a normal-looking man to a half state, where both bones and flesh were visible, then to the dreaded form of the Grim Reaper in his tattered black robe. He unfolded his arms and extended his left hand, plucking his scythe out of the aether.

The scent of urine, only faint in his current form, wafted toward Dax. The detective had pissed himself. Dax groaned internally. He'd have to mop it up himself. He couldn't ask his people to do it. They cleaned up enough human grossness in the restrooms on the regular. The detective had found another way, though unintentional, to spite him yet again. The detective couldn't see the sneer on his face since there was no skin or muscles over the bones of his skull.

"Pathetic." Dax's voice rasped forth like chains over a broken gravestone. He took a step closer, sending flames burning along the edge of his scythe. "I have had enough of you, Detective Randall Ryan. This is the last day you will ever bother me."

Dax adjusted the scythe so the tip of the blade pointed straight at the detective's chest. Reducing on the solidity of the weapon, Dax let the blade slip mostly into the aether, though it was still visible, if mostly transparent, to the detective.

"P-p-please…" Ryan whimpered. "I-I don't want to die."

Dax laughed, the sound multi-harmonic and disharmonic at the same time. "We all die, but annoying little gnats die sooner. That's all you are, Rand Ryan. A little, annoying, buzzing, biting bug. Easily squashed and forgotten about."

The cop whimpered. The pee pooling around the detective seemed to be growing. Dax hoped none of it soaked into the hem of his robes.

"Oh, you won't be so fortunate to die today. Instead, you will get to live a while longer, knowing what a weak, corrupt, piece of garbage you are." Dax set the pointed tip of the scythe blade against the man's chest and pushed.

The detective drew in a gurgling, wheezing breath, his eyes rolling up into his head. Dax pushed the blade in slowly, so the cop would feel it and so he didn't accidentally kill the cop. When and if he claimed the pig's life, it would be purposeful and intentional. Once the thrumming power of the cop's heart vibrated through the blade and into his hand, he stopped, only letting the tip puncture the edge of the cop's heart slightly.

His mouth worked like a fish's out of water, and his body shook with a steady tremor. Dax hoped no one would walk in and startle him, or he might be in serious trouble with the fire department outside and a dead cop on the floor. With his free hand, he grabbed the detective's jaw and locked the flaming pits of his eye sockets with the fear-filled eyes of Ryan.

"You have one chance to save your miserable life. Do you understand?"

The cop nodded vigorously.

"Good. You will swear to never bother me or any of my associates—past, present, or future—again."

"I promise," Ryan squeaked out.

"You're also going to report this as an arson, which it is, by your little motorcycle thugs. Which is all true and can be attested to by many witnesses. It might be pleasant to actually speak the truth for a change."

"I don't control—"

Dax cut him off by giving the scythe the barest of twitches.

"I swear! Arson, bikers. Please." Tears streamed down the cop's cheeks, and snot bubbled from one nostril.

"Oh, I know you will make it happen. And to ensure you don't go back on your word, I've marked your life thread. I'll feel any mischief you attempt against me. I'll also give you a little gift—free time."

"W-w-what?"

"The stresses of the job are becoming too much for you to handle. I'm going to make sure you get the free time you need to think about your…sins." It wasn't a term Dax thought in. As the ultimate arbiter of Death, he just claimed the lives of those who'd been called by the universe. He didn't care what happened to their souls or where they went. It was up to the gods humans had conjured from their own beliefs to deal with that. *But sin* was a powerful word, especially to someone raised in a place steeped in the myths of Christianity.

"I swear. Whatever you want. You'll never see me again. Just… just don't kill me," Ryan pleaded.

Dax laughed, and the cop tried to cringe away from the terrifying sound. "Death is too easy for you." His grip still strong on the detective's life thread, he pulled it toward himself and drew it taught against the sharp edge of the scythe. Ryan wobbled in place, unable to resist the power of Dax manipulating his thread. "Don't move anymore, Rand Ryan, or you'll meet your eternal punishment earlier than planned by the universe."

Concentrating on the thread, Dax slipped it along the blade carefully. As each tightly wound strand popped, he had to be even more cautious as the energy stored in the cop's life thread was unleashed. Once he figured he'd cut about halfway through, leaving the central core still intact, he moved the thread away from the scythe's blade.

The detective paled as his body slumped. He started panting harder, little whimpers falling from his lips on quick exhales. Then he grunted in pain. As Dax let go of the thread, returning control of the cop's body to him, Ryan clutched his chest with his right hand as his left arm hung limp.

Dax withdrew the blade from detective's chest, and he collapsed on the floor and landed in the puddle of his own urine, a tremor running through his body.

"Heart…heart attack." After managing to get the words out, Ryan grunted and clawed at his shirt collar and the buttons keeping it closed.

Taking a step back, Dax pulled in his human flesh and let his robes and scythe return to the aether. "Huh. I guess you're going to need medical leave."

He sighed and took a wide berth around Ryan. Opening the door, he was greeted with Tomi arguing with a voice he didn't recognize. Likely a firefighter.

"Look, the cop said he didn't want to be disturbed," Tomi lied.

"Tomi, let them through. Detective Ryan just collapsed. I think he's having a heart attack." He didn't sound as concerned as he should have, all things considered. "Hurry!" he added for good measure.

He stepped out of the way, and two men in fire gear jogged into the tearoom.

"One of you go outside and get the EMT, and tell them to bring a stretcher," one of the firefighters called.

"I got it," Tomi said, running out the front door.

Careful to stand out of the way, Dax peeked in to watch the firefighters work on the detective. They'd pulled his shirt open but weren't doing much else. As soon as couple people dressed as EMTs ran into the room with a gurney, the others stepped out of the way.

"Watch it," one of the firefighters said. "He's lying in a pool of his own piss."

"Great," one of the EMTs said. Together, they lifted the detective onto the gurney and strapped him down. "Hold on, Detective, we've got to get you to the bus and the defibrillator.

Ryan groaned but didn't move. Dax pushed his back into the wall the as the EMTs pushed the gurney out of the tearoom, down the hallway, and through the scattered, charred debris of bar's tables and chairs. He followed them out of the tearoom at a slower pace but stopped by the bar. Firefighters were wandering around, checking for any signs of embers or hot spots that might flare up again.

Dax cringed when one of them swung his fire axe into the wood under the bar several times, no doubt looking to see if there were any hidden hot spots.

"You finding anything?" a fire person near the door asked.

"Nah, they appeared to get it all." He looked up from the bar, noticing Dax standing there. "Sir, you're going to have to wait outside."

"Right. Thanks," Dax added the second word as he walked through the mess of his business.

THIRTY-SEVEN
DAX

The fresh nighttime air felt good after the scent of the detective's urine and the smell of burned wood, plastic, and other crap. He stopped on the curb outside the bar and inhaled deeply. Once he exhaled, he spotted Tomi standing in front of Minh's convenience store with her. Off to the side of the bar, red lights flashed on the fire engine and the ambulance. A moment later, the bus took off, its sirens screaming.

It was now up to medical science if the detective survived or not. Dax hadn't intended to give the man a heart attack, but it would likely punctuate the encounter and keep the detective honest. That was assuming he even recovered enough to return to active duty. It almost made him want to smile, but the smoldering ruin of his and Tomi's business put a quick damper on his mood.

Dax crossed the street and stepped onto the sidewalk, joining his friend. Tomi handed him a water bottle. Before he said anything, he opened it and took a deep drink of the cold water, then sighed after he swallowed.

"Thanks. That helps wash the taste of char out of my mouth." Dax took another drink.

"What did you—" Tomi interrupted himself. "What happened to old Randy Ryan?"

Dax caught Tomi's eye and held it for a moment before answering, "He had a heart attack."

"Good. The son of a bitch deserves it." Minh, folding her arms over her chest, spoke with uncharacteristic heat. "Bastard has extorted a lot of money from us over the years. I hope he chokes on it all."

"Did he, uh, pee his pants?" Tomi asked, a grin slowly spreading across his face.

Dax nodded.

Tomi chuckled. "I couldn't quite hear what the EMTs were saying, but I thought that's what I overheard."

Boudreaux strolled around a couple firefighters as they jogged back and forth between their truck and the bar's door. He'd been standing where the ambulance had been parked. Dax guessed he probably knew the EMTs, since the bus looked to be from the same company he worked for.

"How was our nearly departed detective?" Tomi asked once Boudreaux stopped in front of them.

"Alive-ish. He'll probably pull through. As long as he gets a competent ED doctor. Though he's a cop, so they'll probably drag someone good in to make sure he lives."

"That's unfortunate," Minh said.

"Damn, your girl's got some fangs, Tomi." Boudreaux chuckled and shook his head. "Though I guaran-damn-tee you she's not the only one holding those sentiments. That cop was crookeder than a dog's hind leg."

"And based on his bathing habits, probably had twice as many fleas." Tomi snorted, then bumped Boudreaux's knuckles in acknowledgement of the joke.

"I'm surprised his greasy hair didn't catch on fire when he walked through the bar," Minh said.

A moment later, the door to the convenience store burst open and Minh's father, Thuc, stomped out, his jaw clenched and his eyes fit to shoot fire. "Minh, what are you doing getting involved in this mess? With that dirty cop? You're going to get us in trouble."

"Father, that pig can fuck off. And so can his thug biker flunkeys. I'm not going to be chased out of another home by authoritarian goons. Not again."

Thuc shifted to Vietnamese—a language the biker's brain Dax inhabited didn't know, and one his former self didn't have access to while trapped in this mortal shell. Tomi, Boudreaux, and Dax stepped away from the arguing father and daughter as their voices rose and they gesticulated wildly at each other and the nearby buildings.

Dax nudged Tomi gently with his elbow. "So... You and Minh, eh?"

A goofy grin spread across Tomi's face. "Mind your own business, Dax. Speaking of which..." He gestured with his head at an official-looking man walking toward them.

"Which one of you is Dax Smith?" the man asked.

Tomi and Boudreaux both pointed at Dax.

"That would be me."

The average-looking white man with brown hair stuck out his hand. "I'm Bill Preston, Fire Marshal. I need to collect your statement and those of any other witnesses."

Dax took a step closer to the inspector so he wouldn't have to raise his voice over the noise of the fire department working. "Well, it was a normal evening service, when a rock broke the window. Someone had tied a note to it saying we had five minutes to evacuate the customers. So we did, then stepped out. There was a motorcycle gang waiting."

"The Black Suns," Tomi said.

Dax nodded. "A couple of them ran up and threw Molotov cocktails into the broken windows, and some others started throwing fists at our customers. We did our best to defend ourselves. Then when they heard sirens, they all bailed."

The marshal jotted down some notes on a pad. "Where did you get the fire hose? Is that how you put out the fire?"

Tomi chucked his chin at the arguing father and daughter

standing in front of their store. "Minh, who runs the convenience store, had one. So we borrowed it and put out the fire."

"That's pretty dangerous. You should have waited for the professionals."

Dax scoffed. "They didn't seem to be in a hurry to get here. If we'd waited, there'd have been nothing left for you to inspect."

The fire marshal eyed the front of the convenience store. "I'm going to need the footage from that security camera."

As one, Minh and Thuc said, "It doesn't work."

Bill rolled his eyes. "Of course."

Geoffrey, who'd been standing out of the way quietly, stepped up, his hands in his pants pockets. When he brought them out, they no longer had bloody brass knuckles on them. "Hi. I witnessed the whole thing. I can corroborate Mr. Smith's statement."

Distracted momentarily from the camera, the marshal took Geoffrey's details and statement. When he finished with Geoffrey, he worked his way through the rest of the people who all confirmed Dax's story from their points of view.

Looking around for a moment, Bill turned to Dax. "I heard there was a cop on the scene. Where did he go?"

Dax tried to keep the smile off his face. "He was taking my statement when he suffered a heart attack. He was taken away by an ambulance. I'm not sure what hospital he was taken to. If he survives, he'll confirm the details."

"Did he give you a card?"

"No. But I didn't need one. I've known him for years. Detective Randall Ryan. I'm sure if you call the police, they can direct you to whichever hospital he's in."

Nodding, the fire marshal wrote down the name. "Is there anything else you'd like to add before I go take a peek inside the building?"

Dax and Tomi exchanged looks and shook their heads at each other. "Not that I can think of."

Bill reached into his pocket and pulled out a card and handed it to Dax. "If you think of anything, please call me."

As soon as the fire marshal stepped into the building, Boudreaux and Tomi made eye contact and started laughing. Both of them pantomimed air guitars.

"You need to get some Wyld Stallyns for the juke box," Boudreaux said, with a big grin on his face.

Dax looked at both of them, wondering what the joke was. "I've never heard of them. What kind of music?"

That started Boudreaux and Tomi laughing again.

"You should go ask Fire Marshal Bill what the joke is." Boudreaux tried to keep a straight face.

Before Dax could do anything—not that he was going to bug the man while he inspected the damage—Tomi put a hand on his forearm as he guffawed. "No, don't ask Fire Marshal Bill."

That started the two men laughing again. Dax was getting annoyed at not being in on the joke, though he was pretty sure they weren't laughing at him. Human humor was one of the things he still didn't quite understand, at least not to its fullest depths. He laughed at things and made the odd humorous statement now and then, but he had no idea what had the two grown men laughing hysterically. Their antics had even put a pause on the argument Minh and her father were having.

Once they recovered, Tomi wiped the tears from his eyes and exhaled through a smile. "We'll leave the fire marshal alone, because I'm sure he's heard all the jokes before."

"What jokes?" Dax asked, crossing his arms over his chest.

"You're going to have to get your boy up to date on some pop culture references." Boudreaux slapped Dax on the back in a companionable manner.

"I guess I'll start him on *Bill and Ted's Excellent Adventure*," Tomi said. "*In Living Color* might take a little more time."

Pop culture was another thing he was woefully inadequate at. The body he'd hijacked had only a limited frame of reference for such things. Or at for least the things Tomi liked to reference. Fortunately, Dax's best friend was more than happy to be a good-natured teacher. Together, they'd watched all kinds of movies and TV shows in the five-plus years they'd known each other. Though that was hardly an adequate time to pick up on all the things humans seemed to know. Dax was definitely not tapped into the cultural zeitgeist.

"When we have time, I'll put myself at your disposal." Dax sighed as his thoughts returned to the burnt husk of his business. "We're going to have to see if we have enough money to hold us over until we can get any kind of insurance payout."

"Speaking of which, you sure Ryan is going to actually play along?"

An evil grin spread across Dax's face. "Oh, yeah. He will."

THIRTY-EIGHT

DAX

Dax's phone wouldn't stop vibrating. At one point, Morty had hissed at it and left the bedroom. Dax couldn't blame him. That shit was annoying. Finally with a put-upon sigh, he grabbed it and answered. "What the fuck do you want?"

"Damn, a bit grumpy this morning?" Tomi asked.

Dax took a moment to collect himself. "Sorry. What time is it, anyway?"

"Just after eleven."

Dax dragged his hands over his sandy eyes. "Why are you calling me this early?"

Generally, Tomi never called before noon or one p.m., if he could help it. Especially if Dax had been at the bar late for the closing shift. They'd all been there late last night dealing with the aftermath of the bikers and the fire.

"Um, have you heard from Jamie?"

"What?"

"Jamie? Cute kid, drives delivery for us. Popped a cap in your ass." Although Tomi was being humorous, even through his fog of sleep, Dax could hear the worry threading through his tone.

"I don't know. I've been asleep. My phone has been vibrating off the hook. Maybe one of them is her. Let me check." He attempted to swipe the phone app away but ended up hanging up in his tired clumsiness. Oh well, he'd call Tomi right back.

Looking through his missed calls and messages, he found none from Jamie. Once he double checked to make sure he hadn't missed something in his haze, he decided to look at his emails as well just to be thorough. Nothing there either. He called Tomi back. All the calls and messages had been from Tomi and Suzie.

"Ya got anything?" Tomi asked by way of greeting.

"Nothing. What's going on?"

"Fuck."

He rubbed his eyes again, concern doing more to wake him up than the vibrating phone had. "Did you check in with Suzie?"

"She's the one who woke me up. Said Jamie wasn't home when she got home, and she still hasn't seen her. Isn't answering her phone either. Suzie swears she saw Jamie drive by the restaurant last night when they were evacuating the bar."

"Shit. Do you think she went to ground after seeing the bikers?" Dax staggered into the kitchen and fumbled for his bag of coffee beans. Morty, who had his face planted in his food bowl, huffed and wandered back into the bedroom. Apparently, Dax was cramping his style.

"Where would she go that's safe? She wouldn't go to her mom's. She's not at your place."

Dax turned around and looked into the living room to make sure she wasn't on the couch. "Nope. Just me and the cat."

"She's not at Suzie's. Where else does she have to hide?" Tomi's voice had become increasingly worried. Since Jamie had started working at the restaurant and living with Tomi's cousin, he'd fallen into his old patterns and started looking after the young woman like he had Dax when he'd first showed up in Red City.

Mama Adele had raised a compassionate man who took care of his people, and now Jamie was one of his people, which despite all Dax's efforts to maintain a barrier between himself and the woman who'd shot him, she'd become one of his people too.

"Damn it."

"Hold on. I've got a call coming in from Suzie. Call you back." Tomi hung up.

The bag of coffee still in his hand, he stumbled over to the coffee grinder and threw in some beans. A few minutes later, he sat at the table in his underwear, the glorious sent of coffee drifting up to his nose. He was glad he'd finally let Tomi talk him into getting better coffee for the bar. He'd used the wholesale discount he paid for the bar to upgrade his home beans as well.

When the phone rang a few minutes later, he picked it up on the first ring.

"Dax, we got trouble. Suzie just got a message that was time stamped last night. Jamie went after the bikers."

Air whooshed from his lungs. "What the fuck was she thinking?"

THIRTY-NINE

DAX

Suzie had been riding Dax's ass the entire way out. Tomi, who knew his cousin best, insisted she follow Dax instead of racing ahead in her souped-up Honda Civic. Dax was of the same mind as her, though, he wanted to mash the gas pedal and get out there as fast as possible. But instead, he reminded himself to be patient as he stared at the approaching mark on his map app. Tomi, sitting in the passenger seat, stared out the window at the passing scenery.

She'd wanted to take off as soon as it had been confirmed that no one had seen Jamie, but he and Tomi had calmed her down and worked to pull together a few people as quickly as possible under the circumstances. Times were too dangerous for going off half-cocked.

Dax's eyes drifted up to the rearview mirror, fascinated by Suzie shifting forward and backward in the lane as she repeatedly got too close then backed off some, only to start the whole process again. Forcing his gaze back to the road, he started checking for any signs of activity or places where they could safely pull off. They were getting close.

"Tomi, you better be ready to hop out and grab Suzie in case she dashes off." Dax checked the map again.

"Right. I'm not sure I've ever seen her keyed up this much. I guess she's gotten quite attached to Jamie."

Dax chuckled. "Suzie is a Chenevert through and through."

"What's that supposed to mean?" Tomi raised an eyebrow.

"Don't worry. I'm not saying it as a bad thing. Y'all adopted Jamie, gave her a job, and provided a roof over her head. Suzie made the girl her friend. Your family takes their responsibilities seriously when it comes to the people you welcome into your community. I should know. You did the same to me when I showed up in Red City."

Tomi slowly nodded. "I guess you're right. She's become mama's new project." He laughed and winked at Dax. "One more skinny stray who needs some more meat on their bones."

"She hasn't succeeded at putting more flesh on this frame, though I'll let her keep trying. Her cooking is just too damned good."

Tom laughed and patted his stomach with both hands. "This was honestly earned."

Dax needed the bit of levity. He'd started feeling too grim, even for himself. Even if he thought he had a right to be. The bikers had burned down his business, nearly killed him, his employees, and his customers, and kidnapped his...

But what was Jamie to him? At this point, he had to admit she'd become his friend. He huffed quietly in amusement. From nearly killing him to his friend in less than a year.

"Alright, get ready," Dax said. He'd spotted a turnout that was close enough they could walk the last couple hundred yards. He could see the reflection of the sun shining off a small car. It appeared to be the Corolla.

He slowed and pulled off the road, stopping at the end of the turnout to leave space for Suzie to park behind him. Before he even had the engine off, Tomi jumped out and placed himself so he could intercept Suzie if he needed to. Fortunately, she didn't come out of her car hot and take off, instead walking over to join them. Delphine appeared from the passenger side looking a little shaky.

"You OK?" Dax asked her.

"The ride was...exciting."

Suzie looked contrite. "Sorry, manman."

"No worries, cher. You're worried about your friend." Delphine reached into a backpack she'd brought and pulled out a bottle of water. She sighed happily after taking a couple drinks and putting it away.

"I guess you're the first person who needs to weigh in, Delphine." Dax gestured at the road in front of them and the car in the distance. "Sensing anything in the magical realm?"

"I'll take a look. But does everyone have their luck gris-gris on and have they been properly fed recently?"

They all nodded. Once she was ready, she closed her eyes and concentrated for a few moments. With an audible exhale, her body untensed and she opened her eyes. "No. Nothing I can pick up."

Dax nodded. "My turn."

He closed his eyes and reached into the aether. Searching through the nearby threads, he looked for any vibrations or deviations that might mean impending doom or harm. Everything that he could see seemed calm, without so much as a ripple to worry him. "Nothing here either."

"Somehow that doesn't actually make me feel better." Tomi's eyes shifted around nervously.

Suzie pursed her lips. "Me either."

"What can I say? I guess we'll just keep being careful." Dax's phone vibrated in his pocket, so he pulled it out and checked it. "Boudreaux and whoever he was able to pull together in a hurry are waiting on the other side of the car. They'll hang back unless they're needed."

Dax and Delphine could handle most of what might come at them on the magical side, while Boudreaux and his people could handle more mundane violence if the situation called for it. Dax waved everyone to follow him. Of all the people there, he could probably take the most physical and magical damage, so if there was something either he or Delphine missed, the others wouldn't pay the price.

He walked carefully, looking around the grass along the roadside for disturbed spots that might point to a boobytrap or other skullduggery, while keeping one eye peeled in the aether for anything concerning there. Although it was painstaking work, they arrived at the car without incident, though it didn't seem to relax anyone. Too many eyes were focused on the shattered driver-side window and the broken glass all over the road.

Dax texted Boudreaux to let him know they needed him. He pulled up in the black Sprinter van a couple minutes later, parking across the street. It had a more clearance underneath than Dax's car, so they were able to move off the road safely.

Boudreaux emerged with a bag and joined them near the car, pulling out a mirror on a telescoping pole. He walked around the car, looking in the wheel wells, under the body, and into the engine compartment without touching the car. When he finished, he poked the mirror into the interior via the broken window, looking at every nook and cranny he could reach. It had been his suggestion to do it all. He'd seen too many IEDs during his time in the army to feel safe letting them check the car out without a proper inspection first.

"All clear as far as I can tell," he said, putting his tool away.

Now that they were closer, Dax and Delphine did another round of checks, similarly finding nothing. The lack of bad news only served to ratchet up everyone's anxiety as they stood around the car staring at it.

"I guess I'll take a closer look. Everyone step back." Dax gave everyone a moment to move to whatever their perceived safe distance was. Once they stopped, he poked his arm into the broken window and pushed the unlock button, a grimace on his face. Nothing happened except the locks clicked like they were unlocked. Next, he found the hood lever and the one for the trunk, opening them both.

He waited for a second, his eyes squeezed shut except for the right one, which he let open enough to see with. Nothing happened. Exhaling heavily, he relaxed. Backing out, he looked around the cabin of the car, particularly in the area of the driver's side. He didn't see any blood.

The bullet hole in the front windshield was concerning, but it was at the wrong angle to have hit the driver. It was probably a warning shot or a lucky miss.

"Anything?" Tomi called.

"No. No blood that I can see. No weird damage except the broken window and the bullet hole." He poked his head back into the car, trying to guess the trajectory of the bullet, assuming it was fired by a man of average height while standing. If the shooter had been farther away, it would have flattened out the trajectory, and the bullet might have hit the back window, so he looked at the back seat.

Seeing a rip that hadn't been there before—the car had been in great condition when they got it from Boudreaux—he opened the back door and inspected it closer. It looked like a puncture wound in the fabric. He pulled out the switchblade he'd taken off the bikers, flicked the blade out, and probed the hole. The metal of his blade snicked on something metal.

He paused for a moment, his blade sticking in the hole, then sighed in annoyance. They'd have to get the seat fixed anyway. Pressing the blade down, he sawed into the fabric and padding until he had a big enough hole to stick a couple fingers in.

"Damnit." He couldn't get a good grip, and it felt like he was pushing it deeper in. Nor did he like the familiar dark tingle the bullet sent through the skin of his fingertip.

Carefully, he slipped a finger of his other hand into the hole and propped the bottom edge of the bullet against his fingertip and slipped the blade of the knife in at the top, poking it along the edge until the tip of the knife met the tip of the bullet. He concentrated, the tip of his tongue sticking out between his lips as he carefully wiggled the bullet out. A quick look physically and in the aether confirmed that there was no blood or residue of life on the slug of metal.

"What do you got there?" Tomi asked, stepping closer. Everyone had moved closer to the car since Dax hadn't blown up.

He angled the bullet into the sunlight, turning it to see what the light revealed. Intricate scratches covered the bullet. Runes. "Looks like one of their magic rounds. Feels similar too, though maybe a bit more sinister. I don't know."

It could be that the bikers had added more or different runes to increase the potency of their ammunition. Or it could be that the situation—a missing young friend—added weight to the circumstances and made anything the enemy used seem that much darker. After he inspected it, he dropped it into the outstretched hand of the manbo, who gave it her own examination.

"So what do we know so far?" Suzie asked, her arms folded over her chest.

Dax shrugged. "Not much. Someone shot the car, but not her. There's no blood that I can see, so she wasn't hurt in a way that indicates bleeding. The airbag didn't deploy, so she didn't run into anything at high speed. Steering wheel looks fine, no signs of a crash." He walked to the front of the car and looked at the bumper and hood. Everything looked perfectly normal. "No damage here."

Boudreaux had walked into the road and stood in the middle of the broken glass. "Looks like the window was broken here. They probably pushed the car off the road and just left it."

Tomi opened the trunk. "Oh, god, that stinks." He coughed a couple times. "Looks like the rats are still alive, but being in a hot trunk sure makes for a stink factory."

Jamie had provided a cage for the rats to ride around with her, so she always had a few available if she came across an opportunity to plant more GPS tags. And in a pinch, she could release them and get aid from The Rat. Dax was glad the rats hadn't died in the warm trunk. The Rat was a good ally and loved his little furry minions. Two or three dying in their service wouldn't have made him happy.

Suzie poked her head into the trunk. "Poor little guys drank all their water. Manman, do you have a bottle you could spare?"

The manbo pulled one out of her backpack and handed it to Suzie, who used it to refill the waterer hanging off the outside of the cage. As soon as she replaced it, the sound of rat tongues flicking across the little metal ball at the end of the spout drifted over to him.

"Car coming," Boudreaux said, strolling out of the road.

They all stopped what they were doing and let the car pass. Once it was out of sight, they looked at each other, unanswered questions in their eyes.

"Now what?" Suzie asked. "We found the car, but do we have anything more than that? We still don't know where Jamie is."

"I'd say we have a bit more than that." Dax moved around to the back of the car where everyone else stood. "We know she's likely alive and not hurt too badly, if at all. We saved the rats, which we can get back to The Rat. It's unlikely, but maybe one of them heard or smelled something that can help."

Tomi reached out and squeezed his cousin's shoulder. "We can check the locations on the active GPS tags and see if we can find something that way. Do we know if Jamie had one on her?"

"No idea. She used up all the old batch, so we can check the new batch and eliminate what we have here and see if that narrows it down. Other than that, I guess we regroup and go from there." He turned to Boudreaux. "Does your van have enough power to pull this thing back onto the road?"

"Yeah, we can provide an assist." He jogged over to the van and said something to the man in the driver's seat, then pulled a towing chain from the back of the van. "One of you is going to need to drive and guide the car."

"Suzie is probably the best driver here," Tomi said, patting her on the back. "Tell her what you need her to do." He sighed. "Too bad we don't know any other wolf shifters. Having one to do some tracking would sure be nice."

Dax agreed with him. The work Jamie had done for them with her nose had helped a lot, but all the other wolves they knew were out of town. Thinking about it, he only knew two other wolves—Ragnar and his father Gunnar. Dax had just assumed that the rest of the members of Ragnar's band were wolf shifters as well. Not that it mattered. Ragnar was in Texas last time they'd called him, and Gunnar had made his views about helping them out clear.

They were on their own.

FORTY

JAMIE

J amie woke up, stiff, sore, and with a blinding headache. When she tried to open her eyes, only one responded, and that one she quickly slammed shut when the light stabbed her brain like a red-hot icepick.

As more awareness seeped into her foggy brain, she realized her arms and ankles were tingling—not tingling but burning. She must've been lying on them funny, and they'd gone to sleep to create the worst case of pins and needles she'd ever had. She tried to shift but couldn't. Nearby, someone chuckled.

She wanted to shake violently and move, but her sluggish brain took long enough to get there that her higher reasoning perked up. She took several calming breaths before exploring what was going on with her wrists. The slight clink of metal on metal told her she'd been cuffed. The burn was silver.

Then her last memory slapped her in the face. Ivar had punched her in the side of the head. That would explain the nonresponsive eye. Now that she was aware of her situation, all the pains redoubled their efforts.

"Our little wolf is awake," Ivar said, his voice low and lazily sinister.

She gave her restraints another shake, then pulled with all her might, the cuffs burning and biting into her flesh. Finally, she stopped with a grunt and a whimper, collapsing from the effort. The cuffs and the chair she was strapped to kept her upright.

"Do you think we don't know how to keep a wolf shifter contained?" Ivar scoffed. "You are a stupid little mongrel."

He walked over to her, his treads sounding heavy on the concrete as the chains on his boots jingled and the leather stretched around his ankles. She opened her functioning eye a slit. He stopped in front of her, his feet spread to shoulder width.

He grabbed her chin, and she yelped in pain as he twisted her head up, so she was facing him as he bent over her. She had no idea how long she'd been unconscious, but her face shouldn't be hurting so much. He must have hit her with all his strength. She was lucky he hadn't killed her with the hit. As he jerked her again, the cuffs dug into her skin, twisting and burning.

Maybe the silver also inhibited her healing. She'd never had prolonged contact with it. Her earrings were barely decent steel; there was no way her parents could have bought something as fancy as silver, not that they would have, since the whole wolf-shifter thing.

He let go of her head and turned around before whirling and unleashing a casual backhand across the bad side of her face. Lights exploded in her brain, and she screamed.

Ivar chuckled cruelly. "Did you think you could get away with betraying the Black Suns and not pay the price?" He tsked. "We collect our debts. You should have learned that from your father. Or at least his corpse."

He'd given her a few moments before speaking, letting her brain recover just enough from the hit to be able to comprehend him. "But I'm not a cruel man. I'll make it easy on you. You tell me what I want to know, and I'll take this gun"—he slowly pulled a pistol from out of a shoulder holster under his leather vest and placed the barrel against her forehead—"and put one round right here. It's far too kind, considering your crimes against the Black Suns."

He flipped the gun in his hand so he held the barrel and reared back to hit her with it. She cringed. He started the swing but aborted halfway.

"Better not. This is my favorite gun. Wouldn't want to break it on your head." Instead, he whipped his arm around and gave her a brutal open-handed slap across her good cheek.

The crack of skin on skin echoed around the large concrete room. Now both sides of her face throbbed. She panted hard, her head hanging and her chin resting against her chest.

He chuckled and held his hand in front of her face. "You actually made my palm red." He inhaled heavily, then sighed contentedly. "I don't often get to do the fun work anymore. You know. The price of leadership. You should feel honored. You get the personal touch."

He rammed a fist into her stomach, and the air exploded out of her lungs.

She struggled to pull in air as her stomach muscles cramped in agony, drool falling from her lips to land on her T-shirt. Once she had enough breath to spare, she whimpered, tears burning against two beat-on cheeks.

"Oh, come now. We're just getting started. Or you can take the easy route. The smart route. And end this all now." He leaned down in front of her, shoving his face into hers. "Tell me what I want to know. Tell me where that piece of shit who burned down my bar lives. Give me the names and addresses of all his known associates. That's it. Just a few names and addresses. Easy. Then it can all end." To emphasize his point, he slapped her again.

After she caught her breath again, she lifted her head slowly, her neck sore and painful from being wrenched around so much. "Go. Fuck. Yourself."

FORTY-ONE

Jamie hadn't managed to get more than a wink or two of sleep in the last…day? She didn't know how long she'd been strapped in the chair, going through alternating cycles of beatings and unconscious moments when her brain retreated from what was happening.

Ivar took his time through it all, waiting for her to be coherent enough to really feel the pain he inflicted on her. Every now and then, he'd pause and ask the same string of questions. Where does Dax live? Who are his friends? Where do they live? Where do they work?

They knew about Dax's bar and had, according to him, burned it to the ground. But they couldn't discover where he lived. She knew it was warded and protected magically. She didn't know how exactly though, because it wasn't any of her business or even a topic she had any knowledge about. He asked politely, sounding like betraying her friends was the kind and reasonable option. His offer of release was presented like sweet relief. The thing any smart person would accept.

Her response was always some variation of her original answer—go fuck yourself.

The entire time, he'd been patient, enjoying inflicting pain and stringing it out. He'd only lost his temper once, screaming and backhanding her so hard he knocked her over. She'd lost consciousness when her head had hit the concrete.

When she'd gradually come to, she realized she'd been left lying on her side. At least the concrete was cool against her skin. She hurt all over, but the worst spots were her face—particularly her cheekbones—and her stomach. She'd taken multiple blows to both places. He'd probably broken both cheek bones, her eye sockets, and maybe her jaw. She no doubt probably had internal injuries from the repeated forceful punches to her gut. But her wolf healing, even in its diminished form, kept her put together just well enough to receive more punishment.

Somewhere in the distance, vague murmurs brought her out of the latest round of beatings.

"She won't give me anything."

She forced a crusty eye open. Ivar paced on the far side of the room, a phone held to his ear.

"Fuck you. I haven't lost my touch." Someone on the other end yelled, and he held the phone away from his ear. "She's a tough bitch, I'll give her that. Just give me more time."

Ivar stopped his pacing, listening. She couldn't make out what was being said. Perhaps if she hadn't taken so many blows to the head, her wolf hearing might have been able to pick up the other side of the conversation.

"Fine. No. I heard you." His empty fist clenched tightly, the muscles in his arm straining. "No. I understand. I'll do what I'm told."

His hand holding the phone dropped to his side, and he stared at the wall for a moment. Then a low growl rose from his throat, and he reared back and hurled the phone at the wall. It exploded, sending bits of plastic and concrete dust everywhere. Whatever Ivar had heard had not made him happy. Seeing his frustration brought her a moment of satisfaction until she thought about who could make a man like Ivar follow orders.

He stalked aggressively across the room, stopping in front of her, and dragged her and the chair back to upright. "This is your last chance. Tell me what I want to know. Believe me, what's coming next will be far worse than what I've already given you. Tell me, and it's sweet, gentle relief with one bullet between the eyes." There was a note of desperation in his voice that hadn't been there before. He leaned down so they were face-to-face and tilted his head to the side quizzically.

She smacked her dry lips and gathered the moisture in her mouth, which included a good measure of blood from the last blows to her head. With all her remaining force, she spat it in his face. His reaction was instant. He reared back and delivered a brutal uppercut that rocked her head back and threw her and the chair she was strapped to onto the floor on her back. He stepped up to her, wiped a hand down his face, and flung her own blood and spit onto her, then drew back his foot and kicked her in the ribs. She blacked out.

FORTY-TWO

JAMIE

"What have you done to her?" A new voice asked, drawing Jamie out from the darkness.

The voice sounded odd, but after the pounding her head had taken, she didn't know what anything was supposed to sound like anymore. A dark shadow fell across her face, blocking the light from filtering through her closed eyelids. She tried opening the one that wasn't crusted shut with blood but only managed to part the lid a little. More shadows.

She blinked the eye as best as she could a few times until the picture came into focus, at least more than it had been. Someone in amorphous black robes stood over her. Their face looked odd. Formless. Flat. Reflective.

It took a moment for her sleep-deprived and pain-addled brain to realize they were wearing a shiny metal mask—maybe stainless steel or chrome.

"You've practically beat her to death."

Ivar scoffed, snorting a blast of air through his nostrils. "She's a wolf shifter. She'll be fine. Besides, we owed her that and more."

"Set the chair upright," the masked one ordered. "Now."

Jamie still couldn't figure out what was going on with their voice.

It lay somewhere in a neutral register, neither high or low, but beyond that it came out in an oddly metallic tone, which vibrated and seemed to have some odd harmonics that just didn't quite mesh.

She was wrenched off her back and she, along with the chair, were roughly returned to a sitting position. The sudden shift in position on her concussed brain made her swoon. Not wanting to vomit on herself, she focused on breathing through it. She'd been subjected to enough indignities; she didn't need to create one of her own.

"Bring me some water," the masked one said, walking away from where she sat.

Jamie couldn't remember when she'd last had something to drink. They'd forced a cup into her mouth some time ago to keep her alive and supplied with enough saliva to speak. The water had back-fired. She had just enough hydration to spit in Ivar's face. As far as a moment of defiance went, it hadn't been too bad.

The masked one stood with their back to her, but their robes moved, indicating motion of some sort. Jamie thought she heard the faint sound of glass clinking against glass, but it could've been the glass being set on something.

They held up the glass to the side where she could see it. "Give her the water. And don't spill any of it."

"I'm not her fucking nursemaid."

The masked one's head rotated slowly to face Ivar. "I do not care. Give her the water. Or do I have to remind you for whom I work?"

Grumbling, Ivar took the glass gently enough none of the liquid spilled. He stomped petulantly across the room to her. He bent over and stuck his head near her ear.

"I'll give you one last chance. Give me the information I want, and I'll put you out of your misery. If not, The Warlock gets you, and you'll soon be missing the love taps I was giving you. You'll know pain in new and dark ways that'll tear you apart from the inside."

"Enough," barked the masked one. Were they The Warlock? Or were they some scary intermediary? "I said to water her, not threaten her."

Ivar pushed the edge of the glass between her lips a bit too roughly and some water sloshed over the side, spilling down her chin and onto her sweat-drenched T-shirt. Once the cool water soaked in, it felt like a small relief. But she didn't trust Ivar or this new...thing. She kept her lips clamped tight.

"Listen, little bitch, drink the fucking water, or I'll stomp you, force it down your throat, and clamp your mouth shut until you swallow it or drown. I don't care which," Ivar hissed.

He'd do it too. Reluctantly, she opened her lips and let a little water pass between them. It tasted fine, maybe even carrying a slight sweet note. But it was cool and wet, so she swallowed greedily, letting Ivar tip the rest down her throat. She chugged the water down out of thirst and self-preservation. The water felt like the elixir of life as it passed through her lips, cooling her dry and sore throat.

"Now we wait. Fetch me a chair, and set it in front of her," the masked one ordered.

Ivar stalked off to comply, mumbled curses falling from his lips. A minute later, he slammed a chair down onto the ground in front of her and moved out of her sight. For the first time since she'd woken up in his hell, she felt a little better. A small pinch of the pain throbbing all over her body went away. She even thought her vision in her slitted eye cleared some. Along with the physical improvements, she calmed, her heart rate and breathing slowing.

The water was working miracles on her as she sat in silence. She still felt like one giant block of pain, but some of the intensity had been stripped away. But while she physically felt a little better, nothing was happening. The masked one stood still, appearing to be staring off into nothing while Ivar paced like a caged animal. The anxiety of anticipation grew steadily. If Ivar was in charge, she knew a beating was coming and had yet to be surprised.

But with the masked one, she didn't know what they would do to her. Ivar had probably been saying they were worse than him to frighten her and get what he wanted. He clearly didn't like that the masked one, whoever they were, was encroaching on his territory. And that scared Jamie. Who controlled the masked one? Who could give orders to a nasty biker gang like the Black Suns?

"You may go, now, Ivar."

Ivar surprised her by leaving the room without any snide

comments and only a minimum of grumbling. The masked one waited for a few moments to make sure he'd properly left, and they were alone.

Reaching into their robes, they pulled something out and set it on the floor in front of her. Narrowing her one good eye, she caught a glint of dull light glinting off it. It looked glassy—maybe a crystal. They moved in a circle around her, the starting and stopping of footsteps marking four other drops.

Walking slowly, the masked one stopped in between Jamie and the empty chair, then sat. As they lowered themselves, they mumbled a word Jamie couldn't quite catch.

Something snapped somewhere in the room. She blinked her eye a few times, and realized the lines she thought she was imagining really existed. They crept across the room, forming a circle. Then more lines formed, connecting points across the circle. Each time the lines connected to one of the five points, the air in the room shifted. She couldn't see any changes, but the air thickened and became more potent with power.

When the last line clicked into place, the room pulsed. Then nothing happened. The masked one stared at her, sitting up rigidly in the chair, their black gloved hands folded in their lap.

Jamie's breathing shallowed as the tension of waiting thickened, and her body seemed to be on the precipice of shifting into fight-or-flight mode. Since she could do neither in her restraints, she had to force herself not to try tearing at them to get free. It took all her will to remain still.

"Now, we are going to have a little chat," the masked one said, their voice drilling into her brain. "Tell me your full name."

She tried to resist. She had no plans to give in to whoever this ghoul was. After taking the beatings from Ivar, whatever this person offered couldn't be worse.

Slowly, sweat broke out across her body. Her veins burned hot, the heat spreading to every neve in her body. Clenching her teeth, she tried to grit her way through the growing agony.

"What is a name? 'Tis a simple request." The words weren't spoken out loud but had been projected into her brain.

Her muscles flashed in a cramp, then released. Then again. On the third time, they didn't release. If she ground her teeth together any harder, she'd shatter them. A scream bubbled up from deep inside her gut, rolling up her throat, and finally out her lips, forcing her mouth open. She felt her throat nearly tear from the force of it.

"Your name."

"Jamie. Rosalita. Rodriguez." The pain disappeared, and she slumped against her restraints, panting hard. A bead of sweat rolled down her forehead, collecting on her brow before continuing its journey down her nose to fall and land on the concrete floor. She stared at it. It gleamed like a small round gem on the ground.

"How old are you?"

"Eighteen."

"Where were you born?"

"Redemption City."

FORTY-THREE

DAX

The Rat hadn't needed any additional enticement to venture out of his tunnels to come pick up his three furry friends—mentioning that Jamie had been kidnapped was enough. But since The Rat was coming, Dax invited Manman Delphine over to join them for tea. That seemed like the best way to have a discussion with the other magical people he knew. Although he didn't know precisely what The Rat was, magically speaking.

Manman Delphine had agreed to host, since the bar and the tearoom were strictly off-limits until inspections could be done on the building. Dax missed his tearoom. He hadn't even gotten a chance to inspect his teas to see if any had sustained any damage from the fire or smoke. The room hadn't smelled smoky, but it was hard to tell when there were so many strong smells coming from the charred ruins of his bar. So, he had to make do with a tea set from his house and one of the varieties he'd brought home.

Balancing the box tea supplies on his hip, he pulled open the door and slid into Madame Thibodeaux's, as the sign on the outside of Delphine's magic shop read. She sold supplies to the local magical community, as well as other curios and occult items to mundanes interested in such things. He'd expressly been forbidden from touching her tarot cards, because his aura tainted them, causing the Death card to always be drawn. She'd given him his own deck so he could do his own readings or use it to have others pull his cards. He wished he had it with him so she could do a reading for him. Or maybe he'd call Tallulah and see if she'd be willing to read them. But his deck was currently behind police tape, sitting on a shelf behind the bar in the tearoom.

He could always buy a new set, but his had been a gift from the manbo and already were starting to build a rapport, or bond, with him. Another option would be to ask the manbo to do a reading after he left, when he was good and far from her store, so his aura didn't fuck up another deck of her cards. He needed to use every tool in his arsenal to find Jamie. Tonight would mark the second night after the bar had burned down. Three days. Three long days since anyone had seen their young friend.

"Dax, it's good to see you." Delphine, back in one of her colorful dresses, pushed away from the counter and smiled at him. Sticking her arm through the beaded curtain separating the front of her shop from her office and stock room, she pulled it open for him. "Table and water are set up in the back."

"Good to see you too. And thanks for letting me do this here." He squeezed through the door sideways so as not to bump her or the box.

"We have to look out for each other in tough times. That's what community is. Any word on when our King of the Rats will join us?"

Dax appreciated the merry twinkle in the manbo's eye. It always lightened the mood when it was needed. He had no doubt positive aura was a big part of the success of the community she'd built among the local voodoo parishioners.

While they waited, he set up the tea service and filled the electric kettle. He only had to wait maybe ten minutes before The Rat poked his head into the shop.

His eyes zipped around, inspecting the riot of colors and shapes as his nose sniffed vigorously. All the sights and smells were a lot for anyone to take in, but it must've been particularly intense for someone with enhanced physical senses, who was used to the gray and dull world of the tunnels under Red City—though they offered their own unique panoply of sights and smells. Dax's stomach turned a bit remembering the stench of the sewer lines they'd used to break into the bikers' compound to free Ragnar's band mates.

"Come on in, cher." Delphine smiled warmly, beckoning The Rat in.

"I have friends. May I bring one?" he asked, his nose still working overtime.

"As long as they mind their manners, they are welcome," she replied.

Dax waved at The Rat, then walked through the beaded curtain to turn the water on.

"Please lock the door and flip the closed sign ," Delphine instructed before joining Dax in the back room. She waited at the door, holding the beads open.

Again The Rat paused at the door and inspected the back room thoroughly before entering. Although The Rat always looked shabby —his clothes were old, worn, and mostly too big for his small stature —they were always clean. Today was no different, except he'd attempted to tame his messy hair and beard. The hair was slicked back heavily with something that made his hair shiny, and he'd trimmed his beard aggressively. The results were uneven at best, but Dax guessed The Rat had wanted to put his best foot forward as a guest of Manman Delphine Thibodeaux the voodoo priestess.

He entered as the water kettle dinged. Dax filled the cups and the teapot with hot water and let them warm up before discarding the water into a nearby bucket. Dumping the tea into the pot, he filled the pot again with water and let it sit for a few seconds, pouring it off and refilling it. In his head, he counted off to thirty, then poured the brown liquid into the three waiting cups.

"Sorry for the lack of a full, proper ceremony, but most of my equipment is trapped in my tearoom."

Delphine laid a hand on his forearm fondly. "No worries, cher. Tea with you is always welcome, no matter why or how."

"Yes, yes. Many thanks." The Rat flashed him a quick, awkward smile.

"What are we drinking today?" Delphine asked, picking up her cup and sniffing at the wafting steam climbing into the air.

"A Chinese single origin from 'ancient' trees." He smelled it, enjoying the aromas of tropical fruit and earthy notes.

They sat quietly for a few minutes, enjoying their first cup tea. When they finished, Dax prepared the second steeping.

"So, I've asked you here so we can pool our resources and come up with a solution to our problem—our missing friend." Dax poured the tea into their cups.

The Rat, anger washing over his face, reached inside his coat and pulled out a large, brown rat and set it on the corner of the table. He leaned over, placing his lips near the rat's ears. "Now be a good rat, we are guests at this table."

The rat looked up at him, then laid down on its stomach to make a little brown loaf, its pink tail wrapped around its side. Reaching into his pocket, The Rat pulled out a little ceramic dish and set it down in front of the rat. There was a small chip on the edge of the little bowl. He blew on his tea for a few moments and took a sip. He nodded to himself, as he poured a little into the rat's bowl.

"Slow now, still hot. Burn your little ratty tongue."

Dax brought his eyebrows back down. The Rat and his friend were guests and allies, but Dax still wasn't quite used to The Rat's eccentricities. But it was always best to be polite to him since he had a prickly ego, especially when it came to his rat minions.

Delphine smiled and looked over at Dax. "Now we can't say we've never shared tea with a rat." She chuckled warmly.

"That's true." Dax lifted his cup in a friendly salute, first to The Rat, then to his friend.

"We thank you for your politeness." The big, awkward grin returned to The Rat's face. "This is my friend, but he is also a Jamie friend. He was with her when the cruel villains took her. Very smart rat, very loyal. Very angry at the bad man who took Jamie friend."

"Bad man?" Dax asked.

"We know this man. Very bad. Dark aura. Cruel. Vicious. He came into our tunnels the last time he hunted Jamie friend." He sipped his tea noisily. "Yes. Know him. I recall Jamie friend said his name is Ivar. Very bad man. The Rat and my little rats always avoid him."

Dax's stomach sank. He guessed that was likely who had Jamie. "Fuck. She must have followed him when he ducked out early the other night. This isn't good. The last time they had her, they offered to trade her and her family in exchange for me. It didn't go well for the bikers."

He didn't want to say what he was thinking. Knowing how the exchange had gone last time, the bikers might forgo trying it again and just pay her back for all her crimes against the gang. It wouldn't be quick and painless either. He took a drink of his tea, but it tasted of bile in his mouth.

"What can we do to help?" Delphine asked.

"I don't understand quite what your practice entails, Manman Delphine, but whatever you can do would be wonderful." He turned to The Rat. "And you, Mr. The Rat, if you can get your rats to canvas the city and look for any biker." He reached into the box he'd brought his tea stuff in with, pulled out a plastic bag, and handed it to The Rat. "It's some of her dirty laundry. I didn't know if rats could track scents, so I erred on the side of bringing something."

Dax set his empty teacup down. "We'll be continuing to check out all the GPS readings we've collected, but there are a lot of them and not many of us. And if I run into any bikers, well, I'll be using my own resources to investigate any threads that may lead to Jamie."

Manman Delphine and The Rat both nodded at him. The Rat grabbed the bag and tucked it into his baggy jacket.

"If you don't mind," Delphine said, "I'll put out a few vague feelers to some of my more regular customers. There are some who have skills that I don't that might be more useful."

Dax narrowed his eyes and regarded the suggestion. He'd reluctantly let these two into his world of trust, provisionally, though Manman Delphine had repeatedly proven her loyalty to Tomi's family and by extension to Dax. The Rat was still a newer and much more unknown commodity. But he'd come through for them before, despite not wanting to get involved. He seemed to genuinely care for

Jamie. Their time together when she'd been forced to hide in his tunnels had won him over.

But Dax worried that if he kept extending his circle, he'd eventually add someone who couldn't be trusted. Probably sooner rather than later. Trusting people had been a problem for him since his betrayal by someone he trusted almost above anyone else and banishment to the world of humanity.

However, Jamie was only eighteen, and she was in the hands of some truly bad people. For her sake and the sake of all those who'd brought her into their worlds, he couldn't reject Delphine's offer out of hand. "If you keep it vague. See if anyone you know would have the skills to solve our problem. If we need them, we can always bring —" His phone started vibrating. When he sent it to voicemail, it started ringing again. His gut tightened. "Damnit."

"Do you need some privacy?" Delphine asked.

"No, probably not." He stood up and walked toward the back of the room. It was Tomi. "What's up, Tomi?"

"Something's happening with the GPS tags."

"Can you be more specific?" Dax asked.

"They're just…blinking out? I don't know. They're just not showing up on the map anymore. Every few minutes more and more are gone. In ones and twos, sometimes more." Tomi sounded desperate.

Dax dragged a hand over his face. "Fuck. The bikers know about the GPS tags."

"Yeah. This is bad. Real bad."

FORTY-FOUR

DAX

"Dax? Dax."

"Hmm?" He shook himself to attention. "I'm sorry, Delphine."

She scooped up the tarot cards from the counter of her shop. He'd managed to get into the tearoom a couple days after their previous discussion and grab some of the things he'd wanted to retrieve, including his cards. Forming them into a neat stack, she slipped them into the box.

Delphine pursed her lips before speaking. "Since you're elsewhere mentally, I'll give you the gist. Things are confusing, and there's something obscuring our ability to get clarity."

He snorted. "I could have told you that." He sighed. "Sorry, I don't mean to be rude."

"You're just concerned about your friend."

"She's not my friend." It was a reactionary response.

"Really? You're worried about her. You care about her well-being. You're doing everything you can to find her. Sounds like someone you care about." Delphine had a sardonic smile on her face.

Jamie had nearly killed him, but ultimately she was just the weapon pointed at him by someone else. He thought about all their interactions since then. He couldn't pinpoint the moment when it'd happened, but he realized he enjoyed her presence when she was around. She was smart, tough, and brave.

"You're right. We've done everything we can think of. We're truly at a dead end. I'm…I'm scared for her."

"Was that so hard to admit?" She patted his hand.

"I don't know. Maybe 'hard to admit' isn't the right way to express it. Fear is not something I've felt a lot of. I've existed so long outside of that emotion. I knew that I caused it. But felt it? Not until becoming a human." He paused, his brow furrowing. "That's not true, now that I think about it. Fear led me to accepting exile as a human. Fearing the other option was my first experience with the feeling. Now the more I get entangled with all the humans in my life, I find myself fearing what will happen to them if I mess something up. Now I have, and my…f-f-friend is missing, likely kidnapped, and certainly in trouble."

"Friendships and relationships do bring complications into lives."

"Is it worth it though?"

"I know my answer, but you should ask the question to yourself. Do you think it's worth it?"

He looked down at the counter between them. His friendships certainly had made his life more complicated. He had more to worry about than just himself. But the thought of going it alone felt wrong. Empty. Being around the people who'd come into his life made it worth leaving the apartment. Morty was a fine fellow, but he was a shit conversationalist and had no appreciation for a fine tea.

"I guess it is." He shook his head. "Who would have thought it?" He picked up his teacup, lifting it in salute. "Tea with a friend. Simple pleasures. But what can I do? We've exhausted everything can think of to find her."

"Well, that's why I called you today. One of my customers returned my call and said they might be able to help you."

He narrowed his eyes. "A customer? What kind of a customer?"

"The magical kind. She's a powerful witch who runs one of the covens in town." She tipped her mug back, then went into the stock room to turn on the kettle before reemerging. "Of the people who we might work with, she is probably the most likely to succeed in getting us actionable information on where Jamie might be."

"I need more tea before we continue." He finished the last swig and went to the back to prepare some new leaves for steeping. Once they had two fresh mugs of a nice Indian black tea, he leaned against the counter, looking toward the door. "Do you trust this witch?"

Delphine clicked her tongue. "I don't distrust her. It's a fine distinction to make, I know. I don't know her well enough to say I have formed a bond of trust with her. She's been a customer since I opened the shop, but we've never broken bread or worked magic together."

"What about her reputation?" He was nervous about working with someone other than Manman Delphine. She'd come to him through people he trusted fully. She'd given him her honest assessment, but he'd have make up his own mind.

"Not bad. Covens guard their secrets. I've known some to do so violently. She is respected among the other covers, at least the ones I've talked to. My other customers. There's always a healthy mix of respect and fear when she's mentioned. No one has spoken ill of her, but as far as I can tell, she doesn't have any alliances with any of the other covens in Red City."

He let Delphine's words ruminate in his head as he enjoyed the aroma of his tea. "That's not a lot to go on. Either she doesn't play well with others and they're afraid to say anything that might get back to her, or she prefers independence or thinks her coven is strong enough to stand alone."

"Pretty much my thoughts as well." She blew over the top of her hot mug. "But a big factor in her favor... She offered to help and thinks she might be able to help us."

He exhaled noisily, staring at the beaded curtain behind Delphine. "That is a big pro in her column. Damnit. I don't want to make a rash choice."

"If it helps your decision, I'll go with you to talk to her and make sure there's no magical skullduggery." She squeezed his hand, the gesture reassuring him of her willingness to help.

"We really can't afford to take time to think about it or look for other alternatives. My friend needs help now." He rubbed his hand over the rough texture of two days of stubble on his chin. "Call the witch."

FORTY-FIVE

Jamie dreaded peeling back her eyelids. She could already tell she'd been moved yet again. She had no idea how many days they'd had her. She'd marked the wall in her first windowless cell to try to tally the time, but she'd only been there two sleeps before she woke up in a new cell. They'd drugged her food or water.

At first, she was grateful they were providing for her basic needs, even if they fed her like an animal by sliding a couple pet bowls through a small flap at the bottom of the door. She'd even thought about shifting to her wolf form to make drinking from the bowl easier, but when she tried to shift, she couldn't. Something about the rooms prevented her from accessing her wolf.

Unfortunately, she couldn't find what was causing the issue. She was kept in almost total darkness except for whatever light leaked through the cracks in and around the door. She was just happy today's cell had a cot in it. A couple of the rooms she'd been kept in hadn't, and she'd been forced to sleep on the hard floor, which wouldn't have been terrible. If she'd been able to shift over.

She didn't know what they wanted anymore. After her first meeting with The Warlock, no one had spoken a word to her. It had actually been pleasant to be left alone so she could heal from the beatings Ivar had given her. She was still sore in some spots, which she thought odd.

Either Ivar had truly beat her within an inch of her life, or whatever was preventing her from shifting was also slowing her healing. She couldn't tell which. If she'd had access to as much food as she wanted, she'd have a better idea. But they were barely providing enough to sustain her. It certainly wasn't enough calories to meet her wolf's healing needs. She pretty much always had a low pang of hunger in her belly.

She'd thought about testing her strength and trying to break out, but her body hurt so badly, the thought made her cry. So she rested and waited and tried to keep her fear and growing loneliness in check. She'd just gotten used to being around people who enjoyed her presence and who she liked seeing. After finally feeling a bit of emotional satiation, she'd been forced back into starvation mode. But now she didn't have Cory or even the disinterested neglect of her parents to keep her company.

Once she'd woken up in yet another new location, she decided to test her jail quietly. She still couldn't shift, but she felt better than she had in days.

Starting with the flap they used to give her meals, she pushed against it with her feet, gradually increasing her pressure against it. It barely budged. She didn't want to try kicking it hard unless it felt like she had a reasonable chance of breaking out. She didn't want to attract the attention of her jailers and incur new hardships.

She tried to tell herself she needed to be patient and vigilant. Patience she had in reasonable amounts, at least for someone her age. But it was hard to be vigilant when you were regularly unconscious.

FORTY-SIX

DAX

Dax rolled to a stop on his motorcycle by the long, black classic car, turned the motor off, and waited for the window to roll down. He was still using the other bike he'd recently stolen, while the one with the fancy paint job was with Boudreaux. The search for Jamie had sidetracked everyone, including Boudreaux and his crew, and anything besides paying gigs had been put on the backburner.

"Are you sure about this, Dax?" Tomi asked from behind the wheel of Dax's 1965 Lincoln Continental, leaning out the open window. Minh—Tomi's girlfriend, Dax had to remind himself—sat next to Tomi in the passenger seat.

Apparently the inner circle of trusted people now included her. He'd saved her life from the cages of The Collector, and she'd repaid him by hooking him up with security footage from her convenience store's supposedly nonfunctioning video cameras. And she'd saved his bar and the building which included several apartments and Mama Adele's restaurant from burning to the ground. He didn't know much about her beyond she was dating his best friend and she was some sort of supernatural who could manipulate water.

"I don't see we have much of a choice. We need to know where these bikers have Jamie. The longer she's gone, the higher chance of her not coming out of this alive, and we owe her the effort of doing whatever we can. Also, we can't let the bikers start picking us off one by one. You and I have people to take care of. Lives to protect."

Tomi clenched his jaw and nodded tightly. Two of those lives were family—his mother and his cousin. They were both glad his younger sister was out of state on a scholarship. She hadn't come home this summer because of an internship. It was a small boon there wasn't another target to worry about. "I still don't like it."

"Me either. But the manbo will be there with me."

"And I can't talk you into letting me come with you?" Tomi asked.

"No. I need a getaway driver ready to go." Dax smiled warmly at his friend. Tomi didn't have any supernatural powers, but he'd done well so far, and didn't back down easily when his friends and family were involved. Dax had never met someone as steadfast and loyal as the human sitting behind the wheel of the Lincoln.

Minh reached over and squeezed Tomi's shoulder. "I can step in if he needs a little extra help."

Dax didn't know what that might mean, but her confidence bolstered his own mood. Even if it only meant blasting the witches with water, it would provide a necessary distraction if he needed to make a run for it.

"And don't forget, we've got Boudreaux and his boys standing by. I doubt even witches could withstand that many bullets fired by trained hands."

"That's true. I just don't trust witches. Too many good houngans and manbos have been killed by covens looking to take out rivals," Tomi said.

Dax would have to ask Manman Delphine for a bit more of that history. He knew the manbo sold witchcraft supplies to this coven and others in Red City. He knew too little about the supernaturals of the world. Before his exile, he'd never cared about what the reaped were in life. They all fell to his powers and were collected by whatever psychopomp matched their beliefs and their afterlife destinations. His purpose wasn't to care about such things. Occasionally when he'd joined The Morrigan, she told him some of the workings of the Celtic afterlife she presided over, but that was about it.

Tomi glanced down the road toward the fenced compound on the edge of town. "At least I don't have to crawl up the sewers to get to the compound this time. I still haven't forgiven you for that."

"Yeah, this is the less fragrant option. Didn't think we'd be back here so soon."

"And I don't want to be here much longer." Tomi pulled his phone out of his pocket. "Almost time. Shit, where's the manbo?"

As if to answer, a taxi stopped behind him and disgorged Manman Delphine. Unlike her normal colorful dress, she wore black, including the wrap that hid her hair. The taxi pulled back onto the road and drove off, leaving a dust cloud from its desire to return to a safer and more profitable part of town.

"Good evening, cher." Delphine stepped between Dax's motorcycle and the car and kissed him on the cheek. "Tomi, always a pleasure to see you. How's Adele doing?"

Tomi chuckled. "Pissed off and ready to go to war against everyone messing with her boys and her business."

Delphine laughed. "So about the same? I'm glad no one was hurt."

"Me too. It could have been a lot worse if Minh hadn't stopped the fire."

Delphine bent over and looked into the car. "Avek plezi, Minh." She straightened up. "I wish you'd told me you were bringing an extra person; I would have made up a gris-gris for her."

Minh replied in what Dax guessed was French, then shifted to English. "It's alright, manman. I can handle myself."

The manbo smiled. "I bet you can." She reached into her flowy black dress and drew out a couple of gris-gris, handing one to Tomi and one to Dax. "Just for a little extra luck and protection."

Dax took it gratefully. The gris-gris she'd made previously had helped, including saving him from a stabbing from a magical switchblade. He took the new bag in both hands and held it to his lips, then blew into the small bag. Tomi did the same thing. After they finished their exhales, they both dropped the cords around their necks.

"Are you ready?" Delphine asked.

"I guess so," Tomi said.

Dax simply nodded and started the engine. Delphine hiked up the material of her skirt, revealing combat-style boots and threw her leg over the back of the motorcycle. Wrapping her arms around his midsection, she squeezed when she was ready to go. He waited until Tomi had the window rolled up so he didn't spit dust into his own car, and took off. Checking the mirror, he made sure Tomi was right behind them.

FORTY-SEVEN

DAX

Out of the corner of his eye, he saw Tomi turn off the road onto a side street. He'd wind his way through the neighborhood until he reached the spot where he'd hang out, waiting in case they needed a hot ride out of their meeting.

Dax didn't plan on leaving his motorcycle behind, but if he had to, it was better to have a backup plan. At least it wasn't the one with the nice paint job. He wouldn't regret having to leave a stolen bike behind if they had to hustle out of there.

He took one hand off the handlebars and checked his watch. He normally didn't bother with one, but he'd left his phone behind to keep it out of unwanted hands. It was approaching midnight. He goosed the engine and sped up.

After a few gentle curves, he slowed the bike as they approached the abandoned compound and its collapsed buildings. It had been a few weeks since Dax had last been here, and he'd been the one to collapse the buildings. He found it fitting that he'd be able to use the site of the bikers' most recent defeat at his hands to strike another blow against them.

During the time the lot had sat empty, no one had come to install a new gate. The last one had been torn apart by an explosion he and the rat had set to open the compound so their allies could join them.

With a slow bank, he turned into the compound, avoiding the crater the bomb had made, turned in a tight circle, and parked the bike near the gate with the front pointing toward their escape route. He'd have loved to leave the engine running, but that would likely be viewed by the witches as an insult or at the very least untrusting. But since he needed this to go well, he turned the motor off and waited so Delphine could get off first. Once it was clear, he dismounted and stood by her side.

Something felt odd to him.

He looked around, and his eyes narrowed as he sent out gentle feelers into the aether. A vague sense of nearby power tickled the edges of his awareness, but he couldn't be sure if it was the manbo, all the gris-gris he and no doubt she were wearing, or the witches. But he didn't see them. The compound was empty save for him and Delphine, his bike, and the three collapsed buildings.

A small shadow passed through the light cast from a nearby light pole, drawing his eye. Running along the top of the fence near the back left corner of the compound was a rat. It was accompanied by several friends. There was no doubt many more moving about where he couldn't see. The other backup plan was in place.

He ground his teeth in annoyance. He didn't like to be kept waiting, especially if he didn't know the other party. It didn't help with his trust issues. Leaning closer to Delphine's ear, he pitched his voice low enough that he thought only Delphine would be able to hear him.

"Where are they?"

Delphine opened her mouth.

"Right here." A white woman in a dark flowy dress stepped out of thin air about fifteen feet in front of him, between where he and Delphine stood and the largest of the collapsed buildings—the one where the bikers had kept the hostages, Ragnar's bandmates.

Dax tensed and reached into the aether for his scythe, though he left it there—invisible. It was ready if he needed to go into action.

The shadows behind the woman shifted and broke apart like a

mirage cloud, revealing six other women, all white, of varying ages. A small smile spread across the lead woman's face.

"I hope you'll pardon the display." The woman tilted her head in a nearly imperceptible gesture. "Delphine, it's always a pleasure to see you."

"Grizelda, same, as always." The normal note of wry humor was turned down a little, with a bit of wariness replacing it. She gestured at Dax. "This is my friend, Dax Smith. He's the one who needs your skills."

"Mr. Smith, it's a pleasure to meet you. I'm Grizelda."

Dax nodded and tried to release the tension from his jaw.

"Not too loquacious, is he?" She directed the question to Delphine.

The manbo chuckled humorously. "That he isn't."

The witch clapped her hands together lightly. "So, on to business then, since we're not really here for conversation anyway."

Dax held up a hand. "Is this likely to draw attention? Creating lights? Noises?"

"We can handle that," Grizelda replied, raising her hand above her head.

Several more witches stepped out of the shadows. A quick survey noted five spread about the compound spaced equally apart. If he were to draw lines crossing the compound from person to person, they would form a rough pentagram. Grizelda and her six other companions—coven mates—would be roughly placed in the center of the pentagram.

"My five sisters will take care of glamouring the lot. While it won't make us totally invisible, it'll muffle any lights and sounds and will also deter people from investigating."

Dax nodded, casting a quick glance at Delphine, who gave him a nod to acknowledge the witch's words. "OK. What else do you need?"

"We need something belonging to those you wish to contact."

He spread his arms out and looked around. "Everything here. The soil has drunk of their blood. Their souls were ripped from their corpses here." He pointed to a chunk of dust-covered metal. "Some of their motorcycles were destroyed here. That's why I selected this place. It's isolated on the edge of town and was the site of their last extended occupation."

Grizelda raised a questioning eyebrow. "I'm not sure motorcycles are going to be personal enough."

"Oh, they're personal enough if you know motorcycle club culture. Their bikes are probably their most prized possessions. It's wrapped up deeply in their self-identity. The club and the motorcycles are what matters most in their lives." Dax folded his arms over his chest.

Grizelda nodded. "Very good. If that's the case, then the parts will work nicely. If you'd fetch any of the scraps that look relevant, we'll put them in the center of the formation."

He walked over to a piece he'd pointed out earlier and hooked a boot-covered toe under it and kicked it over. It was a bent piece of a rear fender. Picking it up, he brought it over to Grizelda and set it at her feet, then went to look for a couple more chunks of debris that had been left behind.

"Ick, rats. Disgusting," one of the witches near the fences grumbled in the background.

A smirk spread across his face. Most humans found rats to be disgusting, disease-carrying vermin, but he'd kind of grown fond of them since meeting The Rat and his minions. The little creatures had helped him out more than once, including saving his life and protecting his friends. They were useful allies, and in this case, their reputation was also useful.

If the witches decided to turn on him for whatever reason, the fear and disgust they felt for rats would make the rats' attacks much more potent. And he had no doubt The Rat was nearby. Although he wasn't sure where or how, since the sewer access tunnel had been thoroughly damaged when Tomi and The Rat had exploded a bomb in it to escape the bikers sent after them and their rescued hostages.

The bomb had been meant as a deterrent. What they hadn't expected was for the opening and closing of the sewer hatch to mix in the right amount of oxygen to turn the sewer gas into a massive explosion. None of the bikers who'd gone in survived. Tomi, The

Rat, and the hostages had just barely made it out of the explosion's range.

Once he'd gathered a few more pieces and placed them near Grizelda, he stood back and waited with his arms crossed while Delphine and Grizelda squatted down and looked over the debris, picking them up and inspecting them.

"These should work well," Delphine said.

"Agreed. Excellent psychic resonance." Grizelda plunged her hand into the gravel and scooped up a handful, bringing it up to her nose to sniff. "I can still smell the blood in the soil." She looked up at Dax. "Are you sure this is their blood?"

"Yes. None of our blood was spilled here, and besides that, very little was spilled on our side. We were fortunate."

An eyebrow shot up toward her wavy raven black tresses. "Against a gang of violent, white supremacist werewolf bikers?" She looked him up and down, her eyes narrowing speculatively. When she finally broke her eyes away from his, she tossed the handful of gravel and dirt onto the ground and brushed her hands off, leaving a small cloud of dust around them. "Very good. This should work well for what we need. Are you ready?"

Dax thought about it for a second. This was his last chance to back out without becoming entangled in yet another magical connection in Red City. But right now, with his bar filled with ashes and debris and his friend missing, he didn't know how much caution he could afford. Whatever costs might rack up in the future would have to be a problem for tomorrow's Dax.

"I am. Where do you need me?" He'd ensured Delphine made it explicitly clear that he wouldn't provide any of his own DNA of any type. No hair follicles, no spit, no blood. If they couldn't work their magic without it, he wouldn't participate.

Grizelda stepped aside and gestured toward the six other witches standing behind her in an almost complete circle. On cue and in unison, the witches backed up two steps each in a display designed to be a little creepy while recognizing his need to feel as safe as possible, all things considered.

He nodded and stepped into the middle of the circle, nervously licking his lips.

Delphine grasped her hands behind her back and gave Grizelda a nod. The manbo looked as if she was signaling to a student to start their presentation. He wanted to chuckle but kept it to himself. He wouldn't lessen the effect of her little display of power and self-confidence.

Bowing her neck gracefully toward the voodoo priestess, the witch spun just quick enough to set the diaphanous material of her dress to twirling and floating around her as she stepped into the open space left for her by her sisters.

As soon as she joined the circle, the witches, save for their leader, raised their arms above their heads and out to the side.

Grizelda smiled mischievously and winked at Dax. "Here. We. Go."

FORTY-EIGHT

DAX

As soon as Grizelda's hands rose into the air, the five witches on the perimeter of the compound barked out a word and began chanting in low voices. The darkness surrounding the compound shifted and bent like heat waves pouring off a desert highway. Dax found their coordination and the clear display of their power spooky, as it was probably meant to be.

When he'd agreed to seek help from the coven, he'd expected a display of power, and he wasn't disappointed with what they'd shown him so far. He believed that little things done well and with the same level of attention and detail as the important things boded well for the success of the big pieces.

His ears popped as the illusion or glamour snapped into place, and the air solidified, looking slightly glossier than a velvety, dark sky usually did. He wondered if there was a similar, slightly off-textured dome barely visible if someone was looking at the lot from the outside, or if it was just the inside that took on the effect.

As soon as the glamour squad finished their incantation, they dropped elegantly to the ground and sat cross legged in unison, resting forearms on their knees with their palms up, their thumbs and middle fingers touching. Eyes closed in concentration, their lips moved as they continued their chant at such low volume that he doubted even Jamie with her enhanced wolf ears could have heard their words.

As the glamour squad quieted, the inner seven started their own chant in a low tone. When they finished their first…verse—he wasn't sure what to call it, he couldn't understand what they were saying, but he felt the building power of their words—their arms snapped down to their sides with their wrists bent to press their palms flat to the ground. Their last word cracked like lightning through the compound.

The circle rotated two steps counterclockwise. The hairs on his arms rose, as did the ones the back of his neck, and a tingle ran over his scalp. He wasn't sure if it was the gathering and release of power or the spooky coordination.

He was considered to be a spooky bastard by most people he knew, though they used the phrase with a tone of friendliness, respect, and a touch of fear. The witches, so far, were impressing him, at least aesthetically.

He thought about peeking into the aether to see if he could figure out what they were trying to do on a level he knew they couldn't see, but ultimately, he wasn't sure what the results would be if he poked his nose in. It was possible he could mess up their spell and ruin the effort. He needed the information too much to risk the results over what he decided to term professional curiosity.

With their hands still down, the witches started another verse, the volume rising with each word until it crescendoed with another release of power. They extended their arms out perpendicular to their bodies and took another two steps counterclockwise.

This power release sent electricity buzzing through his body and vibrations through the ground. Eddies of dust swirled around them. He clenched his jaw as a few small mounds puffed up from the ground. Narrowing his eyes, he realized the little swirls of dust weren't from mundane dirt but were pieces of life force and death force. A translucent hand clenched into a claw poked out from the surface before the breeze teased it apart and it disappeared. Farther away, a half-visible head appeared before being blown away.

Another verse fell from the witches' mouths, rising in volume and power as had the previous two. This time when the last word activated, the witches alternated their arm positions, half of them holding their hands up, and half down. Beneath him the earth trembled.

He looked around the debris and collapsed-building-strewn compound, but nothing rattled or shook. There wasn't so much as a shimmy or a vibration. The trembling was magical.

His heart rate picked up, and his breathing grew shallower as his eyes flicked about. Instead of partially formed hands and heads, torsos appeared to be pushing themselves out of the ground. He could still see through them. Then a gentle gust of wind frayed their edges and allowed them to dissolve again.

He caught Grizelda's eye just as her brow furrowed and her eyes narrowed in annoyance. Apparently, they should be further along. She barked out a quick command in the language they were using.

The seven witches took one step forward. This time, their chanting started louder. Pressure squeezed around his body, pushing against his chest and making it harder to draw in a good breath. Teeth clenched, he waited, ready to spring into action if he needed to defend himself.

He hoped the glamour was working, because the verse was practically being shouted. This time, the seven brought their arms forward, clapping sharply.

Grizelda called out a solo line loudly. Her six sisters responded with a different line. Their arms still in front of them, they lifted them some. Clap.

Another solo line. Another response. A slightly higher, louder clap.

On the next line, Grizelda had almost reached the volume of a yell. Power swirled around Dax and the lot. His heart thundered in his chest. The six called out their response and all seven of them raised their hands above their heads for another clap.

The sound cracked throughout the compound, rebounding off the walls of the glamour to stir the power pulsing about into a roiling boil. More figures appeared to be trying to push themselves out of the ground.

The witches rotated their circle another two counterclockwise steps and repeated the previous sequence—Grizelda with her call and her sisters with the response, punctuated with a clap above their head. The spirits climbed to their feet but still felt entirely too insubstantial.

They repeated the process once more, even louder. He almost wanted to cover his ears. With their combined claps, the compound rang like a struck bell, and the figures congealed and formed into one nearly solid figure in the middle of the circle.

FORTY-NINE

DAX

The coven held their position in the circle, their arms held in the air.

"Ask your questions," Grizelda gritted out through clenched teeth.

Dax nodded, taking a step toward the partially translucent figure. It had a long beard and wore the typical biker getup—leather vest, motorcycle boots, jeans, and in this case a ratty looking T-shirt. Or it might have been the ghostly nature of his appearance that made it look ratty.

Dax exhaled slowly before beginning. "Where can I find the Black Suns?"

The ghost barked a spectral laugh. "We are everywhere. We are nowhere."

He cast a side eye toward Grizelda, but she only gave him a strained shake of her head. He didn't know this process, so he didn't know if this was more difficult than normal, but from what Delphine had said, part of spell compelled the ghost to answer.

"Where is the main base of the Black Suns?"

"Fuuuuuck. Yooooouuuuu."

"Are they keeping the girl there?"

The ghost flipped him off, his laugh floating on the wind.

"Damnit," Dax mumbled. "Fine. You want to do this the hard way."

He reached into the aether to find the ghost's life thread but had difficulty pinning it down. It had been hauled from deep out of the ethereal realms. Hel had harvested the souls of the bikers here. She was renowned for her tenacity and control over that which she took. No wonder the witches were struggling.

Within the aether, he brought his scythe into contact with the knotted end of thread. "Tell me what I need to know or—"

"Or what? You'll destroy my soul?" A malicious grin spread across his face. "Be my guest. I would welcome nothingness after Hel and Hel's dominion."

Dax returned the sinister smile. "No. I'll cut your tether and unleash your soul onto the earth as an unhoused spirit. You'll haunt this patch of dirt, slowly going insane from the pain of being an untethered ghost until the sun swallows this planet, millions of years from now. And then, you'll be detached from this world and cast forth into the nothingness." He paused and quirked an eyebrow up. "That's what."

The ghost took a step back, but Dax hooked a finger into his spectral thread and tugged him closer. "Now answer my questions. Where is the main base of the Black Suns? Is the girl being held there?"

The ghost hesitated, so Dax pressed the edge of his scythe into the knot tethering the spirit to the afterlife. The ghost biker paled, becoming slightly more translucent. He rolled his eyes into the back of his head. They were white and milky, where a moment before they had at least appeared mostly like they had in life.

"Hurry," Grizelda grunted.

Nodding at her, he put more pressure on the blade.

The ghost groaned. "Rocks. On the rocks… Where the birth of death was birthed. On the rocks… Where death meets death. On the rocks… That is all I know, all I can give. Release me."

The witches, their arms still above their heads, clapped once and spoke a word of power that throbbed through the circle. One by one the witches turned their backs and faced the outside of the circle, crossing their arms in an X over their chests. When it came to Grizelda's turn, she clapped once more, repeated the word of power, and turned.

The ghost disappeared, and the power held in the circle winked away as if it were a candle being snuffed out in a breeze.

Dax stared at the spot where the ghost had been. He had no idea what the ghost's words meant. They sounded like a prophecy. They were probably meaningless until they could be filtered through hindsight, which would result in a variety of likely interpretations that would fit the narrative the interpreter needed or wanted. Utter bull shit.

He wanted to spit invectives but restrained himself in front of the strangers.

"I'm sorry it didn't work as well as it should have." Grizelda, a fine sheen of sweat on her brow, stepped up next to him. "Usually we have more control over our subjects. But the spirit did speak true. His words have meaning and significance. What that is, I'm not sure since the words were yours to hear."

Delphine had joined him. She squeezed his shoulder. "We'll have to reflect on them and see what meaning we can ring from them."

Grizelda nodded, giving Delphine a tired smile. "If it's OK, I'd like to pack up the ladies and go home. That was far more tiring than our usual seances."

Dax nodded absentmindedly as he pondered the words.

"I'll see you the next time you need supplies, Grizelda." Delphine shook the witch's hand.

"I look forward to it. I'm only sorry we couldn't get a clearer answer for you. Whatever had hold of the spirit was unhappy about our handling of it. It was all we could do to get it solid enough and keep it here."

"I really appreciate it." Delphine nudged Dax softly with her elbow.

He stuck his hand out to shake Grizelda's hand. "You have my thanks as well. We were at a dead end, but this at least gets us a clue to go on."

"It was educational and interesting to have met you, Dax. May the goddess watch over you." She turned and issued instructions to her coven. The glamour covering the lot disappeared, and the witches burst into action. Within a few minutes, they'd packed up and disappeared.

Dax stared at the empty lot, trying to force the ghost's words into some meaning he could use until The Rat emerged from the shadows, flanked by dozens of his furry minions.

"Very interesting. Good show." The Rat chuckled as he scratched the rat in his arm's ears.

"Indeed. I've never seen that kind of magical working before." Delphine removed her phone. "Did you hear what the ghost said?"

The Rat shook his head. "Too spooky, but too far. Rats not good with those details."

The thought of getting spy-level details from the rodent made Dax laugh and pulled him out of his brooding. Taking his phone from his pocket, he texted Tomi to move closer.

"We should get out of this lot and go discuss this somewhere more suitable. The bar—" He cut himself off, rubbing his eyes. A burnt-out husk wasn't a better location.

"Diner? Coffee? The Rat knows a place." He gave them the location.

"You'll have to ride with Tomi," Dax said. "You too, Delphine."

"I'll ride with you," she said.

"Are you sure? The car is more comfortable." He gestured to the car as it drove in carefully to avoid the biggest holes in the lot.

She smiled at him. "It's a nice night for a ride."

FIFTY

JAMIE

When Jamie woke up this time, something felt different. For one, she wasn't as groggy as she normally was after she'd been drugged. Second, a slow drip provided a new sound she hadn't heard before. Third, this new cell was a bit brighter than the last one, thanks to a few more cracks around the door that let in the light. And last, she'd woken up in a small bed with a blanket.

She let her eyes adjust, hoping there'd be enough light she could make out some details. Staring into the gloom of the ceiling, she thought she could make out markings. Carefully, she stood up and climbed on to the foot of the bed, where she hoped it would be more stable than the middle, because of the frame.

Indeed, there was a large pentagram on the ceiling surrounded by markings that looked like other symbols, but she wasn't familiar with them. She tried reaching up to the ceiling but couldn't quite touch it. When she sniffed the air, she caught the faint odor of chalk.

She lowered herself to the floor, then she sat on the bed, thinking. All the pieces of the puzzle whirled in her head until they clicked into place. They'd made their first mistake. She just needed to be bold enough to capitalize on it.

Looking around the room, she found the dripping noise. A small puddle had formed in a dip on the floor. Nearby on the ceiling, a slow, steady drip of what smelled like water fell from the ceiling.

She grabbed the blanket off the bed and set it under the drip in the corner. While she waited for it to soak up enough water, she paced around the room. Now that she could see a path forward, her patience had evaporated. Every fourth or sixth time across the room —on one occasion she'd made it ten times—she stopped to check the blanket. It had to be the most wicking blanket she'd ever seen. It seemed determined to spread the water evenly through the material so it was only slightly damp right under the drip.

Once the blanket felt wet enough for her plan, she laid down on the floor by the door and placed her ear near one of the wider cracks near the floor where the old wood had split. She counted to one hundred in her head, but didn't hear so much as a peep outside.

She checked the blank and was happy with its moisture levels. Grabbing it, she climbed back on top of the bed and tried to balance on the metal bar that constituted the "headboard" of the bed. As much as she tried, she just couldn't quite reach the chalk marks on the ceiling, even with one hand on the wall and standing tiptoe on one foot. She was going to be forced to try a less-quiet option.

She stepped down onto the bed, the springs squeaking under her weight. Crouching down, she sprang up and swiped at the ceiling with her wad of wet blanket. When she landed, she tried to control the squeaking. She'd smeared the chalk slightly.

As much as she wanted to keep jumping and wiping at the chalk, she let her better reason stop her. It wouldn't do any good if she was too noisy and got caught, so she waited and listened to see if she'd gone unnoticed.

When she heard nothing, she gently released a sigh of relief and jumped again. More of the chalk smeared. She wasn't sure how much of the circle and symbols she'd need to destroy to access her ability to shift and all the abilities she gained with it, but more would always be a good option. So she kept at the process—jump, swipe, wait, listen, repeat.

When she thought she had enough of the magical circle erased, she slipped off the bed and quickly took off her clothes. But before she shifted, she cast a small prayer to whatever gods were kind enough to be listening and willing to help. One. Two. Three. Shift.

She transformed into her wolf with only a slight hesitancy that spoke to the potency of the dark magic still exerting its influence over her, even in its partially destroyed form. But her wolf had come to her. She wanted to lift her muzzle and howl in triumph but resisted the urge. Even if she had access to her wolf, she was still locked in a sturdy room.

Laying down in front of the door, she perked her ear up next to a crack and waited. Still nothing.

Wherever they'd moved her to, they seemed to think it was secure enough to leave her alone, though the room didn't seem as strong as the last few places she'd been in. She wondered if they were running out of suitable places, and that was why this location felt a bit more slapdash. Now for the problem of the door.

FIFTY-ONE

Jamie stared at the door, waiting. They'd have to bring her food soon. Her stomach told her that it was indeed ready. They probably cared less about maintaining her health and more about maintaining her drugged state. Whatever they'd given her had kept her docile and unable to change.

She had no idea how it worked—if it was mundane drugs, or magic, or some combination. But the symbols on the ceiling had definitely been magic. It wasn't supposed to work well on wolf shifters. They were resistant. But whatever they'd done to her made the magic particularly potent. She wished she knew more about the subject.

But at this point, it didn't matter. The door was mundane and locked and certainly too heavy for her to muscle it open in either form. For one, it swung into the room, which meant it had all the structure around the frame and wall to bolster it. So, she decided on a different tactic.

Her ears perked up at the sound of footsteps on the hard floor. They grew slightly louder as they approached. When fingers scrabbled against whatever was keeping the flap at the bottom of the door closed, she backed up and waited. The sound of a tray being set down put her on alert. She hunched down, muscles taught and ready, mouth open.

The tray scraped along the floor as it was shoved in. As soon as the wooden pole being used to push the tray entered the hole, she sprang forward. She clamped her teeth down on the pole and leapt back, shaking her head violently like she was trying to snap a creature's spine.

Her jailer hadn't been expecting that. The other end of the pole hit something fleshy—someone grunted in pain—then clacked to the ground. Letting it go, she lunged to grab it farther up the shaft and backed up quickly, pulling the rest of it into the room.

"You fucking bitch. You're going to pay for that."

Jingling keys and a steady stream of profanity and threats were the sweetest music she'd heard in ages. Picking up the pole in her teeth, she backed into the corner nearest the door handle and waited.

As soon as it opened and she saw a leg coming into frame, she leapt forward and thrust the stick at the legs. Her aim was true. The pole tangled up in the man's legs and he tripped, falling forward. His face slammed into the door on his way down.

With hesitation, she jumped on his back, clamped her powerful jaws on his neck, and shook her head as hard as she could until she heard cartilage and bone grind and snap. The body went limp. She gave one last shake to further damage his snapped neck out of pure anger, then let go. Her tongue fell out of her mouth as she drooled saliva and the man's blood.

Controlling her urge to gag and throw up, she lowered her head and listened. No heartbeat. She'd been lucky. When he'd hit the door, it had stunned him just enough that she'd been able to dispatch him without him screaming. That didn't mean nobody had heard anything, but it was something. Turning her head to point an ear out of the room, she waited and listened for a few moments, the last of her patience struggling against the urge to bolt and run.

As she waited, her stomach grumbled, and her eyes drifted toward the tray of food that had miraculously not spilled in the tussle. She needed food, but what was on the tray was no doubt tainted and would put her under. She tore her eyes away from the tray and concentrated.

When she felt safe, she shifted back to her human form and rifled through the man's pockets. She found a wad of cash she wished she could take out of spite but had nowhere to carry it as a wolf. What she didn't find was an extra set of keys. So the ones stuck in the lock were likely the only ones she needed. She snatched them out of the door lock and carefully placed them between her front teeth and lips.

She shifted back to her wolf, focusing on keeping the keys in her lips until she was once again on all fours. This room was much bigger than the cell she was abandoning but was lit only slightly better. A lone bulb hung from the ceiling. It didn't provide much light. Trotting across the floor to the next door, she kept her ears peeled. Once she reached the door, she pressed her ear against it. So far, luck was on her side.

FIFTY-TWO

JAMIE

Jamie had made it through a couple doors and up a set of creaky wooden stairs, shifting back and forth from wolf to human whenever she needed to use her human hands with their magical opposable thumbs. She could have snuck along in her human form, but she wanted full access to all her wolf abilities.

She could hear better than mundane humans in her human form, but not as well as a wolf, and she needed every advantage she could get right now.

Once she made it to the top of the stairs, she crept along on her belly with each paw carefully placed so she made absolutely no sound. She could smell and hear people in the distance. There were no other doors or halls, so she was forced to move toward them.

If she encountered someone, there would have to be no hesitation. She would not get another chance to escape. They'd make sure of that. If they even let her live.

A door opened in front of her, and she froze. A man with a thick beard and leather vest stared at her, his mouth open in shock. She stared back, unmoving. Then her eyes caught the Black Suns symbol on the chest of his black leather vest and something in her snapped.

She sprang at him, her teeth clamping around his throat. A quick shake and she ripped his windpipe out. Spitting it out, she heaved once before she got herself under control.

"Hey, Leif, quit fucking around and shut the door." Another biker came into view.

Before he could swing his eyes to her, she darted forward, hamstringing. He went down with a scream of pain and a thump. He only yelped once before she ripped his throat out. She was done. She had no more mercy in her young heart for these pieces of shit who'd done nothing but make her life hell.

"What the —"

"Holy fuck…"

Several burly men pushed away from a table in the middle of the room, a couple of the chairs tipping backward and clattering to the floor.

She looked around the room quickly, spotting the door. She'd dropped her keys to take out the first man, so if the doors were locked, she'd have to worry about that later.

A deep, rage-filled growl rumbled in her throat. Bunching her muscles, she sprang at the nearest biker, her mouth open and teeth glistening. Flecks of blood-stained drool splattered on the man's face as he cringed away from his attacker. It was the last thing he ever did. Using her momentum, she bounced off his chest and onto the table, scattering bottles and ashtrays.

Out of the corner of her eye, she saw a man pulling a gun. She spun and leapt at him. Twisting away, he brought the butt of the gun around as her teeth narrowly missed his throat. The butt of the gun glanced off her head and sent her tumbling away. She landed on her side, the air whooshing from her lungs.

Before someone could take advantage of her fall, she rolled to her stomach and jumped at the nearest biker. But this time, she aimed low instead of attacking their throats. Her teeth clamped around a denim-covered knee. She shook her whole body, destroying the joint. The man fell backward, screaming and flailing. His large body crashed onto the table. The poorly constructed table cracked and splintered, dumping the man on the floor in a pile of debris. His screams filled the room as he thrashed around.

The remaining men backed away, reaching for guns. She counted three still standing. The man with the destroyed knee would be out of it for a while. Even with wolf-shifter healing, he'd probably never walk quite right again. The thought brought a smile to her wolfish maw as she added more heat to the growl coming out of it. She'd know him by his limping.

She had to do something. She had no desire to feel what it was like to be shot. Making a snap decision, she lunged at the two men who were closest. Counting on the first guy's reaction and the gun in his right hand, she aimed for where she'd guess he'd turn. She sprang off his chest at the other man. But he'd pulled back as well, raising an arm with a gun in his hand. Taking the target of opportunity, she sank her teeth into his arm and savaged it as they tumbled to the ground.

As soon as they landed in a heap, she jumped off, snapped her teeth at the third man, and ripped into the flesh of his calf muscle. She let go after a couple of vicious shakes and darted away from the bikers.

As she'd been jumping around, she'd spied an escape route. She just hoped it wasn't a modern double-pane window. As she neared it, a bullet flew over her head, smashing into the glass and sending shards flying. She jumped and hit the old, wooden crossbar and the top of the shattered glass. She felt a ribbon of pain snake down her back.

Another shot rang out, missing her. Her feet touched down on dirt. Skidding to a stop, she turned and ran along the side of the building so she'd be out of the way of the window and any easy potshots. To her right were trees. She didn't see any fences.

She slid to a stop and whipped her head around, surveying her surroundings, then picked an angle that looked good and sprinted toward the woods with all the speed she could muster. She'd worry about where she was after she got away.

FIFTY-THREE

DAX

Dax stared up at the ceiling, refusing to get out of bed. Not even the shrill cries of Morty yelling in his face for his morning breakfast could move him. Was this what humans called depression?

It had been three days since the seance, and they still had no leads. They'd wrangled over the words spoken by the ghost at the all-night diner until the sun came up, then in frustration, they'd called it quits. Everyone promised to keep thinking through the words in case they had some revelatory inspiration.

Dax still hadn't had any. And judging by the lack of calls from Delphine and The Rat, neither had anyone else. He rolled over to stare at the wall, hoping the change of vista would make a difference. He just wished there were flowers to count.

Finally, when Morty took to slapping and biting his nose, he relented and dragged himself out of bed. The sound of kibbles hitting the bottom of the bowl brought a loud purr from the kitten. And since Dax was up, he might as well have coffee.

They couldn't find Jamie. They'd checked every address they'd noted from the GPS tags, but when the tags went dark, they had nothing left to check. Dax had taken to driving around town looking for any motorcycle he could find. None of the few he'd seen belonged to the Black Suns.

The ball was out of his proverbial court.

He was still waiting for more red tape to clear on the bar before they could begin the long process of rebuilding, assuming they got the insurance payout. Fortunately, the restaurant had been allowed to reopen. He owed Minh for whatever she'd done to save the majority of the building.

As he sat on his couch in his underwear drinking coffee, he fixated on and worried about Jamie. He wondered when he'd decided it was his duty to help protect her. Probably when he'd made the decision to forgive her for shooting him, whenever that was. It had seemed a gradual process of getting used to her being involved in his fight against the Black Suns, because they kept dragging her back into it.

She'd been his enemy—not by choice—before he even knew she existed. Then she'd been the enemy of his enemy. Now... Now she was a part of his circle of people. His crew, as Boudreaux or Tomi might call it.

When the phone rang, he let it go for several rings before sighing and picking it up. As sad and frustrated as he was and as much as he didn't want to be disturbed so he could wallow in those feelings, it might be news or some new idea on how to find his wayward young friend.

"Dax." It was Tomi.

"What?"

"You need to get down to the restaurant. We got a message about Jamie."

He sat up, spilling hot coffee on his leg. "Fuck, ow, fuck." He sloshed more over his other leg, then got control of himself and set the coffee down on the coffee table.

"You OK, dude?" Tomi asked.

"Spilled coffee on bare leg. Hold on." He got up and found a towel in the kitchen to wipe himself off.

He had a couple red splotches on his legs where the coffee'd scalded him, but it appeared the burns hadn't caused any real damage. He'd been brooding for long enough for most of the coffee's heat to have wafted away on the steam. Putting on the water to boil for another cup, he took the towel with him and dabbed up the bit that had dripped onto the upholstery of the couch and the floor. He still had half a cup left, but that wouldn't be enough. Hopefully, Tomi would be quick so he could make himself a second cup.

"OK. Back. What's going on?" he asked.

"We got another note tied to a rock. Right through the window at Mama's restaurant. They say they've got Jamie, and they want to deal."

Dax dragged a hand down his face. He guessed the deal would involve turning himself over to the dirtbags. "The bikers?"

"Don't know. Didn't hear any bikes or see any before the brick was thrown." Tomi sounded annoyed.

"Call the glass company. I'll be down there shortly."

"I already did. And…shower and put some clean clothes on."

He sighed. "Fine." He hung up and did as Tomi instructed.

A quick shower and some fresh clothes later, he locked up his apartment and stalked down the hall to the elevator. When the door dinged and opened on the lowest floor, he stepped out into the apartment's parking garage.

"Go!"

A body slammed into his side, and something was dragged over his head. It felt damp against his skin and smelled weird and potent. Magic. He twisted and thrashed, smashing someone with his elbow. A grunt and a whoosh of air out of someone's lungs brought a brief feeling of satisfaction. Throwing more elbows, he tried stomping and kicking blindly, hoping to get another blow. Another body grabbed him and struggled with him up until his arms were immobilized.

All three of them went down, landing on the hard concrete of the garage's floor. One of his tacklers wrapped their legs around his. A moment of separation was followed by a brutal punch to his guts. He gasped for air, drawing in the sickly scent of herbs coupled with something dark tainting them.

Reaching into the aether, he tried to grab his scythe, but his hands passed through the shaft with only the slightest resistance. His head began to spin and swim. Each breath drew in more of whatever the bag had been soaked in, and each breath took more of the fight out of him until he could only breathe and twitch. Then he knew nothing.

FIFTY-FOUR

JAMIE

Jamie stumbled, her legs exhausted and her head drooping. Her tongue lolled out, and she panted. She was almost there.

She'd run through the woods as hard as she could. It took a while for the man left alive and uninjured to rally anyone to chase her. By the time he did, she could barely hear their shouts. She hoped kept trying to chase her in their human forms. She could easily outrun bikers wearing motorcycle boots in the woods. But eventually smarter heads prevailed and changed into their wolf forms. Then they'd be able to track her.

She relied on her woodcraft and all the years of playing hide-and-seek in the woods as a wolf with her friend Cory. Only one biker managed to track her down, but despite the earlier evidence of it, he underestimated her ruthlessness and let her get the jump on him. She left him bleeding out, and now he was likely dead. She didn't stop to make sure. He was out of the chase for a while…or permanently.

If she'd had a full belly—water and food—and she didn't have to sneak around town because she was a wolf, she might have already arrived at Mama Adele's restaurant. Fortunately, it was dark enough that she could dart through the shadows. Most citizens of Red City probably had no idea what a wolf looked like in real life. They probably just thought she was a large stray. Still, she didn't want someone to call animal control on her.

She hid in the bushes across the street, making sure the way was clear. They'd covered one of the windows with a sheet of plywood. Wondering what happened to the window, she sat down. Though the blinds were drawn, she could see plenty of light in the building. It looked like they'd closed earlier than usual.

This didn't seem normal. A bit of adrenaline slipped into her already stressed and exhausted system. She looked around once more. She didn't see any headlights, and people rarely took strolls in Red City this time of night.

Instead of sprinting across the street, she jogged across on all fours, looking like a dog or coyote just moving through the neighborhood. She stopped at the door and pawed at it, whimpering loudly. When no one came to check out the noise, she repeated it and added a bark.

"Berta, go see what that is, and if it's a stray, chase it off." It was Adele.

"No, I'll check it," Suzie said.

Jamie's heart rate picked up, and she pranced in place, excited that her friend was there. When Suzie opened the door, she yelped and clutched her chest. Jamie hopped up on her hind legs, placed her paws on Suzie's shoulders, and licked her face, wagging her tail furiously.

Suzie, laughing at the ridiculous animal and trying to gently swat her away, staggered under Jamie's wolf weight.

"Stop that you silly… Oh, shit! Is-is that you, Jamie?" Suzie stumbled back into the restaurant.

Jamie fell back onto all fours and yipped happily, nodding her head. Once she cleared the doorway, she kicked back with one of her hind legs and pushed the door shut. Berta had backed herself up against the counter and looked terrified. Mama Adele stared out the pass-through window from the kitchen.

"What the hell is a dog doing in my restaurant, Suzanna Marie Chenevert?"

Yikes. She'd gotten the full name treatment.

"It's not a dog, Auntie Adele. It's… Well, I think it's Jamie."

Jamie nodded her head again.

"Jamie? What?" Adele came out of the swinging doors from the kitchen, her eyes narrowed as she stared at the wolf in her front of house. "Damn, Tomi did say she was a werewolf."

Jamie peeled back her ears but stopped the annoyed growl before she could release it. Being called a werewolf was a minor annoyance, and something she'd take up with Tomi later. It wasn't Mama Adele's fault.

"She a what?" Berta yelped, edging along the counter to the end so she could get behind it.

"Don't worry, Jamie isn't going to hurt anyone," Suzie said over her shoulder before returning her gaze to Jamie. "Why don't you change to your — I don't know what you call it. Your people suit?"

Jamie reached out and caught the hem of Suzie's shirt in her teeth and shook her head gently.

"What? Oh! Shit." She started laughing. "We got anything she can wear? She's naked under her furry costume."

Jamie huffed and deflated a little. She'd get Suzie back for that comment. Mama Adele disappeared into the kitchen and reemerged a moment later with one of her spare chef's shirts. Suzie took it and dropped it across Jamie's back. Turning around gently so as not to dislodge the shirt, she shifted but made sure she stayed on her hands and knees, so the shirt didn't slide off her back. Once she'd completed the shift, she took hold of the shirt's lapels and pulled on it on, buttoning it up the front.

It was much too large for her, but it would do the job. Mama Adele was a robust woman with what Jamie had once read was called a "matronly bosom." She stood up slowly, her legs shaking. It felt good to be back on two feet, but she was drained.

"Water? Please," Jamie croaked. She sniffed the air, the beautiful aromas making her body try to force some saliva into her mouth. "And food?"

"Suzie, get her some sweet tea. She'll need a little boost. I'll fix up a plate for her real fast." Adele disappeared into the kitchen.

Jamie worried her knees would buckle, so she grabbed a chair from the nearest table and sank into it, sighing in relief. Once Suzie set the large, rough-textured, red-plastic glass in front of her, she pulled the straw from the wrapper with shaky hands and pushed it into the tea. She took down about half of the large glass before coming up for air. Suzie was ready with a pitcher and topped her off.

"That's the best-tasting glass of tea I've ever had. Thanks." Jamie went back for another drink, though this time she kept it more reasonable.

"A bit thirsty, eh?" Suzie asked.

"You can say that. I had to move hard and fa"—a massive yawn cut her last word—"fast. Damn, I'm tired." She perked up a bit. "You can relax now, Berta. I'm not going to bite you. I wouldn't as a wolf either."

Berta nodded nervously, her eyes still wide. Jamie was too tired to deal with her any more than she already had. She let her eyes drift to the plywood and the broken window with a hole in the middle. "What happened there?"

Suzie snorted. "You did. Kinda. Your kidnappers threw a rock through the window offering a trade. You for Dax." She looked around nervously. "Did… Did, uh, you see Dax?"

Jamie narrowed her eyes and shook her head. "No. I didn't see anyone but some b-bikers and someone called The Warlock."

"Berta, why don't you go home early. Full pay though. We'll talk about this later. OK, dear?" Adele called from the kitchen.

Berta didn't say anything. She just grabbed her purse from under the counter and headed to the front door. Suzie opened it for her and waved as Mama Adele's employee left.

Laughing, she sat down. "Poor Berta is going to need a stiff drink or two tonight."

Jamie nodded, saying nothing. She didn't like scaring people, especially people she worked with and kind of liked. She'd leave it to Mama Adele to sort it out. Jamie neither had the energy nor brain space for it now.

"So, you haven't seen Dax at all?" Suzie leaned on the table with her elbows.

"No. Not since the night I was captured."

"Well, fuck."

"Suzie Girl, watch your language," Adele called from the kitchen.

"Sorry, Auntie." Suzie rolled her eyes and winked at Jamie. "Crap." She said it quieter, though so far Mama Adele had only objected to the "f" word. "He was supposed to meet us here. So we could sort out how to get you back. He never showed up. Tomi's trying to track him down."

"Damn. That's not good." If they'd gotten to Dax, it would be a huge blow to their continued survival. Dax was a scary man, especially to the dirtbag bikers. Now this The Warlock character... What was it with people and definite articles in their names? It was almost like Red City was turning into a comic book.

"No. Tomi's got the word out to Manman Delphine and Boudreaux." She shrugged in frustration. "But no one has found anything."

Adele emerged from the kitchen and set down a steaming hot plate of red beans and rice with a side of collards, before taking a seat at the other end of the table

The spicy aroma made Jamie swoon. "Thank you, Mama Adele."

"You're welcome, child. Enjoy."

Jamie dug in, blowing on her food perfunctorily before shoving it in her mouth. It was still too hot. She dropped her jaw open and tried to breathe it cooler. Suzie chuckled. Jamie resorted to a quick drink of the sweet tea to cool her mouth. On the second spoonful, she was more careful. It took all her restraint to keep cooling her food, but she didn't want to add a badly scalded mouth to her list of issues. When she finished, she pushed her plate away and sighed happily, proud she hadn't picked up the plate and licked it clean.

"OK. You've got food and water. Now are you going to tell us what happened?" Suzie sounded stern, but the twinkle in her eyes and the grin on her lips belied her tone.

"I don't know where Dax is, but I think I met the person who's been pulling the bikers' strings." She yawned.

Suzie leaned closer.

Jamie shook herself, trying to keep from passing out. "It's... I don't know. Some magician or mage or something. All I know is they gave me something to drink that might have been a potion, then made a giant pentagram on the ground with some crystals." Jamie swallowed, her brow furrowing. Her stomach clenched in shame. "They started asking me questions. And I answered. I couldn't stop myself."

Mama Adele squeezed Jamie's shoulder reassuringly. "We'll want to get the details to the manbo so she can sort it out. But there's no shame in answering questions when you were forced to."

Jamie sniffed loudly, her body trembling. "He hurt me. Hit me. Over and over." A sob escaped her lips. "I didn't give him anything. Not a word." Tears burned down her cheeks. "Then… The Warlock made me drink something. I tried to resist." She sobbed. "But it hurt so bad. My veins burned under my skin." Her whole body shook. "All my muscles cramped. So much p-p-p." She started to pant. "They asked me for my name. Just my name. I said it. And the pain disappeared."

She broke down, sobbing violently, and covered her face with her hands.

Mama Adele stood up and moved around the table. Dropping down next to Jamie, Mama Adele pulled the teen girl into a firm embrace, stroking her hair. The Black woman made comforting sounds and held her tight. Suzie moved to the other side of the table and took the chair next to Jamie and rubbed Jamie's back soothingly.

The sudden affection and embrace redoubled her crying. She couldn't remember the last time she'd felt loving arms around her. Judgement-free arms. Soft and kind words.

When she'd cried herself out, Suzie fetched her a clean, damp cloth to wipe her face with. While Jamie got herself back together, Mama Adele called Manman Delphine. After she hung up, she went behind the bar and grabbed a bottle of bourbon and three glasses, setting them down on the table.

"Manman Delphine is calling everyone and telling them to hunker down for the night. And you need to sleep, young lady." The large, Black woman poured three healthy glasses of whiskey.

Jamie reached for the glass, her hand shaking but not as badly as before. "But Dax…"

FIFTY-FIVE

DAX

The soft murmuring of voices drifted into Dax's foggy mind as he came to. The sickly scent of the hood still teased at his nostrils. His tongue felt like sandpaper in his mouth, and there was an odd bitter taste that mingled with the unctuous aroma.

"He stirs."

Dax couldn't tell who the voice belonged to. He didn't recognize it. But more than that, it sounded weirdly neutral and unnatural. It was neither high nor low, and there was a hollow quality to it that obscured its true nature. It felt like a wholly false voice, designed to keep its speaker disguised.

Dax tried to reach out and feel for the life threads flowing around him but found nothing—not a single trace. What he heard could've come from a speaker, and the person was somewhere else. But this didn't feel like when there was no one around with a life thread to feel. It felt different. More empty. More closed.

His ability to touch the aether was completely gone. He could find neither his skeleton nor his scythe. Not only were there restrains on his wrists and ankles, but they'd found a way to restrain his supernatural abilities.

"Remove his hood. I want to see him." This voice sounded more natural. It was on the more masculine side. It might have sounded familiar, but he couldn't be sure.

Someone roughly yanked the hood off his head. It caught on his nose and dragged roughly across it, scraping against his skin. Dull light flooded into his eyes, and he clamped them shut, squinting after a moment of letting them adjust.

Fresh air smelled and tasted so good. At least it was fresher than being inside the bag and whatever it had been dosed with to knock him out. He could taste the polluted air of Red City. He was still well within its limits.

It was difficult to see where he was. A light was aimed at him. He could make out a few faint lines though, and he guessed he was in some large, empty industrial building. Maybe a warehouse.

"This is the man who's been creating chaos in our city?" the masculine voice asked.

"Yes, sir," replied the false voice. "He won't take the hint and die."

The masculine voice laughed. "How dare he."

As Dax's eyes adjusted more, he could see shadows just out of the light. One stood, shapeless and more shadow than solid form. Some light glinted off the space where its face might be. They might be wearing a metallic mask. The other shadow sat in a chair. They looked a bit more real, though they too were mostly dark and formless.

Dax couldn't pick out any other features.

"And you think you can finally accomplish it? So we can return to our business at hand?" The masculine voice asked.

"Yes. He is not a complex problem, just an overlooked one. He will cease to be." This new, third, deep voice resonated with power. More power than Dax had felt in a long while.

He doubted this other individual was mortal, but if they were, they'd be a truly powerful practitioner. Apparently Dax had worked his way up the food chain and whoever was pulling the strings of the Nazi bikers had grown tired of their continued inability to kill the target. But three voices and three vague shapes were not enough to build his case on. Getting to the bottom of the biker well wouldn't stop the attempts to end his existence.

"You have nothing to say for yourself?" asked the masculine voice.

"What's the point. It's not like this is a trial and you're a jury of my peers. Not that it matters in the injustice system in this country and corrupt city."

"Corrupt?" The masculine voice laughed. "Redemption City runs exactly as it's designed to. Until little wrenches like you gum up the works. Then we have to call mechanics. But you've been a slippery little wrench. You've wasted a lot of money and time." The one with the masculine voice rotated in their chair a little. Dax got the impression of hands being steepled in front of a face.

Dax snorted. "Sorry to be a bother. But you can just fuck right off." He let a sinister grin play across his face. "You've made a mistake—letting me know you exist. Now you'll have to spend every day looking over your shoulder, because when I get out of this, I'm coming for you. And I won't rest until you're gone, and I'm left standing."

The shadow in the chair gestured to the one who looked like they wore a mask. The mask twitched, and the bag was dragged over his head by some nearby goon. The bag was damper than it had been a few minutes prior and smelled much stronger. They'd renewed whatever potion or enchantment they'd put on it. He felt his awareness start to drift.

"You're mistaken, my good sir. After tonight, I will think on you no more."

FIFTY-SIX

JAMIE

Jamie had slept like the dead, which felt entirely too appropriate, all things considered. Suzie had forced Jamie to take the bed, and she'd been too tired to argue.

She could hear Suzie moving about out in the living room, but she didn't want to acknowledge her own awareness. The bed was soft, and the covers were so cozy. She really needed to get a bed of her own and an apartment to put it in. But when the aroma of coffee drifted into the room, she groaned and forced her feet to swing off the bed. Besides, her bladder was becoming quite insistent. She'd put down a lot of sweet tea the previous night in her need to slake her thirst.

As soon as she stepped out of the bathroom, Suzie handed her a giant mug fixed up the way Jamie liked it.

"You're the best," Jamie said, wafting the mug under her nose.

"I was about to get you up! We're being called to a meeting," Suzie said, returning to the coffee pot to fix herself a cup.

"Where? The bar is burned down." Jamie thought about risking the hot coffee but decided to let it cool more.

"We're meeting at Dax's house. They want to start the investigation there."

"OK. Let me finish this cup and grab a shower. I smell rank."

Suzie chuckled. "Don't worry, you've got an hour. I picked you up a bagel and lox."

"Damn, you're the best roommate ever."

"Don't I know it." Suzie took a drink of her coffee, sighing happily.

Jame took her time to enjoy her coffee and bagel, then took a steamy hot shower, putting her damp hair up in a bun to get it out of the way. With a full, caffeinated belly and a shower, she felt better than she had in days. She was still tired and kind of hungry. She'd been short on sleep and food for days while she'd been in captivity. Whatever they'd drugged her with hadn't created restful sleep, just unconsciousness.

She opted for comfortable, dark workout clothes she could easily strip off if she needed to shift. And thinking of it just before stepping out the door, she turned around and snagged her bathrobe. It would let her shift in a more public setting and allow for some privacy.

They jumped into Suzie's Honda Civic and zipped away.

"Hey, um, what happened to the Corolla?" Jamie felt bad for going off on her own and losing the car. Not to mention the broken and shot windows.

"We got it back when we went looking for you. Boudreaux has his crew fixing it."

She exhaled in relief. "That's good. I was worried about that."

"Don't worry. You'll be delivering Auntie Adele's fine food again in no time."

"Can't wait." Speaking of food, a thought occurred to her. "Does anyone have a key to Dax's apartment? I gave mine back when I moved in with you."

"Yeah. Tomi does. Why?"

"We'll need to feed Morty. Dax has been gone for almost a full day. Poor kitty is probably hungry."

"Good thinking. I'll get to meet the infamous Morty the Kitten." Suzie parked.

They were the first to arrive because of Suzie's general disdain for the rules of the road, so they both stood on the sidewalk, leaning up against the car where they could see the front of the building.

Tomi and Manman Delphine were the next to arrive. Suzie waved, and she and Jamie walked over to join them.

"Hey, cuz, give Jamie the keys to Dax's apartment. She wants to feed the kitten." Suzie hitched her thumb over her shoulder at Jamie.

"Smart thinking." He fished the keys out of his pocket and sorted through the keyring until he found the one he wanted. "This one."

"Who else is coming?" Jamie asked.

"Just Boudreaux. Figured we didn't need to have too many people tromping around. Besides, it would attract attention. But we've got Boudreaux's crew geared up and on standby."

"Why don't you wait out here for Boudreaux, and I'll go in with the ladies and start my investigation," Manman Delphine said.

Tomi chuckled. "You just want to play with the cat."

Manman Delphine raised an eyebrow and smirked. "Your point being?"

Jamie headed to the building's front door, unlocking it. The manbo and Suzie followed her in. The elevator had an out of order sign on it, so they were forced to take the stairs. They didn't pass anyone in the halls. It was the middle of the day and probably most people were at work.

Jamie unlocked and opened Dax's door, stepping out of the way to let Suzie and Manman Delphine in.

FIFTY-SEVEN

JAMIE

"Holy shit!" Suzie squealed, backing up hard into the wall just inside the door.

Jamie darted in, tossing her bathrobe onto the back of the recliner. "What?"

A little kitten skeleton hopped across the floor with his back arched, hissing and growling. Normally, this was his cute, tough-cat act. But as a skeleton with the weird freaky harmonics that sounded similar to Dax in his Grim Reaper mode, it actually was scary. Ish. It was still a tiny kitten.

Jamie squatted down in front of the kitten and scooped him up. In her revulsion, she almost launched him into the air. He was actual bones. She thought his flesh and fur might have just been invisible, but they were truly not there.

"This is freaky as fuck," she mumbled, holding the skeleton close to her face. He'd stopped hissing and was now purring and kneading at the air. "Dax told me about this, but I still wasn't expecting... I don't know what I was expecting."

"You could have warned me." Suzie sounded annoyed but was panting a bit.

"Sorry, I thought Tomi or Dax would have told you."

Suzie snorted. "Those boys aren't really what you call communicative."

The manbo leaned in close, looking at the kitten. "Do you mind if I hold him?"

"I mean, that's up to him really." Jamie held him out to her. "If he starts squirming, put him down. Those claws are sharp." She stared at the tiny little scythes at the end of his toes. "And who knows what they can do in this form."

"I'll be careful." Manman Delphine held her hand in front of the kitten's nose. Morty extended his neck to bring his face closer to her hand. He kept purring, so she gently took hold of him and began examining him. "Interesting."

Suzie, who'd gotten over her fright somewhat, moved closer to the manbo to inspect the kitten. "How long has Dax had him?"

"I don't know," Jamie said. "I think he told me he got him the first time he got shot."

"That was several months ago," Manman Delphine said.

"Shouldn't he be bigger by now? He still looks like he's only a few months old." Suzie reached out and touched his skull, then pulled back and shook her hand, a look of disgust on her face.

"Did it hurt?" Jamie asked.

"No! It's a skull. Like bone."

Jamie chuckled. "I almost tossed him when I picked him up. I thought he might still be furry and stuff, but invisible, you know?"

Suzie nodded vigorously.

"I wonder if the kitten is intentionally staying this small because he knows it's his cutest phase." Manman Delphine turned the kitten in her hands so she could look at various parts of his body. "The little shit is even cute like this." She set the kitten down. "I guess we better start our investigation."

"I'll go feed him and give him some extra, in case we're not able to get back quickly. Then I'll shift and sniff around."

"Suzie, you can assist me and watch what I'm doing. I know you've been avoiding it, but it's time to start your training. You have too much innate power to let it lie fallow, especially as dangerous as it has become for our community," the manbo said.

Suzie huffed and folded her arms over her chest. "Fine. I guess I was getting bored with how I was before, anyway."

Jamie snickered to herself as she got out the cat food. Suzie had been avoiding the conversation since the manbo first showed an interest in her. Now it looked like she wouldn't be able to pretend to be mundane any longer.

After she filled the bowl and added a second one near it, Jamie topped off Morty's water and added another bowl as well, in an over-abundance of caution. But thinking about it, would he really need food? He was a skeleton cat, at least some of the time. But Dax needed food, so who knew.

With a shrug, she stripped down and set her clothes on the counter. As soon as she shifted, she gagged, making a horking noise.

"You OK in there?" Suzie asked from the bedroom.

Jamie shifted back. "The litter box is rank, and my wolf nose did not like it."

So she scooped the box, washed her hands, and shifted back. The odor was marginally better. She joined them in the bedroom, starting with the bed, then sniffed her away out into the living room and kitchen. Once she'd covered the small apartment, she shifted back.

"He hasn't been here in a while. Maybe a day? I'm still not that good at tracking. All I know is his scent isn't as fresh as Morty's or ours. It's strong enough to be recent compared to some of the older traces, but we already know he's been gone since yesterday mid-day sometime, when Tomi talked to him."

"Yeah. I'm not seeing anything that contradicts what you're saying," Manman Delphine said, taking a moment to speak quietly to Suzie in what could best be described as a teaching tone. "Also there are no other magical traces that don't belong to him or the kitten." She quirked up an eyebrow and looked at the kitten, who was back in his fur, as he played with one of his toys. "I'd love to investigate those traces more, but we are on a bit of a time crunch here. We should follow Dax's out in the hallway and see where they go."

"I'm glad I didn't get dressed. Let's hope no one pops out of their apartment and freaks out about the wolf. Someone bring the robe." Jamie shifted back to the wolf and headed to the door.

Suzie picked up her robe and the manbo opened the door. Putting her nose to the floor, Jamie followed Dax's scent, focusing on the freshest line. When she stopped at the elevator, she looked back and gestured toward the stairs leading down to the parking garage. Suzie jogged over to the door and opened it for Jamie.

She put her nose back down just to be on the safe side and headed toward Suzie and the open door. There might be a familiar scent or one that would be handy later. Once they emerged from the stairwell, she headed to the elevator. She found Dax's scent immediately, as well as four others and something else that pinged a note of familiarity in her mind.

She moved around the area , sniffing back and forth, and focused first on the four scents intermingled with Dax's. She didn't recognize any of them, but if she caught their scents again, she'd recognize them right away. Once she was satisfied, she focused on the familiar scent. It smelled vaguely herbal and a bit sweet, with an undertone she couldn't quite place. But that didn't matter; she'd recognized it.

It was very similar to the scent of the water she'd been forced to drink by The Warlock.

"Boudreaux is here. I'll text Tomi that we're out in the garage." Suzie's thumbs flew over her phone's screen.

Wanting a moment to think about her water discovery, Jamie followed the scent of the four others to a spot outside on the sidewalk by the street. That was where the scent trail ended. They'd loaded Dax into a vehicle and driven off. She returned to the garage where the manbo and Suzie stood. Grabbing the robe in Suzie's arms with her teeth, Jamie gave it a little shake.

Suzie draped it over the wolf's back and stepped away. Jamie shifted, poking her arms into the robe, and quickly stood up and belted it closed. Boudreaux and Tomi walked in a minute later.

"Find anything?" Tomi asked.

Jamie nodded. "Yeah. Four men abducted him outside the elevator. They took him out to the curb and drove off."

"Were the men supernatural?" Manman Delphine asked.

"I don't know. They weren't wolf shifters, but they also didn't quite smell fully mundane human either." Jamie shrugged. "I don't know. I'm still learning about tracking and scents and stuff. But there was something else that was familiar. I caught a scent that was very similar to the water…potion The Warlock forced me to drink when I was captured. It felt more potent though. Much more."

"The Warlock?" Tomi asked.

She filled them in on what had happened, giving a brief version.

"I don't like this," Tomi said, pacing.

"Me either," Boudreaux said. "Wolf shifters are bad enough. Now we have some comic book villain called 'The Warlock'? Nope. Don't like it."

The manbo's lips were pursed as she tapped her chin with her finger. "Just thinking out loud here, but you escaped yesterday morning, right?"

Jamie nodded.

"Probably about the time they delivered their rock for a hostage swap. Then they discovered they no longer had their hostage, so they sent some goons here to snatch Dax."

"That's what it sounds like," Boudreaux said.

Tomi, his brow furrowed, stopped pacing. "Do we have any other clues? Do you know the scents, or did you get anything else? Do you remember where you were held?"

"I remember where I escaped from. But I doubt they'll be there anymore. They moved me several times, and the last place looked the least permanent. They've probably already cleared out and moved on," Jamie said.

"Fuck." Tomi kicked at a nearby pebble, sending it skittering away.

"The only clue we have that's still not accounted for is the message from the seance," Manman Delphine said.

"Seance?" Jamie asked.

"When we couldn't track you down, we called in a little outside magical help," the manbo said, briefly filling Jamie in on what had happened.

"'Rocks. On the rocks. Where the birth of death was birthed. On the rocks. Where death meets death. On the rocks,'" Jamie mumbled to herself, pacing as she thought about Manman Delphine's words. She sighed and turned to face everyone. "I know where we need to go. I know where's he's being held."

FIFTY-EIGHT

DAX

Dax woke to a gentle, cool breeze brushing across his face. It smelled fresh in the way that indicated he was outdoors and outside of city limits, although an undertone of pollution could still be detected. He wasn't that far out of town.

He forced himself not to move until he could gain more awareness. Reaching out, he looked for the aether. But like the last time he'd come to, he was completely blocked from it and sat inside a space devoid of power.

After checking a few more times and trying some different methods, he gave up on reaching his power. He moved on to figuring out his restraints. His hands were behind his back and cuffed, the back of a heavy metal chair separating them from his body. His ankles were cuffed together and bound to something. Probably the legs of the chair he sat on. He shifted a little, and the chair wobbled.

Once he reached the end of what he could tell by using small motions, he opened his eyes, leaving his chin pressed to his chest. He shivered as the late summer breeze turned cool. He looked down. They'd stripped him down to his underwear. Symbols had been drawn on his body in a dark ink that had a bit of iridescence to it.

Sweeping his eyes around, all he could see were large rocks and small boulders. On the rocks surrounding him were symbols painted in white. He didn't know what they were, and without his connection to the aether, he couldn't access any of his old memories or examine them at the magical level.

He lifted his head to see the last traces of the sun set. It was a spectacular one, thanks to the pollution of Red City creating beautiful reds and oranges, with darker blues and purples fading into the dark of the night sky. It would have been lovely to sit and watch it if he wasn't strapped to a chair inside some sort of magical equation.

The falling sun left just enough light to see more symbols and lines painted on the rocks extending farther away from him. He sat in the center of a large pentagram filled with all kinds of drawings he didn't understand. As if to make it more ominous, off in the distance several crows squawked and bickered in their birdy manner as they settled down for the night.

Dax couldn't see anyone, at least within the arc of his vision. There might be someone standing directly behind him in his blind spot. He couldn't see or hear anyone, nor did he have access to his magic that would let him see people's life threads in the aether.

He tried to keep his calm—panicking wouldn't save his life—but his heart rate and breathing increased. He didn't know how he was going to get out of this situation. Whoever had captured him hadn't put him in the middle of a giant pentagram filled with magical symbols as an art installation.

For the first time since he'd been forced to live as a weak human, he felt truly powerless.

FIFTY-NINE

JAMIE

Jamie waited across the street from the fence protecting the quarry with Boudreaux's crew of about thirty people, the manbo, and Suzie. She hadn't been there in months. Not since she and Cory had gone there to practice shooting the handgun Ivar had given her to murder Dax. But here she stood after what had already been a long, busy day that promised to only get more intense in a place she'd hoped to never revisit. It was where the birth of the death of Death had begun. At least the sunset had been spectacular outside the lights and noise of Red City.

And if Manman Delphine was to be believed in her interpretation, the quarry would be the place where Death died.

At hearing that, Tomi had gone into a panic about not having tried to find him the previous night, but the manbo calmed him down. If they were going to kill him using magic, the probable method based on being abducted by someone named "The Warlock," they would wait until the moon was at one of its power points. Likely since they were trying to end Dax, they'd do it the last night before the new moon phase began, which was tonight.

The manbo had explained that many in the magical world believed rituals performed at the new moon drew the energy of new beginnings, so if they wished to end Dax, the best time would be at the very end before the new beginnings of the new moon. She also added that she'd not felt any magical ripples the previous night. The death of someone like Dax would have been felt by every magic-sensitive person in the Red City basin.

That had calmed Tomi enough to get him focused on helping Boudreaux coordinate all the equipment and people they'd need to prepare on the mundane side. While they let the guys attend to that aspect, Jamie got into the cramped back of Suzie's civic on the driver's side. Even though Suzie was short, there was barely enough room for Jamie's legs behind her. Manman Delphine got to ride shotgun on the way back to her shop. If Jamie had to sit behind the long-legged manbo, it would have been a horrible ride back.

As soon as they'd entered the manbo's shop, Manman Delphine had relocked the door and put up a note that said the store was closed due to a family emergency. Then she, with Suzie's help, began mixing up some gris-gris and some magical oils. Jamie'd stood out of the way and watched with fascination as the manbo quickly explained everything to Suzie as they worked. Education under fire.

When Manman Delphine and Suzie had finished, Jamie helped them pack up all the magical goodies they'd made and carried them out to Suzie's trunk so they could proceed to the rendezvous point near the quarry. It had been a quiet ride without the usual good-natured banter Jamie normally shared with Suzie.

Sighing, Jamie checked the time on her phone and then fingered the array of gris-gris lying against her skin under her shirt. Nearby, one of Boudreaux's people was operating a drone as they tried to survey what might be waiting for them. But all they saw was an empty quarry full of rocks.

"Are you sure this is the right place?" Tomi asked her.

Jamie'd felt much more confident earlier in the day when, she'd declared the quarry as the spot. "As sure as anyone can be in this situation."

Manman Delphine held her nose up and sniffed, a slow grin spreading across her face. "This is it. I can taste the magic on the wind. It says glamour. And it's a powerful one."

She squatted and opened her backpack, pulling a black automatic pistol from it and strapping it to her stretchy-yoga-pants-covered thigh. Once she was satisfied with its positioning, she pulled out one of the bottles of oil blends she'd made.

She unscrewed the lid and tucked it away in one of her pockets. "Everyone line up. I'll need to anoint you all with a bit of my own creation—True Vision Oil. It'll allow you to see through most glamours."

"Most?" Boudreaux raised an inquisitive eyebrow.

The manbo grinned wickedly. "I guess we'll see who has the more powerful magic, them or me."

Boudreaux laughed but tamped it down to a quiet chuckle. They wanted to go in quietly after all.

As everyone lined up, Manman Delphine dabbed some oil on her thumb, and like a priest on Ash Wednesday, she made a line starting in the middle of their foreheads, and brought it down between their eyes, stopping just below the bridge of their noses.

When it was Jamie's turn, she closed her eyes and waited for the pressure of the thumb. As it glided down her skin, the oil tingled and smelled pleasantly fragrant. She opened her eyes, and everything appeared sharper, almost like the landscape was in high definition. She wondered if it was affecting everyone else in a similar way, or if it was interacting with her innate wolf-shifter abilities.

After the manbo finished with everyone, she put away her oil and slung on her backpack. Boudreaux stepped over to her and asked for her gun. She raised an eyebrow but pulled it out and handed it to him, butt first. He took it and popped out the magazine. With a practiced hand, he removed all the bullets and gave them back to Manman Delphine. He grabbed some different ones from out of one of his pockets and refilled the magazine.

He winked at her, a smirk spreading across his face. "Hollow points."

The manbo chuckled. "Smart."

"Yeah. We need to even the odds." He turned to the rest of the people clustered around. "Chest and head if you have a good shot. But don't go for the headshot unless it's an easy one. Better to put one center mass and knock them out of the fight. Remember, these fuckers are fast and strong. Show no mercy. Take them out and move on."

A petite but muscular-looking Latina woman raised her hand. "Should we John Wick them?"

Boudreaux chuckled. "If it doesn't endanger yourself or others, go for it. But remember, we only have so many hollow points before we have to fall back on standard rounds."

Jamie leaned over to Tomi and whispered, "'John Wick' them?" She hadn't seen the movies.

Tomi smirked. "John Wick puts a bullet in their heads after he's taken them down to make sure they don't get back up again."

"Ah."

Suzie leaned in from the other side. "You haven't seen the John Wick flicks? We'll get some snacks and do a movie marathon soon."

Jamie smiled at her friend. "Sounds good."

Though she was still super nervous, she also felt more confident than ever before in their ongoing fight against the bikers. She was surrounded by competent people who didn't look at her as a liability, but as someone with unique skills who would benefit the team and help them achieve their goal.

Suzie squeezed Jamie's arm. "Good luck! Stay safe."

Jamie nodded. Suzie wasn't going with them. She didn't have the necessary skills and would be more valuable watching over the vehicles and fleeing for help in her souped-up Civic if it was needed. She'd been given a list of contacts for the members of Boudreaux's crew who weren't here for various reasons but could come if things got dicey.

Looking around the crowd, Jamie wondered just how big his "crew" was. There were nearly thirty people of various races and genders assembled here, all with military experience. How many more were there?

Suzie turned to Tomi, who held the spear he'd taken from the assassin. "You don't do anything stupid, cuz."

Tomi rolled his eyes. "I'm not going to. I've been training, and I know my limitations. But Dax is my best friend. Besides, someone has to be the robe person for Jamie."

Suzie looked at Minh. "You keep an eye on him."

Minh nodded once, a slight smile on her beautiful face. Jamie didn't know the pretty Vietnamese woman other than by sight. They'd never exchanged more than a few greetings in passing. But she held herself confidently and apparently had some sort of water magic that had allowed her to save the bar and the building from burning completely down. All Jamie could tell was that she was some kind of supernatural, but she didn't know what kind. She'd never encountered anyone with her scent before.

"Alright, everyone. This is it. Keep radio chatter and talk to a bare minimum. Use hand signals if you can. Our adversaries have enhanced hearing." He turned to Jamie. "Any other tips we should know?"

Jamie swallowed, suddenly put on the spot. "Um, pay attention to the wind. They have enhanced senses of smell. If you can, keep the wind in your face. If it shifts behind you, try to get behind a bush or something. It might obscure your scent some."

Boudreaux nodded. "Right. Jamie will be helping Alpha group with counter detection and tracking. Bravo group, pay attention to your surroundings."

The petite Latina woman spoke up. "I'll take care of it for Bravo."

He raised an eyebrow but nodded. "Thanks, Marisol."

Jamie tried to casually check out Marisol. She hadn't stood close enough to the woman to check out her scent. But Jamie hadn't been subtle enough, and Marisol was making hard eye contact, a smirk on her face. She nodded once.

Surprised, but pleasantly so, Jamie resolved to introduce herself after they freed Dax, assuming they all survived, and they succeeded. She pushed those thoughts away, not wanting any doubt to take hold. She needed her confidence.

"Alright, everyone lock and load." Boudreaux chopped his hand toward the fence blocking access to the woods around the quarry.

Their little army shifted into professional-soldier mode and moved across the highway. The first one to the fence held back the cut section that Jamie and Cory had made months ago when this all started. One by one, they moved through the opening and cleared the way, setting up a semicircular perimeter with guns pointed toward the woods.

Soon it would be her turn, and there'd be no going back. Minh winked at Jamie, then ducked through the opening. Tomi followed. Next, it would Jamie's turn.

After she made it through, she ducked out of the way and moved up next to Tomi and Minh. "Robe please."

Minh took it from Tomi and held it up so it blocked everyone's view of her, and Tomi turned his back. A moment later, she stripped down and made the shift quickly. She could have changed before entering the quarry and left her clothes with Suzie, but she liked having her clothes available if she needed to shift back to communicate or use her hands.

A world of scents and sounds opened to her enhanced wolf senses. She was ready to hunt.

SIXTY
DAX

Dax waited patiently, not that he had a choice. Strapped to the chair, his body grew stiff from the inability to move and adjust it. He was almost constantly in a state of goosebumps and shivers from the breeze. Normally, it would be a pleasant, summer-night breeze…fully clothed.

Still no one had appeared. Nor had he thought of a way to escape. He was good and truly captured, restrained, and fucked.

"Good evening, Mr. Smith." A voice, the same odd, false voice he'd heard from the masked being, came to him from out of the darkness. A person drifted through an invisible wall of shadow. They moved as if almost floating and wore a shapeless black robe, its hem reaching the ground. It was hooded, and their face was covered by a shiny steel or chrome mask. "We thank you for your presence here this evening."

He ignored his desire to make a snarky response. He really wasn't in the mood for banter, not that he usually was anyway. The masked entity didn't wait for or seem to care about not getting a response. They raised their arms to shoulder height, hands open and palms face up.

Out of the same line of shadows, more people in black robes and masks emerged at steady intervals and took their places around the outer circle of the pentagram. There were two circles, the space between forming what looked like a walkway around the pentagram. He imagined there were a few people in his blind spot as well. By his calculation, there were likely to be thirteen people in total. A full coven.

A massive hit of adrenaline dumped into his veins. He looked around the circle nervously, hoping the extra fear of imminent badness—although how bad, he wasn't sure, but he doubted the results would be good and for his benefit, since he'd been abducted, drugged, stripped, and strapped to a chair—would inspire him to find some new solution he hadn't thought of or seen before. It didn't.

His friends probably knew he was missing. He hadn't shown up when Tomi had called him, and Tomi would have definitely come looking for him.

Dax couldn't tell what time it was, but based on the sunset and the length of time he'd been sitting there, it had to be close to midnight. At least within an hour or so.

The amorphous witches or wizards or whatever—he didn't know if the different terms were interchangeable or meant something different in context—began chanting, the one with the hollow voice rising loudest and strongest. The others functioned more as an accompaniment and undertone. Unlike their leader, their voices sounded more natural and feminine. He couldn't find any voice that sounded masculine.

The chant rose in volume and tone until it reached a crescendo. With a final power word, the white lines painted on the rocks glowed brilliantly, flooding the circle with their glare. He clenched his eyes shut, but they throbbed from the sudden assault.

Once his brain collected itself, he noticed the power pulsing around him. He opened his eyes carefully. The light had rescinded to a bluish-white glow, illuminating the circle, pentagram lines, and symbols. But it didn't brighten anything beyond the wall of shadows surrounding the circle. The coven had emerged through a glamour and were maintaining it to keep their works hidden. There must be more witches nearby who were handling that.

He breathed tightly through his nose and kept his teeth clenched to keep them from chattering in the wind and the power flowing around him. He waited for them to move, but they all stood motionless.

Finally, the one in the mask stepped forward, breeching the line of the outer glowing circle. The figure stopped before crossing into the inner circle where the pentagram was.

The leader started another chant, but this one was a call and response. They'd chant their lines, then the rest of the coven chanted different lines back. After several verses of back and forth, the leader responded with a final line and a word of power.

An invisible force pressed against his body from every angle, squeezing him firmly after the first round of chanting. He could breathe, but barely.

The one in the mask started again. After the second round, nonexistent needles pierced his skin everywhere, lighting his nerves on fire. A scream of pain and agony bubbled up deep from within him, finally bursting through his clenched teeth.

He barely noticed when they started a third round. The pain seemed to go on steadily, as if it never intended to let him go. The final word of power cracked through the inner circle like a bolt of lightning and stripped away his flesh. He'd thought the previous pain couldn't be topped, but he'd been wrong.

He blacked out as his mortal body dissolved and disappeared. Now that he didn't have lungs and air that could run out, his scream could continue into infinity. The quarry filled with the minor harmonics and disharmonies of his voice.

Just when he thought his screams would tear apart his being, turning his bones to dust, they stopped and along with it, the pain. His tattered robe dropped over him. Their magic had forcefully summoned the Grim Reaper form he'd been forced to use as part of his exile.

The pressure holding him in place disappeared, and he slumped as much as the restraints allowed. He panted despite his lack of lungs, his bony jaw clacking against his collar bones. Gradually his awareness reassembled itself in bits and fractured pieces.

The witches stood statue still, waiting for something.

Once he thought he had enough awareness to do so, he reached out to the aether, hoping that by forcing him into this form they'd opened a path for him to find his power. But they hadn't. He couldn't even find the door into the aether. He was still just as helpless as he'd been in his human body.

Whatever the witches were waiting for occurred. They started chanting again, this time in unison. At first, they started low, gradually rising in volume, then once again descending to a quiet point. The chanting continued in this way, rising and falling, rising and falling. He felt like a ship on a sea heading into a storm, riding up the crest of the wave and falling down into the trough, with each wave getting higher and higher.

Power rose around him, lapping at him. When it reached the point where it felt like it was up to his neck, they stopped their rising and falling chant. A moment of pregnant silence felt entirely too dense, then the one in the mask sang out a new chant, and instead of a call and response, they passed the chant to the witch on their right, and it went around the circle in a counterclockwise wave.

The chanting increased in volume and power, moving around the circle faster and faster, sending the power swirling like a violent whirlpool. Then he felt it. With each circuit, the chant picked at his essence, pulling little pieces away. He could do nothing to stop it. He stared at the being in the mask, looking at the cold, steel face of his own oblivion.

He sagged, his eyes lowering. The gods and psychopomps who'd sought his destruction were going to get their wish.

As his mind drifted, growing more fuzzy as the whirlpool of power plucked at him, he saw a little bobbing shadow near the back circle of the ring of power. It held something shiny in its…beak. It was a crow.

As it wiggled its head around near the line, he saw tiny sparks burst from the outer circle, where the shiny object rubbed at it. No one but him seemed to notice what was happening, and it was a better distraction than his impending doom. A moment later, the crow cut through the line.

Something changed in the feel of the power whirling around him. A note of wildness slipped quietly in. Either the witches didn't notice or didn't care, because they kept up their inexorable rhythm of their chant.

The crow waited, looking around the circle at the witches. When no one moved or seemed to notice it, it hopped up to the line of the inner circle and started rubbing the shiny bit of whatever it carried in its beak against the line.

With each twitch of the crow's head, the power in the whirlpool slipped the tethers of its tameness just a little more. If he'd had flesh, an eager smile would have slipped across his face.

SIXTY-ONE

At first, their sweep through the woods had gone smoothly. They'd been able to use the terrain and wind to their advantage, sneaking up on the wolf-shifter bikers serving as guards. Each one had been dispatched without a single shot fired.

But one poorly placed foot and a broken stick had elicited a shout and a gunshot from a startled biker. Then all hell broke loose as Boudreaux and his people responded, putting down the sentry with a quick burst of bullets. When the biker went down and stopped shooting, someone walked up and gave him the John Wick special.

Off in the distance, in the direction Bravo group had gone, gunfire pierced the momentary blanket of silence that had fallen after the biker had been executed. Boudreaux barked out a series of commands, and the team returned to readiness, sweeping forward.

The next line of bikers ringing the quarry were grouped together in twos and threes. When she saw someone sneaking up on Manman Delphine as she kneeled and took shots, Jamie burst into action, her muscles bunching as she sprang forward. The biker had a knife raised and was about to plunge it into the manbo's back.

Jamie leapt with a growl and caught the biker's forearm in her teeth mid-jump. She clamped down twisting around in the air until her feet hit the ground. As soon as she could get purchase with her claws, she savaged the biker's arm, shaking her head back and forth as hard as she could. The biker screamed, dropping the knife.

As if she'd practiced it a million times, Manman Delphine rotated on her knees until she'd turned around. She took aim and shot in a split second, hitting the biker square in the chest. The hollow point worked devastatingly well, blasting out the biker's back with a spray of blood. He fell over backward, the momentum of his weight and the power of the shot pulling his arm from Jamie's mouth.

The manbo stood up and walked over to the fallen biker. Aiming carefully, she squeezed the trigger and blasted him in the face. He wouldn't recover from that.

Manman Delphine nodded her thanks to Jamie, then surveyed the area, looking for her next shot. The manbo was frightening enough as a voodoo priestess, but mix in her skill with a gun and her willingness to use it, and it added a whole new layer of scary to the woman. Jamie was glad the manbo was on their side and seemed to like her.

To distract herself from the momentary brush with violence, she sniffed at the dropped knife. It had marks on the blade and handle like those she'd seen on the bullets Ivar had given her and the switchblade Dax had taken off a biker. She sniffed at it but had trouble smelling anything but the biker's blood in her mouth. She focused so she didn't vomit right there.

"Jamie," Minh whispered, kneeling next to her. She pulled out a canteen from her backpack and screwed the top off. She held canteen up and a line of water flew out of the opening like a snake and danced its way to Jamie's mouth.

Jamie snapped at the water, trying to get enough to swish and spit, but had trouble doing it with a wolf mouth. She decided to shift quickly and cupped her hands together. Minh got the hint and directed the small stream of water into Jamie's hands. She sucked it into her mouth and rubbed it over her face, then spit it out onto the ground next to her. She took another handful and repeated it.

"Thanks," she whispered to Tomi's girlfriend. Minh gave a thumbs up, looking for her next move.

Jamie grabbed the knife and put the handle in her mouth, then shifted to her wolf. The fight had moved past them. A stream of gunshots and muzzle flashes about fifty yards ahead indicated the moving battle line.

Minh darted off to help Tomi, leaving Jamie standing still. She needed to get back into the fight. They were likely outnumbered by the bikers and every fighter helped. She followed Minh. Tomi was hiding behind a tree, peeking around it to fire his pistol when he had a shot. To his right, a biker was sneaking around a nearby tree, working his way to Tomi.

Minh changed her course and picked up speed. Jamie stopped, shaking her head lightly. Minh's hair shifted from glassy and black to lighter shade and feathery. Her skin appeared to be mottled and almost scaly. Leaping into the air, she drew back her fist and obliterated the biker's head with it.

Jamie nearly dropped the knife from her jaws. She had no idea what kind of supernatural Minh was, but damn! The Vietnamese woman sprinted into a cluster of bikers and disassembled them with some fancy martial arts moves.

Jamie jogged forward in Minh's wake. In the distance, shouted commands interrupted the sounds of gunfire and fighting. The voice was all too familiar—Ivar. Picking up speed, she used the distraction Minh's ass-kicking provided and moved through the battle line. Once she passed the action, she slowed down and found a bush to hide behind.

Sticking her nose in the air, she got her bearings and figured out what the smells and sounds were telling her. She'd found a pocket of quiet behind the enemy line and the direction of the shouts. It was time to hunt.

She stalked around the bush until she got her nose into the wind. He wouldn't smell her coming. She moved like smoke in the breeze. All the years of wolfy hide-and-seek she and Cory had played were coming in very handy. She stopped behind a scrubby rhododendron bush and laid down on her belly. She could see him—the man who'd put the gun in her hand that had inexorably connected her to Dax—Ivar, the president of the Black Suns Motorcycle Club, Red City chapter.

Her ears perked up. Something in the dynamic of the air had shifted. Power was being accessed, huge amounts of it. A wave of pure, burning anger swept over her. She shivered. She knew the feeling of it. She'd witnessed its owner decimate a bar full of biker wolf shifters. But this felt more potent, more dangerous. Dax...

Calls came from behind Ivar, and he turned to see what was going on. It was her time. She got up and slunk around the bush, creeping slowly toward him so he wouldn't hear her coming. She still had the wind in her face. As she neared him, she broke into a sprint. She was too close for him to evade her.

She leapt into the air and shifted midflight. She caught the dagger in a reverse grip and slammed into Ivar. With a rage-filled scream, she sank the blade into his back above his right shoulder blade.

She gave him no quarter, yanking the knife out and plunging it into his back again and again and again until he stopped moving. Then she pulled it free one last time and gripped the blade in both hands. With a cathartic yell, she slammed the blade through Ivar's skull and twisted it as hard as she could.

She sat on him, breathing heavily and holding the blade in place. Finally, she staggered to her feet, then spat on him. "Heal from that, you fucking piece of shit."

SIXTY-TWO

DAX

With the lines of the pentagram breeched, power surged into Dax's body. He grasped onto a trickle of it and directed it toward the cuffs binding his wrists and ankles, telling the metal to die. The cuffs corroded and rusted away into little flakes floating on the breeze. He stood and sent the chair after the cuffs.

Stretching to loosen his body, he sent a surge of power out all around the circle. The chanting faltered.

The one in the mask raised their arms and screamed, "Don't stop, you fools!" Then they launched into a new chant, which the coven took up hesitantly.

The crow hopped away from the circle and fluttered into the air, but instead of flying away it changed into the form of curvy, pale white woman with her hair pulled back into a braid. The shiny thing she'd been holding in her beak became a short bronze sword of Celtic design. She wore black battle leathers.

Raising her sword, she gave him a knowing smile and saluted him with the blade. Then she disappeared into the woods. A scream of death trailed in her wake. The Morrigan had showed up to do battle. Graciously, she'd left the witches for him to seek his revenge upon.

First, he needed to obliterate the symbols. He raised his arms and reached out for his scythe, drawing it forth from the aether. Once it appeared in his hands, he ignited the blue flames in his eyes and along the blade, stoking his fury into them. They lit up the hollow in the quarry where they'd tried to destroy him.

He moved to take a step forward, but an invisible lasso snagged his arm. Then another one snared his other arm. The witches were trying to regain control.

Drawing in his strength, he stomped on the nearest symbol, sending out a wave of power. The symbols popped, spraying shards of hot rock. The wave of exploding symbols worked outward. When it neared the witches, spraying them with hot shards of rock, the chant faltered and died, releasing him from all their invisible ropes except for one.

The coven's leader kept their steely mask pointed at him, their voice rising in strength as they tried to make up for the coven's absence. Death brought around his scythe and cut the invisible rope. The masked one staggered backward and fell on their butt.

The witches stood motionless, their heads turned to their leader, wondering what to do.

He hadn't felt this much power since before he'd been forced into exile. Drawing it in, he expanded and grew until he was ten feet, then twenty feet tall. As the sensation of being unleashed coursed through him, he laughed, the normally spooky sound coming out as downright terrifying. The witches took a step back.

He pushed the power down into the earth, forcing the rocks he'd been standing on to undergo rapid erosion until they turned to powder. The breeze picked it up and swirled it around him as the wave of destruction flowed away from him. Spotting a witch turning to flee, he swung his scythe and split them in half. He laughed harder.

All the rocks that had made up the painted circle were completely destroyed. He floated in the air above a growing pit of dust and particles. Reaching into the aether, he found the nearest witch and obliterated their life thread, erasing their soul from existence. There'd be no afterlife for her. He found another witch and obliterated her. They'd come here to remove him from existence; revisiting it upon them felt like justice.

He looked around for the one in the mask, but they'd disappeared. By now, the rest of the witches had also disappeared into the woods, away from the approaching sound of gunfire. He bellowed his rage at missing his opportunity to kill the leader.

His anger seethed around him. The wave of destruction found the closest tree, and it turned to rot and collapsed.

Below him, thousands of miles away, sat the earth's core. He could reach down through the earth's layers and snuff it out. Explode it and everything and everyone on this miserable rock.

"Dax." A familiar voice seeped into his awareness. "Dax, buddy."

DEATH brought his awareness back up from the earth's core to see who was speaking the familiar word — Dax.

Dax. That had been his name.

A chubby Black man wearing black and holding a spear stood on the edge of the destruction. Carefully, he set down the spear and held up his empty hands. "Dax. You've got to stop."

DEATH gathered the swirling powder and bound it with his power, forming a bridge between where he floated and the Black man. Tomi. Tomi was his name.

Tomi trembled and looked down at the seemingly insubstantial path. He gingerly placed a foot on it, and when it held, he walked slowly and carefully toward Dax. "Dax. You're going to hurt your friends. Maybe kill them. You have to stop."

Friends? What were they? He stared down at Tomi who now stood at his feet. He towered over the man. He could lift his foot and squash him. Friend?

He shrank down to match the human's height.

"Dax, you need to come back to us. You don't want to hurt your friends. We're all here."

"*FRIENDS*?" The word reverberated with disharmonics.

Tomi covered his ears and shook his head. He clenched his teeth, then looked up, placing his hand on DEATH's robes over his forearm. "It's OK. You're free now. It's time to come back to yourself. I'm your friend, there's no one left here to hurt you."

"Tomi?"

"Yeah, Dax. It's me."

Tomi was his friend. His best friend.

The cool summer breeze whispered across his sweat-drenched skin. He had skin again. "Tomi."

Dax smiled weakly at his friend, then blacked out.

SIXTY-THREE

Jamie sat on the ground under a tree, fully dressed. A massive yawn stretched her jaw. Off to the east, the first hints of dawn were painting the sky. She wiped at her sweaty forehead, drawing away a damp hand covered in dust and grit from the destruction of the quarry.

Dax, still unconscious, lay nearby, a blanket draped over his nearly nude body. The strange woman who could change into a crow stood against a tree, watching over him. Jamie couldn't keep her eyes from drifting toward the scary woman.

For one, she looked like an artifact out of time, dressed in black armor with a sword belted at her hip. She also had black paint on her forehead and under her eyes, streaking down onto her cheek. She looked both badass and scary as fuck. She'd come blasting through the woods, slicing up fleeing bikers as she went, when Jamie first saw her. The sword wasn't an affectation; she swung it with super-human skill and grace.

Suzie emerged out of the woods with a backpack and a couple of tote bags in each hand. She set them down in the area where they'd been gathering supplies. Jamie groaned as she forced herself up to her feet. Staggering a bit, she walked over and found a water bottle. She'd been holding off, letting Manman Delphine and her witch friends use their supply for the wounded. But she couldn't hold off anymore.

Nearly all of Boudreaux's people had wounds, though a good many had gotten off lightly. But the more severe wolf-inflicted wounds required magical medical attention immediately so the injured would be able to recover normally. Only time would tell if the wolf shifters' magic had been transmitted through the bites, making the injured humans into wolves.

But there was no amount of magic that could heal the three who'd been killed.

All things considered, three deaths and a handful of severe wounds weren't bad results, considering most of Boudreaux's crew were regular humans who were outnumbered by wolf-shifter bikers. Still, it felt like a heavy price to pay.

She took a deep drink of water and walked to where Suzie sat next to Tomi, who was propped up against a tree with his ankle wrapped in bandages. He'd broken it somehow.

"You gonna live, cuz?" Suzie asked, handing him a water and some ibuprofen.

"Prognosis is good." He took the water and swallowed the pills. "I hope this takes the edge off until the manbo can get to me. This fucking hurts."

"What happened? Trip over your spear?" Suzie was teasing her cousin, probably in hopes of lightening his mood.

"Ha, ha, ha. No. I fell and landed on it funny. It snapped hard." He looked over at Dax and the woman in black. "Are you sure we can trust her near Dax? He wouldn't want her there, staring at him."

"I don't know what's going on between them, but she helped us." Suzie shrugged. "And I don't mind her there, looking all sexy and badass in her leather and with her sword."

"Keep your eyes on the prize, cuz," Tomi said by way of a reprimand.

"I am!" She punched him playfully in the shoulder while ogling the woman.

Tomi shifted to the side and grunted in pain as the movement moved his ankle. "Careful."

"Sorry."

A tired smile spread over Jamie's face. The lighthearted moment was much needed right now. But what she truly wanted was a shower and a bed. Maybe Suzie would be nice and let her have the bed again, since Jamie had been fighting. It didn't matter, really. She could sleep on a pile of sharp rocks right now. Not that there were many of those left. Dax had turned the quarry, at least a good chunk of it, into a pit of dust and powder.

If a good wind came through, it would coat the whole city in grime, not that anyone would notice. It was a grimy city after all.

A surge of power alerted her to something. A whisper of metal against leather followed it. She leapt to her feet, turning toward the sound. The woman stood over Dax with her sword drawn. But she wasn't threatening the unconscious man. She stood between him and someone in a dark-brown robe that looked like a monk's habit.

"Come no further," the woman said.

"Morrigan, this is none of your business, nor do you want it to be." The voice coming from the hood sounded elegant and bored.

"I've made it my business. Stand back." She raised her sword to a ready position.

The hooded figure took a step back, but a hand emerged from within its sleeve, holding a parchment scroll with a golden wax seal and black ribbons dangling from it. The figure brought out their other hand and formed a cradle with their hands for the parchment.

"Receive this, then I shall depart." The figure stood perfectly still.

"Girl," Morrigan said. "Take it quickly, then move behind me."

Jamie felt compelled to obey. She walked around Dax and Morrigan. Slowing as she neared the robed figure, she stopped as far away as she could and extended her arm, carefully taking the scroll. As soon as her grasp on it was firm, she scuttled backward, nearly bumping into the woman with the sword.

"Your message is delivered, now begone." Morrigan shifted her stance.

The figure bowed their head then disappeared with another surge of power.

Jamie held the scroll out to Morrigan.

"Keep it, girl. It'll be better received coming from a hand that isn't mine." Morrigan looked down at Dax. He groaned softly, moving some. "He will return to the world of the awake soon. I shall depart."

She didn't wait for any kind of response; instead she sheathed her sword and walked away, disappearing behind a tree. A large black crow flapped its way into the air, cawing as it went.

"Damn," Suzie said, her eyes shifting toward where the manbo worked with someone who had a gash in their side. "I used to be a regular old bartender." She gestured around. "Now all this magic shit."

"Still excited to be a manbo?" Jamie asked, dropping to sit next to Suzie and Tomi.

"I never was excited, nor am I now. But an extra pair of healing hands would be useful here." She sighed.

"It won't be that bad, Suz." Tomi patted her knee, grinning impishly. "When you're a powerful manbo, you can flirt with the sword lady."

Jamie snickered but shook her head. "I think that's a bad idea. She scares the shit out of me."

Tomi chuckled. "Me too."

"Spice for the dish," Suzie mumbled, watching Manman Delphine work.

"Who's the witch?" Jamie asked to change the subject, pointing at the woman who was helping someone with a head wound.

"She's the one who did the seance for Dax. Grizelda, I think her name is," Tomi said. "She was late to arrive but caught the bikers on the other side of the quarry and cleared them out."

"Better late than never." Suzie rummaged in her backpack for something, her hand emerging with three granola bars. She gave one each to Jamie and Tomi, keeping one for herself.

"Yeah. All the extra healers were needed." Jamie took a big bite of the bar. When she finished it, she stashed the wrapper in Suzie's bag, since she didn't have one of her own there.

"Gee, thanks."

Jamie grinned, then yawned, her jaw popping. "I'm going to go take a nap under that tree. Wake me up when it's time to go."

EPILOGUE

DAX

Dax squinted against the sun as he bent over to grab a can of beer from the cooler for Delphine. It was a perfect day to be on the roof of their building, and the day called for a celebration. The Black Suns had been driven out of Red City, though not entirely defeated. Quite a few had escaped, and he had no idea how many other chapters there were. The insurance money had come in for the bar. He'd just hired some of Boudreaux's crew to start the work of cleaning up and renovating the apartments and the bar. And now Adele was bringing up a batch of fried chicken and some sides she'd made especially for their little get together.

He opened the can and plucked another one out for himself. Dropping off Delphine's beer, he sank into the camping chair, opened his beer, and took a deep drink. Now that the building had been fully cleared, they could use the roof to gather and watch the fireworks Red City always put on for Founder's Day. They still had an hour before the sun set and another thirty minutes before the fireworks started.

Tomi leaned over and kissed Minh before getting up from his chair. He headed toward the door that led off the roof. He'd probably gotten a message from his mama to go help her bring up the food. Despite the magical healing after the battle, he still had a slight limp. As he exited, Jamie and Suzie came through the door, making way for the big man.

"Hey everyone!" Suzie said, waving. Jamie smiled and waved but didn't say anything.

"Pull up a chair and grab yourselves some drinks." Dax waved at the cooler with the beer in his hand, spilling a few drops down the side. "Oops." To solve the problem, he put the can's opening to his lips and drained some more from it.

Suzie selected a beer from the cooler while Jamie picked a soda. They picked up chairs and walked to where Minh sat.

"So what are the big plans for the bar now that you've got the money?" Delphine asked.

"Definitely converting the alley to a patio. Tired of getting attacked every time I step out the side door. Other than that, I'm going to wait to talk to the construction people to see what we can do to make the space better. We'll have to keep things tight since the check probably won't go as far as we want it to."

She snorted. "Insurance companies never pay out what's deserved."

He nodded. A moment later, his phone vibrated, sliding off the arm of the camping chair and hitting the roof. Groaning in annoyance, he bent over and scooped it up, answering it.

"What's up, Boudreaux?"

"You sound jolly."

"I don't know if I've ever been described as jolly before, but I guess I'm feeling pretty content right now. How are you doing?"

"I'm positively spectacular, and I'm sure you'll be feeling a lot better in a moment after this news." Boudreaux, who always sounded friendly with a note of humor in his tone, practically brimmed positivity.

"That'll be a nice change. Seems like all the news I get is bad."

"Well, let's put it this way. You won't have to worry about cutting corners to finish the bar and building."

"What did you do, rob a lumberyard?" Dax grinned and took a drink from his beer.

Boudreaux laughed. "Not this time. So, you remember that laptop we picked up from that assassin's gear?"

"Yes, I do."

"Well, my girl Claire finally cracked into it and found her bank accounts. Let's just say the assassin was very naughty and very successful. Those were some fat accounts." He laughed again.

"Were?"

"They've mysteriously dried up."

"Shame, that." Dax smiled broadly. If he wasn't careful, his face muscles would get sore from the unfamiliar expression.

"Indeed. We're moving it around a bit. To make sure it comes back clean, if you know what I mean."

"Cleanliness is next to godliness, or something of the sort. How much we talking?"

"If you want, you could open up a few more bars and buy a few more buildings and have plenty left over."

"Damn." He wondered what had been the blood price for his life. Magical assassins who could change their appearance probably didn't come cheap. "Pull ten large from my half as a bonus for Claire."

They'd agreed to split whatever they found on the computer fifty-fifty, since Dax was the reason they had it and Boudreaux knew someone with the skills to attempt the access. A ten-thousand-dollar bonus seemed cheap to build a good relationship with someone with clandestine tech skills.

"That's mighty generous," Boudreaux said. "We'll get together soon and work out the final details so we can keep the money off the radar."

"Sounds like a plan."

"Well, I gots to go. I've got a date waiting for me."

Dax chuckled. "Good luck. Later." He hung up.

"You look…happy?" Suzie said. "That's a new expression for you. Good news?"

"You could say that. We're all getting a little hazard pay for recent events."

"How much?" Suzie waggled her eyebrows.

"Enough that none of us will have to worry about money for a little while."

Suzie nudged Jamie with her elbow. "You'll be able to get your own apartment! If you want to." She looked slyly at her friend. "Or if you wanted to save a little money, we could go halfsies on a two-bedroom place."

Suzie had planned to move after everything was done, since Jamie had been captured and might have spilled their address.

Jamie, normally a serious young woman, grinned happily. "If you don't mind living with me, I'd love to split a place."

Dax was happy to see the joy on his friends' faces. All of them had struggled financially, especially Jamie. For the first time in her life, she might have a little bit of a safety net. It was good that she was going to go in on a place with Suzie instead of going big on her own. The money wouldn't last forever, but it would last long enough if they were all smart with their shares. He planned to split everything evenly among the group. They'd all earned it.

He walked over to Delphine but stopped when she picked up her phone.

"Hello?" After a few moments, her face fell. "My sincerest condolences. Thank you for letting me know. If I can do anything, just call." She hung up, dropping her phone into her purse.

"That didn't sound good." He sank into his chair next to hers.

"It's not." She wiped a tear from her cheek. "Gunnar is dead. He was murdered last night."

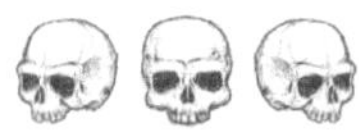

Join Ragnar in his first Red City adventure and preorder Road To Rune!

ROAD TO RUNE

RED CITY RUNESMITH: BOOK ONE

Murder is common in Red City. But this time, someone murdered Ragnar's father.

Ragnar and his band were forced to cancel their tour. The were-wolf bikers tracked them down. But when he got the call about his father's murder, he had to return to Red City fast.

The packless wolf shifters listened to Ragnar's dad, but now they're looking to Ragnar. He's got to protect his community. But he needs to solve his father's murder. The problem is, there are too many suspects in a crime ridden city like Red City.

But if he draws the wrong attention, he risks drawing the wrong eye. And there are too many of those in Red City. If Ragnar can't find his father's killer, he might be next victim...

Preorder Ragnar's first Red City adventure in Road To Rune!

CONTENTS

Content Warning: Gun violence, white nationalism/supremacy, kidnapping

GLOSSARY

Adyeu - Goodbye
Avek plezi - With pleasure
Bon chans - Good luck
Bonswa - Good afternoon/evening
Bourré - A popular card game played in the New Orleans region of Louisiana
Byenveni lakay, zanmi m - Welcome home, my friend
Cher - dear (a term of endearment)
Lwas - spirit, god, saints
Manbo - female voodoo priest
Manman - mother (a term of respect)
Misye Lanmò - Mr. Death
Mwen, oswa chat ou? - Me or your cat?

ACKNOWLEDGMENTS

Thanks to my talented partner Amy Cissell, my ARC team, and all those who helped make this book come alive.

And a special thanks to the newsletter readers who selected the villain name Grinder Sorenson during our name a villain tournament!

ABOUT THE AUTHOR

C. Thomas Lafollette is a student of history and a world traveler. He's dined with a Prime Minister, read poetry with Yevgeny Yevtushenko, and drank beer with monks. He's the author of the action-adventure urban fantasy series Luke Irontree & The Last Vampire War and the Red City Reaper series. Besides reading and writing, he loves a good action movie, be it a Hollywood blockbuster or a classic Samurai flick, as well as the occasional rom-com. He lives in Porto, Portugal with his partner – the devastatingly talented author Amy Cissell – his stepdaughter, and their three jerkface cats.

facebook.com/CThomasLafollette

bookbub.com/authors/c-thomas-lafollette

amazon.com/C-Thomas-Lafollette/e/B09JMTR7W7

goodreads.com/cthomaslafollette

threads.net/@cthomaslafollette

instagram.com/CThomasLafollette

tiktok.com/@cthomaslafollette

ALSO BY C. THOMAS LAFOLLETTE

Luke Irontree & The Last Vampire War

Book 0 - The Centurion Immortal

Book 1 - Dark Fangs Rising - March 22, 2022

Book 2 - Dark Fangs Raging - April 19, 2022

Book 3 - Dark Fangs Descending - May 17, 2022

Book 4 - Blood Empire Reborn - August 23, 2022

Book 5 - Blood Empire Avenged - September 20, 2022

Book 6 - Blood Empire Infiltrated - October 18, 2022

Book 7 - Blood Empire Burning - November 15, 2022

Book 8 - Ancient Sword Falling - March 21, 2023

Book 9 - Ancient Sword Unyielding - August 22, 2023

Book 10 - Ancient Sword Shattering - January 4, 2023

The Luke Irontree Historical Adventures

Rise of the Centurio Immortalis - April 5, 2022

Fall of the Centurio Immortalis - May 31, 2022

The Moonlight Centurion*

The Highway Centurion*

Red City Reaper - A Dark Urban Fantasy Adventure

Book 0 - Dead in Red City*

Book 1 - A Shot For Death - March 26, 2024

Book 1.5 - Death Uncaged - March 21, 2024

Book 2 - Death Orders a Double - July 23, 2024

Book 3 - Death With A Twist - November 7, 2024

Book 4 - Death On The Rocks* - February 25, 2025

Book 5 - A Fifth Of Death*

Book 6 - A Dash Of Death*

Book 7 - A Chaser of Death*

Book 8 - A Nightcap of Death *

Red City Runesmith - A Wolf Shifter Urban Fantasy

Book 0 - Runing With The Wolves* - Fall 2025

Book 1 - Road to Rune* - June 24, 2025

Book 2 - On The Rune Again*

Book 3 - Runing On Empty*

Book 4 - Runing Wild*

*Forthcoming

Titles and release dates may be subject to change.

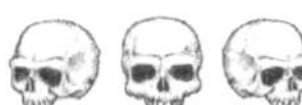

www.ingramcontent.com/pod-product-compliance
Lightning Source LLC
Chambersburg PA
CBHW031209310726

48969CB00001B/276